THE SILVER LININGS PLAYBOOK

Matthew Quick is the author of *The Silver Linings Playbook*, which was made into an Academy Award-winning film, and the young adult novels *Sorta Like a Rock Star*, *Boy21* and *Forgive Me, Leonard Peacock*. His work has been translated into more than twenty languages and he has received a PEN/Hemingway Award Honorable Mention, among other accolades. He is married to the novelist and pianist Alicia Bessette.

ALSO BY MATTHEW QUICK

FOR ADULTS

The Good Luck of Right Now

FOR YOUNG ADULTS

Forgive Me, Leonard Peacock

Boy21

Sorta Like a Rock Star

THE SILVER LININGS PLAYBOOK

MATTHEW QUICK

PICADOR

First published 2008 by Farrar, Straus and Giroux

First published in the UK in paperback 2009 by Picador

This edition published 2014 by Picador
an imprint of Pan Macmillan, a division of Macmillan Publishers Limited
Pan Macmillan, 20 New Wharf Road, London N1 9RR
Basingstoke and Oxford
Associated companies throughout the world
www.panmacmillan.com

ISBN 978-1-4472-8663-9

Grateful acknowledgement is made to the Edward B. Marks Music
Company for permission to reprint lyrics from 'Total Eclipse of the Heart,'
written by Jim Steinman. Used by permission of Edward B. Marks
Company on behalf of Lost Boys Music.

The author would like to acknowledge his first reading of the adage
'You can either practice being right or practice being kind' in
Anne Lamott's excellent essay 'Adolescence.'

1 3 5 7 9 8 6 4 2

A CIP catalogue record for this book is available from
the British Library.

Printed and bound by CPI Group (UK) Ltd, Croydon, CR0 4YY

For Alicia—*la raison*

THE SILVER LININGS PLAYBOOK

An Infinite Amount of Days Until My Inevitable Reunion with Nikki

I don't have to look up to know Mom is making another surprise visit. Her toenails are always pink during the summer months, and I recognize the flower design imprinted on her leather sandals; it's what Mom purchased the last time she signed me out of the bad place and took me to the mall.

Once again, Mother has found me in my bathrobe, exercising unattended in the courtyard, and I smile because I know she will yell at Dr. Timbers, asking him why I need to be locked up if I'm only going to be left alone all day.

"Just how many push-ups are you going to do, Pat?" Mom says when I start a second set of one hundred without speaking to her.

"Nikki—likes—a—man—with—a—developed—upper—body," I say, spitting out one word per push-up, tasting the salty sweat lines that are running into my mouth.

The August haze is thick, perfect for burning fat.

Mom just watches for a minute or so, and then she shocks me. Her voice sort of quivers as she says, "Do you want to come home with me today?"

I stop doing push-ups, turn my face up toward Mother's, squint through the white noontime sun—and I can immediately tell she is serious, because she looks worried, as if she is making a mistake, and that's how Mom looks when she means something she has said and isn't just talking like she always does for hours on end whenever she's not upset or afraid.

"As long as you promise not to go looking for Nikki again," she adds, "you can finally come home and live with me and your father until we find you a job and get you set up in an apartment."

I resume my push-up routine, keeping my eyes riveted to the shiny black ant scaling a blade of grass directly below my nose, but my peripheral vision catches the sweat beads leaping from my face to the ground below.

"Pat, just say you'll come home with me, and I'll cook for you and you can visit with your old friends and start to get on with your life finally. *Please*. I need you to want this. If only for me, Pat. *Please*."

Double-time push-ups, my pecs ripping, growing—pain, heat, sweat, change.

I don't want to stay in the bad place, where no one believes in silver linings or love or happy endings, and where everyone tells me Nikki will not like my new body, nor will she even want to see me when apart time is over. But I am also afraid the people from my old life will not be as enthusiastic as I am now trying to be.

Even still, I need to get away from the depressing doctors and the ugly nurses—with their endless pills in paper cups—if I am ever going to get my thoughts straight, and since Mom will be much easier to trick than medical professionals, I jump up, find my feet, and say, "I'll come live with you just until apart time is over."

While Mom is signing legal papers, I take one last shower in my room and then fill my duffel bag with clothes and my framed picture of Nikki. I say goodbye to my roommate, Jackie, who just stares at me from his bed like he always does, drool running down off his chin like clear honey. Poor Jackie, with his random tufts of hair, oddly shaped head, and flabby body. What woman would ever love him?

He blinks at me. I take this for goodbye and good luck, so I blink back with both eyes—meaning double good luck to you, Jackie, which I figure he understands, since he grunts and bangs his shoulder against his ear like he does whenever he gets what you are trying to tell him.

My other friends are in music relaxation class, which I do not attend, because smooth jazz makes me angry sometimes. Thinking maybe I should say goodbye to the men who had my back while I was locked up, I look into the music-room window and see my boys sitting Indian style on purple yoga mats, their elbows resting on their knees, their palms pressed together in front of their faces, and their eyes closed. Luckily, the glass of the window blocks the smooth jazz from entering my ears. My friends look really relaxed—at peace—so I decide not to interrupt their session. I hate goodbyes.

In his white coat, Dr. Timbers is waiting for me when I meet my mother in the lobby, where three palm trees lurk among the couches and lounge chairs, as if the bad place were in Orlando and not Baltimore. "Enjoy your life," he says to me—wearing that sober look of his—and shakes my hand.

"Just as soon as apart time ends," I say, and his face falls as if I said I was going to kill his wife, Natalie, and their three blond-haired daughters—Kristen, Jenny, and Becky—because that's just how much he does not believe in silver linings, making it his business to preach apathy and negativity and pessimism unceasingly.

But I make sure he understands that he has failed to infect me with his depressing life philosophies—and that I will be looking forward to the end of apart time. I say, "Picture me rollin'" to Dr. Timbers, which is exactly what Danny—my only black friend in the bad place—told me he was going to say to Dr. Timbers when Danny got out. I sort of feel bad about stealing Danny's exit line, but it works; I know because Dr. Timbers squints as if I had punched him in the gut.

As my mother drives me out of Maryland and through Delaware, past all those fast-food places and strip malls, she explains that Dr. Timbers did not want to let me out of the bad place, but with the help of a few lawyers and her girlfriend's therapist—the man who will be *my* new therapist—she waged a legal battle and managed to convince some judge that she could care for me at home, so I thank her.

On the Delaware Memorial Bridge, she looks over at me and asks if I want to get better, saying, "You do want to get better, Pat. *Right?*"

I nod. I say, "I do."

And then we are back in New Jersey, flying up 295.

As we drive down Haddon Avenue into the heart of Collingswood—my hometown—I see that the main drag looks different. So many new boutique stores, new expensive-looking restaurants, and well-dressed strangers walking the sidewalks that I wonder if this is really my hometown at all. I start to feel anxious, breathing heavily like I sometimes do.

Mom asks me what's wrong, and when I tell her, she again promises that my new therapist, Dr. Patel, will have me feeling normal in no time.

When we arrive home, I immediately go down into the basement, and it's like Christmas. I find the weight bench my mother had promised me so many times, along with the rack of weights, the stationary bike, dumbbells, and the Stomach Master 6000, which I had seen on late-night television and coveted for however long I was in the bad place.

"Thank you, thank you, thank you!" I tell Mom, and give her a huge hug, picking her up off the ground and spinning her around once.

When I put her down, she smiles and says, "Welcome home, Pat."

Eagerly I go to work, alternating between sets of bench presses, curls, machine sit-ups on the Stomach Master 6000, leg lifts, squats, hours on the bike, hydration sessions (I try to drink four gallons of water every day, doing endless shots of H_2O from a shot glass for intensive hydration), and then there is my writing, which is mostly daily memoirs like this one, so that Nikki will be able to read about my life and know exactly what I've been up to since apart time began. (My memory started to slip in the bad place because of the drugs, so I began writing down everything that happens to me, keeping track of what I will need to tell Nikki when apart time concludes, to catch her up on my life. But the doctors in the bad place confiscated everything I wrote before I came home, so I had to start over.)

When I finally come out of the basement, I notice that all the pictures of Nikki and me have been removed from the walls and the mantel over the fireplace.

I ask my mother where these pictures went. She tells me our

house was burglarized a few weeks before I came home and the pictures were stolen. I ask why a burglar would want pictures of Nikki and me, and my mother says she puts all of her pictures in very expensive frames. "Why didn't the burglar steal the rest of the family pictures?" I ask. Mom says the burglar stole *all* the expensive frames, but she had the negatives for the family portraits and had them replaced. "Why didn't you replace the pictures of Nikki and me?" I ask. Mom says she did not have the negatives for the pictures of Nikki and me, especially because Nikki's parents had paid for the wedding pictures and had only given my mother copies of the photos she liked. Nikki had given Mom the other non-wedding pictures of us, and well, we aren't in touch with Nikki or her family right now because it's apart time.

I tell my mother that if that burglar comes back, I'll break his kneecaps and beat him within an inch of his life, and she says, "I believe you would."

My father and I do not talk even once during the first week I am home, which is not all that surprising, as he is always working—he's the district manager for all the Big Foods in South Jersey. When Dad's not at work, he's in his study, reading historical fiction with the door shut, mostly novels about the Civil War. Mom says he needs time to get used to my living at home again, which I am happy to give him, especially since I am sort of afraid to talk with Dad anyway. I remember him yelling at me the only time he ever visited me in the bad place, and he said some pretty awful things about Nikki and silver linings in general. I see Dad in the hallways of our house, of course, but he doesn't look at me when we pass.

Nikki likes to read, and since she always wanted me to read literary books, I start, mainly so I will be able to participate in the dinner conversations I had remained silent through in the past—those conversations with Nikki's literary friends, all English teachers who think I'm an illiterate buffoon, which is actually a name Nikki's friend calls me whenever I tease him about being such a tiny man. "At least I'm not an illiterate buffoon," Phillip says to me, and Nikki laughs so hard.

My mom has a library card, and she checks out books for me now that I am home and allowed to read whatever I want without clearing the material with Dr. Timbers, who, incidentally, is a fascist when it comes to book banning. I start with *The Great Gatsby*, which I finish in just three nights.

The best part is the introductory essay, which states that the novel is mostly about time and how you can never buy it back, which is exactly how I feel regarding my body and exercise—but then again, I also feel as if I have an infinite amount of days until my inevitable reunion with Nikki.

When I read the actual story—how Gatsby loves Daisy so much but can't ever be with her no matter how hard he tries—I feel like ripping the book in half and calling up Fitzgerald and telling him his book is all wrong, even though I know Fitzgerald is probably deceased. Especially when Gatsby is shot dead in his swimming pool the first time he goes for a swim all summer, Daisy doesn't even go to his funeral, Nick and Jordan part ways, and Daisy ends up sticking with racist Tom, whose need for sex basically murders an innocent woman, you can tell Fitzgerald never took the time to look up at clouds during sunset, because there's no silver lining at the end of that book, let me tell you.

I *do* see why Nikki likes the novel, as it's written so well. But her liking it makes me worry now that Nikki doesn't really believe in silver linings, because she says *The Great Gatsby* is the greatest novel ever written by an American, and yet it ends so sadly. One thing's for sure, Nikki is going to be very proud of me when I tell her I finally read her favorite book.

Here's another surprise: I'm going to read all the novels on her American literature class syllabus, just to make her proud, to let her know that I am really interested in what she loves and I am making a real effort to salvage our marriage, especially since I will now be able to converse with her swanky literary friends, saying things like, "I'm thirty. I'm five years too old to lie to myself and call it honor," which Nick says toward the end of Fitzgerald's famous novel, but the line works for me too, because I am also thirty, so when I say it, I will sound really smart. We will probably be chatting over dinner, and the reference will make Nikki smile and laugh because she will be so surprised that I have actually read *The Great Gatsby*. That's part of my plan, anyway, to deliver that line real suave, when she least expects me to "drop knowledge"—to use another one of my black friend Danny's lines.

God, I can't wait.

He Does Not Preach Pessimism

My workout is interrupted midday, when Mom descends the basement stairs and says I have an appointment with Dr. Patel. I ask if I can go later that night, after I have completed my daily weights routine, but Mom says I'll have to go back to the bad place in Baltimore if I do not keep my appointments with Dr. Patel, and she even references the court ruling, telling me I can read the paperwork if I don't believe her.

So I shower, and then Mom drives me to Dr. Patel's office, which is the first floor of a big house in Voorhees, just off Haddonfield–Berlin Road.

When we arrive, I take a seat in the waiting room as Mom fills out some more paperwork. By now, ten trees must have been cut down just to document my mental health, which Nikki will hate hearing, as she is an avid environmentalist who gave me at least one tree in the rain forest every Christmas—which was really only a piece of paper stating I owned the tree—and I do feel bad now for making fun of those gifts and won't ever poke fun at the diminishing rain forest in the future when Nikki comes back.

As I sit there flipping through a *Sports Illustrated*, listening to the easy-listening station Dr. Patel pumps into his waiting room, suddenly I'm hearing sexy synthesizer chords, faint high-hat taps, the kick drum thumping out an erotic heartbeat, the twinkling of fairy dust, and then the evil bright soprano saxophone. You know the title: "Songbird." And I'm out of my seat, screaming, kicking chairs, flipping the coffee table, picking up piles of magazines and throwing them against the wall, yelling, "It's not fair! I won't tolerate any tricks! I'm not an emotional lab rat!"

And then a small Indian man—maybe only five feet tall, wearing a cable-knit sweater in August, suit pants, and shiny white tennis shoes—is calmly asking me what's wrong.

"Turn off that music!" I yell. "Shut it off! Right now!"

The tiny man is Dr. Patel, I realize, because he tells his secretary to turn off the music, and when she obeys, Kenny G is out of my head and I stop yelling.

I cover my face with my hands so no one will see me crying, and after a minute or so, my mother begins rubbing my back.

So much silence—and then Dr. Patel asks me into his office. I follow him reluctantly as Mom helps the secretary clean up the mess I made.

His office is pleasantly strange.

Two leather recliners face each other, and spider-looking plants—long vines full of white-and-green leaves—hang down from the ceiling to frame the bay window that overlooks a stone birdbath and a garden of colorful flowers. But there is absolutely nothing else in the room except a box of tissues on the short length of floor between the recliners. The floor is a shiny yellow hardwood, and the ceiling and walls are painted to look like the sky—real-looking clouds float all around the office, which I take as a good omen, since I love clouds. A single light occupies the center of the ceiling, like a glowing upside-down vanilla-icing cake, but the ceiling around the light is painted to look like the sun. Friendly rays shoot out from the center.

I have to admit I feel calm as soon as I enter Dr. Patel's office and do not really mind anymore that I heard the Kenny G song.

Dr. Patel asks me which recliner I want to relax in. I pick the black over the brown and immediately regret my decision, thinking that choosing black makes me seem more depressed than if I had chosen brown, and really, I'm not depressed at all.

When Dr. Patel sits down, he pulls the lever on the side of his chair, which makes the footrest rise. He leans back and laces his fingers behind his tiny head, as if he were about to watch a ball game.

"Relax," he says. "And no Dr. Patel. Call me Cliff. I like to keep sessions informal. Friendly, right?"

He seems nice enough, so I pull my lever, lean back, and try to relax.

"So," he says. "The Kenny G song really got to you. I can't say I'm a fan either, but . . . "

I close my eyes, hum a single note, and silently count to ten, blanking my mind.

When I open my eyes, he says, "You want to talk about Kenny G?"

I close my eyes, hum a single note, and silently count to ten, blanking my mind.

"Okay. Want to tell me about Nikki?"

"Why do you want to know about Nikki?" I say, too defensively, I admit.

"If I am going to help you, Pat, I need to *know you*, right? Your mother tells me you wish to be reunited with Nikki, that this is your biggest life goal—so I figure we best start there."

I begin to feel better because he does not say a reunion is out of the question, which seems to imply that Dr. Patel feels as though reconciling with my wife is still possible.

"Nikki? She's great," I say, and then smile, feeling the warmth that fills my chest whenever I say her name, whenever I see her face in my mind. "She's the best thing that ever happened to me. I love her more than life itself. And I just can't wait until apart time is over."

"Apart time?"

"Yeah. Apart time."

"What is apart time?"

"A few months ago I agreed to give Nikki some space, and she agreed to come back to me when she felt like she had worked out her own issues enough so we could be together again. So we are sort of separated, but only temporarily."

"Why did you separate?"

"Mostly because I didn't appreciate her and was a workaholic—chairing the Jefferson High School History Department and coaching three sports. I was never home, and she got lonely. Also I sort of let my appearance go, to the point where I was maybe ten to seventy pounds overweight, but I'm working on all that and am now more than willing to go into couples counseling like she wanted me to, because I'm a changed man."

"Did you set a date?"

"A date?"

"For the end of apart time."

"No."

"So apart time is something that will go on indefinitely?"

"Theoretically, I guess—yes. Especially since I'm not allowed to contact Nikki or her family."

"Why's that?"

"Umm . . . I don't know, really. I mean—I love my in-laws as much as I love Nikki. But it doesn't matter, because I'm thinking that Nikki will be back sooner than later, and then she'll straighten everything out with her parents."

"On what do you base your thinking?" he asks, but nicely, with a friendly smile on his face.

"I believe in happy endings," I tell him. "And it feels like this movie has gone on for the right amount of time."

"Movie?" Dr. Patel says, and I think he would look exactly like Gandhi if he had those wire-rim glasses and a shaved head, which is weird, especially since we are in leather recliners in such a bright, happy room and well, Gandhi is dead, right?

"Yeah," I say. "Haven't you ever noticed that life is like a series of movies?"

"No. Tell me."

"Well, you have adventures. All start out with troubles, but then you admit your problems and become a better person by working really hard, which is what fertilizes the happy ending and allows it to bloom—just like the end of all the Rocky films, *Rudy*, *The Karate Kid*, the *Star Wars* and *Indiana Jones* trilogies, and *The Goonies*, which are my favorite films, even though I have sworn off movies until Nikki returns, because now my own life is the movie I will watch, and well, it's always on. Plus I know it's almost time for the happy ending, when Nikki will come back, because I have improved myself so very much through physical fitness and medication and therapy."

"Oh, I see." Dr. Patel smiles. "I like happy endings too, Pat."

"So you agree with me. You think my wife will come back soon?"

"Time will tell," Dr. Patel says, and I know right then that Cliff and I are going to get along, because he does not preach pessimism like Dr. Timbers and the staff at the bad place; Cliff doesn't say I need to face what he thinks is my reality.

"It's funny, because all the other therapists I've seen said that Nikki wouldn't be back. Even after I told them about the life improvements I have been making, how I am bettering myself, they still were always 'hating on me,' which is an expression I learned from my black friend Danny."

"People can be cruel," he says with a sympathetic look that makes me trust him even more. And right then I realize that he is not writing down all my words in a file, which I really appreciate, let me tell you.

I tell him I like the room, and we talk about my love of clouds and how most people lose the ability to see silver linings even though they are always there above us almost every day.

I ask him questions about his family, just to be nice, and it turns out he has a daughter whose high school field hockey team is ranked second in South Jersey. Also he has a son in elementary school who wants to be a ventriloquist and even practices nightly with a wooden dummy named Grover Cleveland, who, incidentally, was also the only U.S. president to serve two terms that were not back-to-back. I don't really get why Cliff's son named his wooden dummy after our twenty-second and twenty-fourth president, although I do not say so. Next, Cliff says he has a wife named Sonja, who painted the room so beautifully, which leads to our discussion about how great women are and how it's important to treasure your woman while you have her because if you don't, you can lose her pretty quickly—as God really wants us to appreciate our women. I tell Cliff I hope he never has to experience apart time, and he says he hopes my apart time will end soon, which is a pretty nice thing to say.

Before I leave, Cliff says he will be changing my medication, which could lead to some unwanted side effects, and that I have to report any discomfort or sleeplessness or anxiety or anything else to my mother immediately—because it might take some time for him to find the right combination of drugs—and I promise him I will.

On the drive home I tell my mother I really like Dr. Cliff Patel and am feeling much more hopeful about my therapy. I thank her for getting me out of the bad place, saying Nikki is far more likely to come to Collingswood than to a mental institution, and when I say this, Mom starts to cry, which is so strange. She even pulls off the road, rests her head against the steering wheel, and with the engine running, she cries for a long time—sniffling and trembling and making crying noises. So I rub her back, like she did for me in Dr. Patel's office when that certain song came on, and after ten minutes or so, she simply stops crying and drives me home.

To make up for the hour I spent sitting around with Cliff, I work out until late in the evening, and when I go to bed, my father is still in his office with the door shut, so another day passes without my talking to Dad. I think it's strange to live in a house with someone you cannot talk to—especially when that someone is your father—and the thought makes me a little sad.

Since Mom has not been to the library yet, I have nothing to read. So I close my eyes and think about Nikki until she comes to be with me in my dreams—like always.

Orange Fire Enters My Skull

Yes, I really do believe in silver linings, mostly because I've been seeing them almost every day when I emerge from the basement, push my head and arms through a trash bag—so my torso will be wrapped in plastic and I will sweat more—and then go running. I always try to coordinate the ten-mile running portion of my ten-hour exercise routine with sunset, so I can finish by running west past the playing fields of Knight's Park, where, as a kid, I played baseball and soccer.

As I run through the park, I look up and see what the day has to offer in the way of divination.

If clouds are blocking the sun, there will always be a silver lining that reminds me to keep on trying, because I know that while things might seem dark now, my wife is coming back to me soon. Seeing the light outline those fluffy puffs of white and gray is electrifying. (And you can even re-create the effect by holding your hand a few inches away from a naked lightbulb and tracing your handprint with your eyes until you go temporarily blind.) It hurts to look at the clouds, but it also helps, like most things that cause pain. So I need to run, and as my lungs burn and my back rebels with that stabbing knife feeling and my leg muscles harden and the half inch of loose skin around my waist jiggles, I feel as though my penance for the day is being done and that maybe God will be pleased enough to lend me some help, which I think is why He has been showing me interesting clouds for the past week.

Since my wife asked for some time apart, I've lost more than fifty pounds, and my mother says that soon I'll be at the weight I was when I played varsity soccer in high school, which is also the weight I was when I met Nikki, and I'm thinking maybe she was upset by the weight I gained during the five years we were married. Won't she be surprised to see me looking so muscular when apart time is over!

If there are no clouds at sunset—which happened yesterday—when I look up toward the sky, orange fire enters my skull, blinds me, and that's almost as good, because it burns too and makes everything look divine.

When I run, I always pretend I am running toward Nikki, and it makes me feel like I am decreasing the amount of time I have to wait until I see her again.

The Worst Ending Imaginable

Knowing that Nikki does a big unit on Hemingway every year, I ask for one of Hemingway's better novels. "One with a love story if possible, because I really need to study love—so I can be a better husband when Nikki comes back," I tell Mom.

When Mom returns from the library, she says that the librarian claims *A Farewell to Arms* is Hemingway's best love story. So I eagerly crack open the book and can feel myself getting smarter as I turn the first few pages.

As I read, I look for quotable lines so I can "drop knowledge" the next time Nikki and I are out with her literary friends—so I can say to that glasses-wearing Phillip, "Would an illiterate buffoon know this line?" And then I will drop some Hemingway, real suave.

But the novel is nothing but a trick.

The whole time, you root for the narrator to survive the war and then for him to have a nice life with Catherine Barkley. He does survive all sorts of dangers—even getting blown up—and finally escapes to Switzerland with the pregnant Catherine, whom he loves so much. They live in the mountains for a time, in love and living a good life.

Hemingway should have ended there, because that was the silver lining these people deserved after struggling to survive the gloomy war.

But no.

Instead he thinks up the worst ending imaginable: Hemingway has Catherine die from hemorrhaging after their child is stillborn. It is the most torturous ending I have ever experienced and probably will ever experience in literature, movies, or even television.

I am crying so hard at the end, partly for the characters, yes, but also because Nikki actually teaches this book to children. I cannot imagine why anyone would want to expose impressionable teenagers to such a horrible ending. Why not just tell high school students that their struggle to improve themselves is all for nothing?

I have to admit that for the first time since apart time began, I am mad at Nikki for teaching such pessimism in her classroom. I will not be quoting Hemingway anytime soon, nor will I ever read another one of his books. And if he were still alive, I would write him a letter right now and threaten to strangle him dead with my bare hands just for being so glum. No wonder he put a gun to his head, like it says in the introductory essay.

Got Nothin' but Love for Ya

Dr. Patel's secretary turns off the radio as soon as she sees me walk into the waiting room, which makes me laugh because she tries to do it casually, as if I won't notice. She looks scared, turning the knob so gingerly—the way people do things after they have seen one of my episodes, as if I am no longer human, but some wild hulking animal.

After a brief wait, I meet with Cliff for my second session, like I will every Friday for the foreseeable future. I pick brown this time, and we sit in his leather recliners among the clouds, talking about how much we like women and "kicking it like we do," which is another one of Danny's sayings.

Cliff asks me if I like my new meds, and I tell him I do, even though I really have not noticed any effects at all and have only taken about half the pills my mother gave me last week—hiding a few under my tongue and spitting them into the toilet when she leaves me alone. He asks me if I have experienced any unwanted side effects—shortness of breath, loss of appetite, drowsiness, suicidal feelings, homicidal feelings, loss of virility, anxiety, itchiness, diarrhea—and I tell him I haven't.

"What about hallucinations?" he says, and then leans forward a little, squinting.

"Hallucinations?" I ask.

"Hallucinations."

I shrug, say I don't think I have hallucinated, and he tells me I would know if I had.

"Tell your mother if you see anything bizarre or horrifying," he says, "but don't worry, because you probably will not hallucinate. Only a very small percentage of people hallucinate while taking this combination of meds."

I nod and promise I will report any hallucinations to my mother, but I do not really believe I will hallucinate no matter what type of drugs he gives me, especially since I know he will not be giving me LSD or anything like that. I figure weaker people probably complain about their drugs, but I am not weak and can control my mind pretty well.

I am in the basement doing shots of water, taking my three-minute break between crunches on the Stomach Master 6000 and leg lifts on the weight bench, when I smell the unmistakable buttery flavor of my mother's crabby snacks and I start to salivate unmercifully.

Because I love crabby snacks, I leave the basement, enter the kitchen, and see that my mother is not only baking crabby snacks, which are buttered crabmeat and orange cheese on English muffins, but she is also making her homemade three-meats pizza—hamburger, sausage, and chicken—and those buffalo wings she gets from Big Foods.

"Why are you cooking crabby snacks?" I ask hopefully, because I know from past experience that she only cooks crabby snacks when we are having company.

Nikki loves crabby snacks and will eat a whole plate if you set it in front of her, and then she will complain later on the ride home, saying she is feeling fat because she has eaten too much. Back when I was emotionally abusive, I used to tell her that I did not want to hear her complaints every time she ate too much. But the next time Nikki eats too many crabby snacks, I am going to tell her she did *not* eat too much and that she looks too skinny anyway; I'll say she needs to gain a few pounds because I like my women looking like women and not like "Ms. Six O'Clock—straight up, straight down," which is another term I learned from Danny.

And I do hope my mother's making crabby snacks signifies that apart time is over because Nikki is on her way to my parents' house, which seems like the best coming-home surprise my mother could cook up—and as Mom is always trying to do nice things for me and my brother, I mentally prepare myself to be reunited with Nikki.

My heart pounds at least fifty times during the few seconds it takes for my mother to answer my question.

"The Eagles are playing the Steelers tonight in a preseason exhibition game," my mother says, which is weird because Mom has always hated sports and barely knows that football season is in the fall, let alone what teams are playing on a given day. "Your brother is coming over to watch the game with you and your father."

My heart starts beating even faster because I have not seen my brother since shortly after apart time began, and like my father, he said some really awful things about Nikki the last time we talked.

"Jake is looking forward to seeing you, and you know how much your father loves the Eagles. I can't wait to have all three of my men gathered around the couch again, just like old times." My mother smiles at me so hard I think she is going to break out in tears again, so I turn around and go back into the basement to do knuckle push-ups until my pecs burn and I can no longer feel my knuckles.

Knowing that I will probably not be allowed to go for my run later, because we are having a family night, I put on a trash bag and run early, passing my high school friends' homes; passing St. Joseph's, which is the Catholic church I used to attend; passing Collingswood High School (class of '89 rules!) and the house my grandparents used to own by the park before they died.

My old best friend sees me when I run past his new house on Virginia Avenue. Ronnie is just getting home from work, walking from his car to his front door, when I pass him on the sidewalk. He looks me in the eyes, and after I have passed, he yells, "Pat Peoples? *Is that you?* Pat! Hey!" I run even harder, because my brother, Jake, is coming to talk to me; Jake does not believe in happy endings, and I do not have the emotional wherewithal to deal with Ronnie right now, because he never once came to visit Nikki and me in Baltimore, although he promised so many times. Nikki used to call Ronnie "whipped," saying that his wife, Veronica, "keeps Ronnie's social calendar where she keeps his balls—in her purse."

Nikki told me that Ronnie would never visit me in Baltimore, and she was right.

He never visited me in the bad place either, but he used to write me letters about how great his daughter, Emily, was and I guess is, although I have not yet met Emily to verify the letters.

When I return home, Jake's car is there—a fancy silver BMW, which sort of implies that my brother is doing well now when it comes to "pockets getting fatter," as Danny says. So I sneak in the back door and run up the steps to the shower. After I wash and put on clean clothes, I take a deep breath and follow the sound of conversation to the living room.

Jake stands when he sees me. He has on fancy pants, lined with charcoal pinstripes, and a robin's-egg blue polo shirt that is formfitting enough to show that he is still pretty fit. He is also wearing a watch with diamonds all over the face, which Danny would call Jake's bling-bling. My brother's hair has thinned a little too, but his head is gelled and looks swanky.

"Pat?" he says.

"Didn't I say you wouldn't recognize him?" Mom says.

"You look like Arnold Schwarzenegger." He feels my bicep, which I absolutely hate because I don't like to be touched by anyone except Nikki. Since he's my brother, I don't say anything. "You're frickin' ripped," he adds.

I look at the floor, because I remember what he said about Nikki—I am still mad about that—and yet I am also happy to see my brother after not seeing him for what feels like forever.

"Listen, Pat. I should have come to see you more in Baltimore, but those places freak me out and I . . . I . . . I just couldn't see you like that, okay? Are you mad at me?"

I am sort of still mad at Jake, but suddenly I remember another one of Danny's lines that is too appropriate to leave unsaid, so I say, "Got nothin' but love for ya."

Jake looks at me for a second as if I had punched him in the gut. He blinks a few times almost as if he is going to cry, and then he hugs me with both arms. "I'm sorry," he says, and holds me for longer than I like, which isn't very long—unless it's Nikki hugging me.

When he lets go, Jake says, "I got a present for you." He pulls an

Eagles jersey out of a plastic bag and tosses it to me. I hold it up and see it's number 84, which I recognize as a wide receiver's number, but I do not know the name. Isn't that young receiver Freddie Mitchell number 84? I think but do not say, because I don't want to insult my brother, who was nice enough to buy me a present.

"Who's Baskett?" I ask, which is the name on the jersey.

"Undrafted rookie sensation Hank Baskett? He's the preseason story. These jerseys are hot on the streets of Philadelphia. And now you have one to wear to the games this year."

"Wear to the games?"

"Now that you're home, you're gonna want your old seat back, right?"

"At the Vet?"

"The Vet?" Jake laughs and looks at my mother. My mother looks scared. "No—at Lincoln Financial Field."

"What's Lincoln Financial Field?"

"Didn't they let you watch TV in that place? It's the home of the Eagles, the stadium your team's played three seasons in now."

I know Jake is lying to me, but I don't say anything.

"Anyway, you got a seat right next to mine and Scott's. Season tickets, bro. Are you psyched, or what?"

"I don't have any money for season tickets," I say, because I let Nikki have the house and the cars and the bank accounts when apart time began.

"I got your back." Jake punches me in the arm. "I might not have been a good brother for the past few years, but I'm gonna make up for all that now that you're home."

I thank my brother, and then Mom starts crying again. She cries so hard that she has to leave the room, which is weird, since Jake and I are making up and season tickets to the Eagles are quite a nice present—not to mention the jersey.

"Put on your Baskett jersey, bro."

I put it on, and it feels good to be wearing Eagles green, especially a jersey that Jake picked out special for me.

"You wait and see how good your boy Baskett is going to be this year," Jake says in a strange way, as if my future were somehow linked to the Eagles' rookie wide receiver—Hank Baskett.

The Concrete Doughnut

I notice that my father waits until the game is just about to begin before he comes into the family room. It is only preseason, so we do not engage in any of the regular-season game-day rituals, but Dad has put on his number 5 McNabb jersey and now sits on the edge of the couch, ready to jump out of his seat. He nods at my brother solemnly but completely ignores me, even after I heard my mother say, "Please, just try to talk to Pat" when they were arguing in the kitchen. Mom puts the food on folding tables, takes a seat next to Jake, and we all start to eat.

The food is excellent, but I am the only one to say so. Mom seems happy to get the compliment, saying, "Are you sure it's all right?" like she does, because she is modest when it comes to cooking, even though she is a great cook.

"What do you think the Birds will do this year, Dad?" Jake asks.

"Eight and eight," my dad answers pessimistically, like he always does at the beginning of every NFL season.

"Eleven and five," my brother says, to which my father shakes his head and blows air through his teeth. "Eleven and five?" my brother asks me, and I nod because I am optimistic, and winning eleven games would most likely put the Eagles in the play-offs. Since we have season tickets, I know we are assured play-off tickets should the Birds earn a home game, and there's nothing better than an Eagles play-off game.

Now, I admit that I have not been keeping up with the Birds in the off-season, but when the starting lineups are announced, I am really surprised that many of my favorite players are no longer on the team. Duce Staley. Hugh Douglas. James Thrash. Corey Simon. All gone. I want to ask, "When? Why?" but don't, fearing my father and brother will think I am not a true fan anymore, which they said would happen when I first moved to Baltimore with Nikki and gave up my season ticket.

To my surprise, the Birds are also not playing in Veterans Stadium, but at Lincoln Financial Field, just like Jake had said. Somehow they have built an entire stadium since last season, and I must have missed all the hype because I was stuck in the bad place. Still, something does not really seem right to me.

"Where is Lincoln Financial Field?" I try to ask nonchalantly when the commercials come on after the first series.

My father turns his head and stares at me but does not answer my question. He hates me. He looks repulsed, like it is a chore to sit in the family room watching the game with his mentally messed-up son.

"It's in South Philadelphia, just like all the other stadiums," my brother says too quickly. "Good crabby snacks, Mom."

"Can you see Lincoln Financial Field from the Vet?" I ask.

"The Vet's gone," Jake says.

"Gone?" I ask. "What do you mean, *gone*?"

"March 21, 2004. Seven a.m. It fell like a house of cards," my father says without looking at me, just before sucking an orange piece of meat from a chicken bone. "Over two years ago."

"What? I was at the Vet just last . . ." I pause because I start to feel a little dizzy and nauseous. "What year did you just say?"

My father opens his mouth to speak, but my mother cuts him off, saying, "A lot has changed since you were away."

Still, I refuse to believe the Vet is gone, even after Jake retrieves his laptop from his car and shows me a downloaded video of the Vet being imploded. Veterans Stadium—which we used to call the concrete doughnut—falls like a circle of dominoes, gray dust fills the screen, and it breaks my heart to see that place crumble, even though I suspect that what I am viewing is a computer-generated trick.

When I was a boy, my father took me to many Phillies games at the Vet, and of course there were all of the Eagles games with Jake, so it is hard to believe such a big monument to my childhood could be destroyed while I was in the bad place. The video ends, and I ask my mother if I can talk to her in the other room.

"What's wrong?" she says when we reach the kitchen.

"Dr. Patel said that my new medication might make me hallucinate."

"Okay."

"I think I just saw Veterans Stadium demolished on Jake's computer."

"Honey, you did. It was demolished over two years ago."

"What year is it?"

She hesitates, and then says, "Two thousand and six."

That would make me thirty-four. Apart time would have been in progress for four years. Impossible, I think. "How do I know

I am not hallucinating right now? How do I know you're not a hallucination? You're all hallucinations! All of you!" I realize I am screaming, but I can't help it.

Mom shakes her head, tries to touch my cheek, but I swat her hand away and she starts crying again.

"How long was I in the bad place? How long? Tell me!"

"What's going on in there?" my father yells. "We're trying to watch the game!"

"Shhhh!" my mother says through tears.

"How long?" I yell.

"Tell him, Jeanie! Go ahead! He's going to find out sooner or later!" my father yells from the family room. "Tell him!"

I grab my mother's shoulders, shake her so her head wobbles all over, and yell, "How long?"

"Almost four years," Jake says. I look back over my shoulder, and my brother is in the kitchen doorway. "Now let go of Mom."

"Four years?" I laugh and let go of my mother's shoulders. She covers her mouth with her hands, and her eyes are full of pity and tears. "Why are you guys playing jokes on—"

I hear my mother scream, I feel the back of my head hit the refrigerator, and then my mind goes blank.

I Fear Him More Than Any Other Human Being

After I returned to New Jersey, I thought I was safe, because I did not think Kenny G *could* leave the bad place, which I realize is silly now—because Kenny G is extremely talented and resourceful and a powerful force to be reckoned with.

I have been sleeping in the attic because it is so ferociously hot up here. After my parents go to bed, I climb the stairs, turn off the ventilation fan, slip into my old winter sleeping bag, zipper it up so only my face is exposed, and then sweat away the pounds. Without the ventilation fan running, the temperature climbs quickly, and soon my sleeping bag is drenched with perspiration and I can feel myself getting thinner. I had done this for several nights, and nothing strange or unusual happened at all.

But in the attic tonight I'm sweating and sweating and sweating, and through the darkness, suddenly I hear the sexy synthesizer chords. I keep my eyes closed, hum a single note, and silently count to ten, knowing that I am only hallucinating like Dr. Patel said I might, but Kenny slaps me across the face, and when I open my eyes, there he is in my parents' attic, his curly mane of hair haloed like Jesus. The perfectly tanned forehead, that nose, that eternal five o'clock shadow and sharp jawline. The top three buttons of his shirt are undone so that you can see a little chest hair. Mr. G might not seem evil, but I fear him more than any other human being.

"How? How did you find me?" I ask him.

Kenny G winks at me and then puts his gleaming soprano sax to his lips.

I shiver, even though I am drenched in sweat. "Please," I beg him, "just leave me alone!"

But he takes a deep breath and his soprano sax starts to sing the bright notes of "Songbird"—and immediately I'm upright in my sleeping bag, repetitively slamming the heel of my right hand into the little white scar above my right eyebrow, trying to make the music stop—Kenny G's hips are swaying right before my eyes—with every brain jolt I'm yelling, "Stop! Stop! Stop! Stop!"—the end of his instrument is in my face, pounding me with smooth jazz—I feel the blood rushing up into my forehead—Kenny G's solo has reached a climax—bang, bang, bang, bang—

And then my mother and father are trying to restrain my arms, but I'm screaming, "Stop playing that song! Just stop! Please!"

When my mother gets knocked to the floor, my father kicks me hard in the stomach—which makes Kenny G vanish and kills the music—and when I fall back gasping for air, Dad jumps on my chest and punches me in the cheek, and suddenly my mom is trying to pull Dad off me and I'm sobbing like a baby; my mother is screaming at my father, telling him to stop hitting me, and then he's off me and she's telling me everything is going to be okay even after my father has punched me in the face as hard as he could.

"That's it, Jeanie. He's going back to that hospital in the morning. First thing," my father says, and then stomps down the stairs.

I can hardly think, I'm sobbing so loudly.

My mother sits down next to me and says, "It's okay, Pat. I'm here."

I put my head in my mother's lap and cry myself to sleep as Mom strokes my hair.

When I open my eyes, the ventilation fan is back on, sun is streaming through the screen in the nearest window, and Mom is still stroking my hair.

"How did you sleep?" she asks me, forcing a smile. Her eyes are red and her cheeks are streaked with tears.

For a second it feels nice to be lying next to my mom, the weight of her small hand on my head, her soft voice lingering in my ear, but soon the memory of what happened the night before forces me to sit up—and then my heart is pounding and a wave of dread courses through my limbs. "Don't send me back to the bad place. I'm sorry. I'm so sorry. Please," I beg her, pleading with everything I have, because that's how much I hate the bad place and pessimistic Dr. Timbers.

"You're staying right here with us," Mom says—looking me in the eyes like she does when she is telling the truth—and then she kisses me on the cheek.

We go down to the kitchen, where she cooks me some delicious eggs scrambled with cheese and tomatoes, and I actually swallow all of my pills because I feel I owe it to Mom after knocking her down and upsetting my father.

I am shocked when I look at the clock and see it is already 11:00 a.m. So I start my workout as soon as my plate is clean, double-timing everything just to keep up with my routine.

The Dress-up Dinner

Ronnie finally comes to visit me in my basement and says, "I'm on my way home, so I only have a few minutes."

As I finish my set of bench presses, I smirk because I know what that statement means. Veronica does not know he has come to see me, and Ronnie needs to keep it quick if he does not want to get caught doing something without Veronica's permission—something like saying hello to his best friend, whom he has not seen for a long time.

When I sit up, he says, "What happened to your face?"

I touch my forehead. "My hands slipped yesterday, and I dropped the bar on myself."

"And it made your cheek all puffy like that?"

I shrug because I do not really want to tell him my father punched me.

"Man, you really have trimmed down and bulked up. I like your gym," he says, eyeballing my weight bench and Stomach

Master 6000, and then he sticks out his hand. "Think I could come over and work out with you?"

I stand, shake his hand, and say, "Sure," knowing the question is only yet another one of Ronnie's false promises.

"Listen, I'm sorry I never came to see you when you were in Baltimore, but we had Emily, and well, you know how it is. But I felt like the letters kept us close. And now that you're home, we can hang out all the time, right?"

"As if—," I start to say, but then bite my tongue.

"As if—*what*?"

"Nothing."

"You still think Veronica hates you?"

I keep my mouth shut.

He smiles and says, "Well, if she hated you, would she be inviting you over for dinner tomorrow night?"

I look at Ronnie, trying to gauge whether he is serious or not.

"Veronica's making a big meal to welcome you home. So are you coming, or what?"

"Sure," I say, still not believing my ears, because Ronnie's promises usually do not come with specific words like "tomorrow" attached.

"Great. Be at my house at seven o'clock for drinks. Dinner's at eight, and it's going to be one of the wife's formal candlelit three-course meals, so wear something nice, okay? You know how Veronica is about her dress-up dinners," he says, and then hugs sweaty me, which I tolerate only because I am so shocked by Veronica's invitation. With a hand on my shoulder, Ronnie looks me in the eye and says, "Man, it's good to have you home, Pat."

As I watch him jog up the stairs, I think about how much trash Nikki and I would talk about Ronnie and Veronica if apart time were over and Nikki was going to the dress-up dinner with me.

"Dress-up dinner," Nikki would say. "Are we in elementary school?"

God, Nikki hates Veronica.

If I Backslide

Knowing that if I wear the wrong thing, Veronica will say I have ruined her night—the way she did that one time when I wore Bermuda shorts and sandals to a dress-up dinner—I can't stop thinking about what I am going to wear to her dinner party, so much that I don't even remember it's Friday, and therefore, time to see Dr. Patel, until Mom calls down in the middle of my workout, saying, "We're leaving in fifteen minutes. Hit the shower!"

In the cloud room, I pick the brown chair. We recline, and Cliff says, "Your mother tells me you've had quite a week. Want to talk about it?"

So I tell him about Veronica's dress-up party and how my old dress clothes don't fit because I have lost so much weight, and I have no swanky clothes other than the shirt my brother has recently given me, and I am pretty stressed out about going to a dinner party and wish I could just spend some time alone with Ronnie lifting weights, so that I would not have to see Veronica, who even Nikki says is a mean person.

Dr. Patel nods a few times like he does, and then says, "Do you like the new shirt your brother gave you? Do you feel comfortable wearing it?"

I tell him I absolutely love my new shirt.

"So wear that one to the dress-up dinner, and I'm sure Veronica will like it too."

"Are you sure?" I ask. "Because Veronica is really particular about what you should wear to dinner parties."

"I'm sure," he says, which makes me feel a whole lot better.

"What about pants?"

"What's wrong with the pants you have on now?"

I look down at the tan khakis my mom purchased for me at the Gap the other day because she says I shouldn't wear sweatpants to my doctor's appointments, and even though the pants are not as swanky as my new Eagles jersey, they do look okay, so I shrug and stop worrying about what to wear to Veronica's dinner party.

Cliff tries to get me to talk about Kenny G, but I only close my eyes, hum a single note, and silently count to ten every time he says Mr. G's name.

Then Cliff says he knows that I have been rough with my mother, shaking her in the kitchen and knocking her down in the attic, which makes me really sad because I love my mom so much and she rescued me from the bad place and has even signed all those legal documents—and yet I cannot rightly deny what Cliff has said. My chest heats up with guilt until I can't take it. Truth be told, I break down and cry—sobbing—for at least five minutes.

"Your mother is risking a lot, because she believes in you."

His words make me cry even harder.

"You want to be a good person, don't you, Pat?"

I nod. I cry. I do want to be a good person. I really do.

"I'm going to up your meds," Dr. Patel tells me. "You might feel a little sluggish, but it should help to curb your violent outbursts. You need to know it's your actions that will make you a good person, not desire. And if you have any more episodes, I might have to recommend that you go back to the neural health facility for more intensive treatments, which—"

"No. Please. I'll be good," I say quickly, knowing that Nikki is less likely to return if I backslide into the bad place. "Trust me."

"I do," Dr. Patel replies with a smile.

I Don't Know How This Works

After some more lifting in the basement, I put on my trash bag and run my ten miles. Afterward, I shower, spray some of my father's cologne, and walk into the mist—just like Mom taught me to do back in high school. I roll on some underarm deodorant and then don my new khakis and my Hank Baskett jersey.

When I ask my mother how I look, she says, "Very handsome. *So handsome*. But do you really think you should wear your Eagles jersey to a dinner party? You can wear one of the Gap shirts I bought you, or you can borrow one of your father's polo shirts."

"It's okay," I say, and smile confidently. "Dr. Patel said wearing this shirt was a good idea."

"Did he?" my mom says with a laugh, and then she removes an arrangement of flowers and a bottle of white wine from the refrigerator.

"What's this?"

"Give these to Veronica and tell her I said thanks. Ronnie's been a good friend to you." And then Mom looks like she is going to cry again.

I kiss her goodbye, and with my hands full of flowers and wine, I walk down the street and across Knight's Park to Ronnie's house.

Ronnie answers the door wearing a shirt and tie, which makes me feel like Dr. Patel was wrong after all and I am underdressed. But Ronnie looks at my new jersey, checks the name on the back—probably to make sure I am not wearing an outdated Freddie Mitchell jersey—and says, "Hank Baskett is the man! Where did you get that jersey this early in the season? It's great!" which makes me feel so much better.

We follow the meaty aroma through their swanky living room and their swanky dining room to the kitchen, where Veronica is feeding Emily, whom I am surprised to see looking much older than a newborn baby.

"Hank Baskett's in the house," Ronnie says.

"Who?" Veronica answers, but she smiles when she sees the flowers and the wine. *"Pour moi?"*

She stares at my puffy cheek for a second, but doesn't mention it, which I appreciate. I hand her what my mother has sent, and Veronica kisses me on my un-puffy cheek.

"Welcome home, Pat," she says, which surprises me because she sounds sincere. "I hope you don't mind, but I've invited someone else to dinner," Veronica adds. She winks at me and then lifts the lid off the single pot on the stove, releasing a warm tomato and basil aroma.

"Who?" I ask.

"You'll see," she says without looking up from stirring her sauce.

Before I can say more, Ronnie is lifting Emily from her high chair, saying, "Meet Uncle Pat," which sounds strange until I realize he is talking about me. "Say hello to Uncle Pat, Emily."

She waves her little hand at me, and then I have Emily in my arms. Her dark eyes examine my face, and she smiles as though she approves. "Pap," she says, pointing at my nose.

"See how smart my girl is, Uncle Pat," Ronnie says, petting the silky black hair on Emily's head. "She already knows your name."

Emily smells like the mashed carrots that coat her cheeks until Ronnie wipes them clean with a wet napkin. I have to admit that Emily is a cute kid, and I instantly understand why Ronnie has written me so many letters about his daughter—why he loves her so much. I start to think about having children with Nikki someday and I become so happy that I give little Emily a kiss on the forehead, as if she were Nikki's baby and I was her father. And then I kiss Emily's forehead again and again, until she giggles.

"Beer?" Ronnie says.

"I'm not really supposed to drink, because I'm on medications and—"

"Beer," Ronnie says, and then we are drinking beers on his deck as Emily sits in her father's lap and sucks on a bottle filled with watered-down apple juice.

"It's good to have a beer with you," Ronnie says, just before clinking his Yuengling Lager bottle against mine.

"Who's coming over for dinner?"

"Veronica's sister, Tiffany."

"Tiffany and Tommy?" I say, remembering Tiffany's husband from Ronnie and Veronica's wedding.

"Just Tiffany."

"Where's Tommy?"

Ronnie takes a long swig of his beer, looks up at the setting sun, and says, "Tommy died some time ago."

"What?" I say, because I hadn't heard. "God, I'm sorry to hear that."

"Just make sure you don't bring up Tommy tonight, okay?"

"Sure," I say, and then drink a few large gulps of my beer. "So how did he die?"

"How did *who* die?" says a woman's voice.

"Hi, Tiffany," Ronnie says, and suddenly she is standing with us on the porch. Tiffany's wearing a black evening dress, heels, and a diamond necklace, and her makeup and hair look too perfect to me—as if she is trying too hard to look attractive, like old ladies sometimes do. "You remember Pat, right?"

I stand, and as we shake hands, the way Tiffany looks into my eyes makes me feel really funny.

We move back into the house, and after some small talk, Tiffany and I are left alone on opposite ends of the living-room couch as Veronica finishes cooking the meal and Ronnie puts Emily to bed.

"You look very pretty tonight," I say when the silence grows awkward.

Before apart time began, I never ever complimented Nikki on her looks, and I think this really hurt her self-esteem. I figure I can now practice complimenting women on their looks so it will come naturally to me when Nikki returns, although Tiffany really does look pretty, even if she is trying too hard with the makeup. She is a few years older than me, but has a fit body and long, silky black hair.

"What happened to your cheek?" Tiffany asks without looking at me.

"Weight-lifting accident."

She just stares at her hands, which are folded in her lap. Her nails have been recently painted a blood red.

"So where are you working now?" I say, thinking this is a safe question.

Her nose crinkles, as if I had farted. "I got fired from my job a few months ago."

"Why?"

"Does it really matter?" she says, then stands and walks into the kitchen.

I down the remainder of my second beer and wait for Ronnie to come back.

Dinner is elegant, with candles going and fancy plates and special silverware, but awkward, as Tiffany and I are completely silent while Veronica and Ronnie talk about us as if we aren't there.

"Pat is a big history buff. He knows everything about every single U.S. president. Go ahead. Ask him anything," Ronnie says.

When Tiffany fails to look up from her food, Veronica says, "My sister is a modern dancer and has a recital in two months. You should see her dance, Pat. So beautiful. My God, I wish I could dance like my sister. If she allows us this year, we're all going to her recital, and you should definitely come with us."

I nod carefully when Tiffany looks up for my response, thinking I'll go just so I can practice being kind. Also, Nikki would probably want to go to a dance recital, and I want to do the things Nikki likes from now on.

"Pat and I are going to work out together," Ronnie says. "Look how fit my buddy is. He puts me to shame. I need to get in that basement with you, Pat."

"Tiffany loves the shore, don't you, Tiff? The four of us should take Emily to the beach one weekend in September after the crowds have left. We could have a picnic. Do you like picnics, Pat? Tiffany loves picnics. Don't you, Tiff?"

Ronnie and Veronica trade facts about their guests for almost fifteen minutes straight, and then finally there's a lull, so I ask if any of them knows anything about the Vet being imploded, and to my surprise Ronnie and Veronica both confirm that it was demolished years ago, just like my father said, which worries me tremendously because I have no memory of this or the years that have supposedly transpired since. I think about asking how long ago Emily was born, because I remember getting a letter and picture from Ronnie soon after her birth, but I get scared and do not ask.

"I hate football," Tiffany offers. "More than anything in the world."

And then we all eat without saying anything for a while.

The three courses Ronnie had promised turn out to be beer, lasagna garnished with baked asparagus, and key lime pie. All three are great, and I tell Veronica as much—practicing again for when Nikki comes back—to which Veronica replies, "Did you think my food would be bad?"

I know she means it as a joke, but Nikki would have used the question to prove just how witchy Veronica can be. I think about how if Nikki were here, after we went home, we'd stay up talking in bed like we used to when we were both a little drunk—and sitting now at Ronnie's dinner table, the thought makes me feel sad and happy at the same time.

When we finish our pie, Tiffany stands and says, "I'm tired."

"But we've hardly finished eating," Veronica says, "and we have Trivial Pursuit to—"

"I said I'm tired."

There is a silence.

"Well," Tiffany finally says, "are you going to walk me home or what?"

It takes me a second to realize that Tiffany is talking to me, but I quickly say, "Sure."

Since I am practicing being kind now, what else could I have said—*right?*

It is a warm night, but not too sticky. Tiffany and I walk a block before I ask where she lives.

"With my parents, okay?" she says without looking at me.

"Oh." I realize we are only about four blocks from Mr. and Mrs. Webster's house.

"You live with your parents too, right?"

"Yeah."

"So no big whoop."

It is dark, and I guess it's about 9:30 p.m. With her arms crossing her chest, Tiffany walks pretty quickly in her clicky heels, and soon we are standing in front of her parents' house.

When she turns to face me, I think she is simply going to say good night, but she says, "Look, I haven't dated since college, so I don't know how this works."

"How what works?"

"I've seen the way you've been looking at me. Don't bullshit me, Pat. I live in the addition around back, which is completely separate from the house, so there's no chance of my parents walking in on us. I hate the fact that you wore a football jersey to dinner, but you can fuck me as long as we turn the lights out first. Okay?"

I'm too shocked to speak, and for a long time we just stand there.

"Or not," Tiffany adds just before she starts crying.

I'm so confused that I'm speaking and thinking and worrying all at the same time, not really knowing what to do or say. "Look, I enjoyed spending time with you, and I think you're really pretty, but I'm married," I say, and lift up my wedding ring as proof.

"So am I," she says, and holds up the diamond on her left hand.

I remember what Ronnie told me about her husband having passed away, which makes her a widow and not married, but I do not say anything about that, because I am practicing being kind instead of right, which I learned in therapy and Nikki will like.

It makes me really sad to see that Tiffany is still wearing her wedding ring.

And then suddenly Tiffany is hugging me so that her face is between my pecs, and she's crying her makeup onto my new Hank Baskett jersey. I don't like to be touched by anyone except Nikki, and I really do not want Tiffany to get makeup on the jersey my brother was nice enough to give me—a jersey with real stitched-on letters and numbers—but I surprise myself by hugging Tiffany back. I rest my chin on top of her shiny black hair, scent her perfume, and suddenly I am crying too, which scares me a lot. Our bodies shudder together, and we are all waterworks. We cry together for at least ten minutes, and then she lets go and runs around to the back of her parents' house.

When I arrive home, my father is watching television. The Eagles are playing the Jets in a preseason game I did not know was on. He does not even look at me, probably because I am such a lousy Eagles fan now. My mother tells me that Ronnie called, saying it's important and I should call him back immediately.

"What happened? What's on your jersey? *Is that makeup?*" my mother asks, and when I do not answer, she says, "You better call Ronnie back."

But I only lie down in my bed and stare at the ceiling of my bedroom until the sun comes up.

Filled with Molten Lava

The picture I have of Nikki is a head shot, and I wish I had told her how much I liked it.

She paid a professional photographer to take the photo, and she actually had her hair and makeup done at the local salon before going to the shoot; plus she also went to the tanning booths the week before the picture was taken, since my birthday is in late December and the picture was my twenty-eighth-birthday present.

Nikki's head is turned so you see more of her left cheek than you do her right, which is outlined by her strawberry blond curly hair. You can see her left ear, and she is wearing the dangling diamond earrings I gave her for our first wedding anniversary. She had gone to the tanning booths just to bring out the freckles on her nose, which I love and miss every winter. You can see the little freckles clearly in the shot, and Nikki said this was the main idea and she even told the photographer to make the freckles the focal point because I love her seasonal freckles best. Her face is sort of like an upside-down triangle, as her chin is sort of pointy. Her nose is like the nose of a lioness, long and regal-looking, and her eyes are the color of grass. In the picture she is making that pouting face I love—not quite a smile, not quite a smirk—and her lips are so glossy that I can't resist kissing the picture every time I look at it.

So I kiss the picture again, feeling the cold flatness of the glass, leaving a kiss-shaped smudge, which I wipe away with my shirt.

"God, I miss you so much, Nikki," I say, but the picture is silent, like always. "I'm sorry that I did not originally like this picture, because you would not believe how much I like it now. I know that I told you this was not such a great present, back before I started practicing being kind rather than right. Yes, I had specifically asked for a new barbecue, but I'm glad that I have the picture now, because it helped me get through all that time in the bad place and made me want to be a better person, and I'm changed now, so I not only realize but *appreciate* that you put a lot of thought and effort into this present. It's the only likeness I have of you since some bad person stole all the pictures of us that were in my mother's house—because the pictures were in expensive frames, and—"

Suddenly, for some reason, I remember that there's a video of our wedding, and in this video Nikki is walking and dancing and speaking, and there's even this one part where Nikki talks directly into the camera as if she were talking to me, and she says, "I love you, Pat Peoples, you sexy stud muffin," which made me laugh so hard the first time we watched the video with her parents.

I knock on my parents' bedroom door, and then I knock again.

"Pat?" my mom says.

"I have to work in the morning, you know?" my father says, but I ignore him.

"Mom?" I say to the door.

"What is it?"

"Where's my wedding video?"

There is a silence.

"You remember my wedding video, right?"

Still, she does not say anything.

"Is it in the cardboard box in the family-room closet with all the other videos?"

Through the door I hear her and my father whispering, and then my mother says, "I think we gave you our copy of the video, honey. It must be in your old house. Sorry."

"What? No, it's downstairs in the family-room closet. Never mind, I'll find it myself. Good night," I say, but when I get to the family-room closet and go through the box of videos, it's not there. I turn around and see that my mother has followed me down into the family room. She is in her nightgown. She is biting her nails. "Where is it?"

"We gave it to—"

"Don't lie to me!"

"We must have misplaced it, but it's sure to turn up sooner or later."

"Misplaced it? It's irreplaceable!" It's just a videocassette, but I can't help feeling angry, which I realize is one of my problems. "How could you lose it when you know how important it is to me? How?"

"Calm down, Pat." My mother raises her palms so they are both in front of her chest and then takes a careful step toward me, as if she is trying to sneak up on a rabid dog. "Relax, Pat. Just relax."

But I can feel myself getting more and more angry, so before I say or do anything dumb, I remember that I am close to being sent back to the bad place, where Nikki will never find me. I storm past my mother, go down into the basement, and do five hundred sit-ups on the Stomach Master 6000. When I finish, I am still angry, so I ride the stationary bike for forty-five minutes and then do shots of water until I feel hydrated enough to attempt five hundred push-ups. Only when my pecs feel like they are filled with molten lava do I deem myself calm enough to sleep.

When I go upstairs, all is quiet and no light is leaking out from under my parents' bedroom door, so I grab my framed picture of Nikki, take her upstairs to the attic, turn off the ventilation fan, slip into my sleeping bag, set up Nikki next to my head, kiss her good night—and then begin to sweat away some more pounds.

I haven't been up in the attic since the last time Kenny G visited me. I am afraid he will come back, but I also feel sort of fat. I close my eyes, hum a single note, silently count to ten over and over again, and the next morning I wake up unscathed.

Failing Like Dimmesdale Did

Maybe Puritans were simply dumber than modern people, but I cannot believe how long it took those seventeenth-century Bostonians to figure out that their spiritual leader knocked up the local hussy. I had the mystery solved in chapter eight, when Hester turns to Dimmesdale and says, "Speak thou for me!" I know we were assigned Hawthorne's *The Scarlet Letter* back in high school, and if I had known the book was filled with so much sex and espionage, I might have read it when I was sixteen. God, I can't wait to ask Nikki if she hypes up the racy stuff in her class, because I know teenagers would actually read the book if she did.

I didn't care much for Dimmesdale, because he had such a great woman and he denied himself a life with her. Now, I understand that it would not have been easy for him to explain how he knocked up another man's teenage wife, especially since he was a man of the cloth, but if there's one theme Hawthorne hammers home, it's that time heals all wounds, which Dimmesdale learns, but too late. Plus, I'm thinking God would have wanted Pearl to have had a father, and probably counted Dimmesdale's disregard for his daughter as a greater sin than having sex with another man's wife.

Now, I sympathize with Chillingworth—*a lot*. I mean, he sends his young bride over to the New World, trying to give her a better life, and she ends up pregnant by another man, which is the ultimate slap in the face, right? But he was so old and nasty and really had no business marrying a young girl anyway. When he began to psychologically torture Dimmesdale, giving him all those strange roots and herbs, Chillingworth reminded me of Dr. Timbers and his staff. I realized then that Chillingworth was not ever going to practice being kind, so I gave up hope for him.

But I absolutely loved Hester, because she believed in silver linings. Even when that nasty throng of bearded men in hats and fat women were against her, saying she should be branded on the forehead even, she stuck to her guns and sewed and helped people when she could and tried her best to raise her daughter—even when Pearl proved to be somewhat of a demonic child.

Even though Hester did not get to be with Dimmesdale in the end—which is a flaw, if you ask me—I felt like she lived a fulfilled life and got to see her daughter grow up and marry well, which was kind of nice.

But I did realize that no one really appreciated Hester for who she was until it was too late. When she needed help most, she was abandoned—and only when she offered help to others was she beloved. This sort of suggests that it is important to appreciate the good women in your life before it is too late, which is a pretty good message to give high school kids. I wish my high school teacher had taught me that lesson, because I certainly would have treated Nikki differently when we were first married. Then again, maybe this is the sort of thing you have to learn by living your life—failing like Dimmesdale did, and I guess like I did too.

That scene when Dimmesdale and Hester finally stand together in town for the first time made me wish apart time was over already so I could stand with Nikki in some public place and apologize for being such a jerk in the past. Then I would tell her my thoughts about Hawthorne's classic, which would make her happy for sure. God, she is going to be so impressed that I actually read a book written in old-fashioned English.

Do You Like Foreign Films?

Cliff asks about Veronica's dinner party in a way that lets me know my mother has already discussed it with him—probably in an effort to get me to wear the collared shirts she bought me at the Gap, which Mom loves and I do not love. As soon as I sit down in the brown recliner, Cliff broaches the subject, pinching his chin the way he does every time he asks me a question my mother has already answered.

Even though I now recognize Cliff's tell, I am excited to let him know he was right about wearing the shirt my brother had given me. Surprisingly, he does not want to talk about what clothes I wore; he wants to talk about Tiffany, and he keeps asking what I thought about her, how she made me feel, and if I enjoyed her company.

At first I am polite and answer by saying that Tiffany was nice and well dressed and had a pretty good body, but Cliff keeps pushing for the truth like therapists do, because they all have some sort of psychic ability that allows them to see through your lies, and therefore they know you will eventually tire of the talking game and will offer up the truth.

Finally I say, "Well, the thing is—and I don't like saying this—but Tiffany is kind of slutty."

"What do you mean?" Cliff asks me.

"I mean she's sort of a whore."

Cliff sits forward a little. He looks surprised, and uncomfortable enough to make me feel uncomfortable. "On what do you base your observation? Did she dress provocatively?"

"No. I told you already. She wore a nice dress. But as soon as we finished our dessert, she asked me to walk her home."

"What's wrong with that?"

"Nothing. But at the end of the walk she asked me to have sexual intercourse with her, and not in those words."

Cliff removes his fingers from his chin, sits back, and says, "Oh."

"I know. It shocked me too, especially because she knows I'm married."

"So did you?"

"Did I what?"

"Have sexual intercourse with Tiffany?"

At first Cliff's words don't register, but when they do, I become angry. "No!"

"Why not?"

I cannot believe Cliff has actually asked me such a question, especially since he is a happily married man himself, but I dignify the inquiry with an answer anyway. "Because I love my wife! That's why!"

"That's what I thought," he says, which makes me feel a little better. He is only testing my morals, which is perfectly understandable, because people outside of mental institutions need to have good morals so that the world will continue to work without any major interruptions—and happy endings will flourish.

Then I say, "I don't even know why Tiffany would ask me to have sex with her anyway. I mean, I'm not even an attractive guy; she's pretty and could do a lot better than me for sure. So I'm thinking now that maybe she's a nymphomaniac. What do you think?"

"I don't know whether she is a nymphomaniac or not," he says. "But I do know that sometimes people say and do what they think others want them to. Maybe Tiffany really did not want to have sex with you, but only offered something she thought you would find valuable, so you would value her."

I think about his explanation for a second and then say, "So you're saying that Tiffany thought *I* wanted to have sex with *her*?"

"Not necessarily." He grabs his chin again. "Your mother told me you came home with makeup on your shirt. Do you mind if I ask how that happened?"

Reluctantly, because I don't like to gossip, I tell him about Tiffany's wearing her wedding ring even after her husband died, and the hugging and the crying we did in front of her parents' house.

Cliff nods and says, "It seems like Tiffany really needs a friend, and that she thought having sex with you would make you want to be her friend. But tell me again how you handled the situation."

So I tell him exactly what led us to the hug and how I let her get makeup on my Hank Baskett jersey and—

"Where did you get a Hank Baskett jersey?" he asks me.

"I told you. My brother gave it to me."

"That's what you wore to the dinner party?"

"Yeah, just like you told me to."

He smiles and even chuckles, which surprises me. Then he adds, "What did your friends say?"

"Ronnie said that Hank Baskett is the man."

"Hank Baskett *is* the man. I bet he catches at least seven touchdowns this season."

"Cliff, you're an Eagles fan?"

He does the Eagles chant—"E!-A!-G!-L!-E!-S! EAGLES!"—which makes me laugh because he is my therapist and I did not know therapists could like NFL football.

"Well, now that I know you too bleed green, we'll have to talk Birds off the clock," Cliff says. "So you really let Tiffany cry her makeup onto your brand-new Hank Baskett jersey?"

"Yeah, and it's one with stitched-on numbers, not the cheap iron-ons."

"*Authentic* Hank Baskett jersey!" he says. "That was certainly very kind of you, Pat. It sounds like Tiffany only really needed a hug, which you gave her because you are a nice guy."

I can't help smiling, because I really am trying hard to be a nice guy. "Yeah, I know, but now she's always following me all over town."

"What do you mean?"

So I tell Cliff that since the dinner party, whenever I put on a trash bag and leave my house for a run, Tiffany is always waiting outside in her little running outfit and pink headband. "Very politely, I told her that I do not like running with other people and asked her to leave me alone, but she ignored my request and simply jogged five feet behind me for my entire run. The next day, she did the same thing, and she keeps on doing it. Somehow she's figured out my schedule, and she's always there when I leave my house an hour before sunset—ready to shadow me wherever

I jog. I run fast, and she stays with me. I run on dangerous streets, and she follows. She never tires out either—and just keeps running down the street when I finally stop in front of my house. She doesn't even say hello or goodbye."

"Why don't you want her to follow you?" Cliff asks.

So I ask him how his wife, Sonja, would feel if some hot woman shadowed him every time he went for a run.

He smiles the way guys do when they are alone and talking about women in a sexual way, and then he says, "So you think Tiffany is hot?" This surprises me because I did not know therapists were allowed to talk like guys do when they are buddies, and I wonder if this means that Cliff thinks of me as his buddy now.

"Sure, she's hot," I say. "But I'm married."

He grabs his chin and says, "How long has it been since you've seen Nikki?"

I tell him I don't know. "Maybe a couple of months," I say.

"Do you really believe that?" he asks, grabbing his chin again.

When I say I do, I hear the yelling in my voice and even allow the f-word to slip out. Immediately I feel bad because Cliff was talking to me like a friend, and sane people should not yell and curse at their buddies.

"I'm sorry," I say when Cliff starts to look scared.

"It's okay," he says, and forces a smile. "I should believe that you really mean what you tell me." He scratches his head for a second and then says, "My wife loves foreign films. Do you like foreign films?"

"With subtitles?"

"Yes."

"I hate those types of films."

"Me too," Cliff says. "Mostly because—"

"No happy endings."

"Exactly," Cliff says, pointing a brown finger at my face. "So depressing most of the time."

I nod wholeheartedly in agreement, even though I haven't been to see any movies for a long time, and won't until Nikki returns, because I am now watching the movie of my life as I live it.

"My wife used to beg me to take her to see these foreign films with subtitles all the time," Cliff says. "It seemed like every day she would ask me if we might go to see a foreign film, until I broke down and started taking her. Every Wednesday night we'd go to the Ritz movie theater and see some depressing movie. And you know what?"

"What?"

"After a year we simply stopped going."

"Why?"

"She stopped asking."

"Why?"

"I don't know. But maybe if you take an interest in Tiffany, ask her to run with you and maybe to go out to dinner a few times—maybe after a few weeks, she will grow tired of the chase and leave you alone. Let her get what she wants, and maybe she will not want it anymore. Understand?"

I do understand, but cannot help asking, "Do you think that will really work?"

And Cliff shrugs in a way that makes me believe it will.

I Can Share Raisin Bran

On the drive home from Cliff's office I ask my mom if she thinks asking Tiffany on a date is the best way to get rid of her once and for all, and Mom says, "You shouldn't be trying to get rid of anyone. You need friends, Pat. Everyone does."

I don't say anything in response. I'm afraid Mom is rooting for me to fall in love with Tiffany, because whenever she calls Tiffany my "friend," she says the word with a smile on her face and a hopeful look in her eye, which bothers me tremendously because Mom is the only person in my family who does not hate Nikki. Also, I know Mom looks out the window when I go on my runs, because she will tease me, saying "I see your *friend* showed up again" when I return from a jog.

Mom pulls into the driveway, shuts off the car engine, and says, "I can loan you money should you ever want to take your *friend* to dinner," and again, the way she says "friend" makes me feel tingly in a bad way. I say nothing in response, and my mother does the strangest thing—she giggles.

I finish my weight training for the day and put on a trash bag, and as I begin stretching on the front lawn, I see that Tiffany is jogging up and down the length of my parents' block, waiting for me to begin running. I tell myself to ask her out to dinner so I can end this madness and get back to being alone on my runs, but instead I simply start running, and Tiffany follows.

I go past the high school, down Collings Avenue to the Black Horse Pike, make a left and then another left into Oaklyn, run down Kendall Boulevard to the Oaklyn Public School, up past the Manor Bar to the White Horse Pike, make a right and then a left onto Cuthbert, and I run into Westmont. When I get to the Crystal Lake Diner, I turn and jog in place. Tiffany jogs in place and stares at her feet.

"Hey," I say to her. "You want to have dinner with me at this diner?"

"Tonight?" she says without looking up at me.

"Yeah."

"What time?"

"We have to walk here because I'm not allowed to drive."

"What time?"

"I'll be in front of your house at seven-thirty."

Next, the most amazing thing happens: Tiffany simply jogs away from me, and I cannot believe I finally got her to leave me alone. I am so happy I alter my route and run at least fifteen miles instead of ten, and when the sun sets, the clouds in the west are all lined with electricity, which I know is a good omen.

At home, I tell my mother I need some money so I can take Tiffany out to dinner. My mother tries to hide her smile as she retrieves her purse from the kitchen table. "Where are you taking her?"

"The Crystal Lake Diner."

"You shouldn't need more than forty dollars then, right?"

"I guess."

"It'll be on the counter when you come down."

I shower, apply underarm deodorant, use my father's cologne, and put on my khakis and the dark green button-down shirt Mom bought me at the Gap just yesterday. For some reason, my mother is systematically buying an entire wardrobe for me—and every piece is from the Gap. When I go downstairs, my mom tells me I need to tuck in my shirt and wear a belt.

"Why?" I ask, because I do not really care if I look respectable or not. I only want to get rid of Tiffany once and for all.

But when Mom says, "Please," I remember that I am trying to be kind instead of right—and I also owe Mom because she rescued me from the bad place—so I go upstairs and put on the brown leather belt she purchased for me earlier in the week.

Mom comes into my room with a shoe box and says, "Put on some dress socks and try these on." I open the box, and these swanky-looking brown leather loafers are inside. "Jake said these are what men your age wear casually," Mom says. When I slip the loafers on and look in the mirror, I see how thin my waistline appears, and I think I look almost as swanky as my little brother.

With forty bucks in my pocket, I walk across Knight's Park to Tiffany's parents' house. She is outside, waiting for me on the sidewalk, but I see her mother peeking out the window. Mrs. Webster ducks behind the blinds when we make eye contact. Tiffany does not say hello, but begins walking before I can stop. She is wearing a pink knee-length skirt and a black summer sweater. Her platform sandals make her look taller, and her hair is sort of puffed out around the ears, hanging down to her shoulders. Her eyeliner is a little heavy, and her lips are so pink, but I have to admit she looks great, which I tell her, saying, "Wow, you look really nice tonight."

"I like your shoes," she says in response, and then we walk for thirty minutes without saying another word.

We get a booth at the diner, and the server gives us glasses of water. Tiffany orders tea, and I say that water is fine for me. As I read the menu, I worry that I won't have enough money, which is silly, I know, because I have two twenties on me and most of the entrées are under ten bucks, but I do not know what Tiffany will order, and maybe she will want dessert, and then there's the tip.

Nikki taught me to overtip; she says waitresses work too hard for such a little bit of money. Nikki knows this because she was a waitress all through college—when we were at La Salle—so I always overtip when I go out to eat now, just to make up for the times in the past when I fought with Nikki over a few dollars, saying fifteen percent was more than enough, because no one tipped me regardless of whether I did my job well or not. Now I am a believer in overtipping, because I am practicing being kind rather than right—and as I am reading the diner menu, I think, What if I do not have enough money left over for a generous tip?

I am worrying about all of this so much that I must have missed Tiffany's order, because suddenly the waitress is saying, "Sir?"

When I put my menu down, both Tiffany and the waitress are staring at me, as if they are concerned. So I say, "Raisin bran," because I remember reading that cereal is only $2.25.

"Milk?"

"How much is milk?"

"Seventy-five cents."

I figure I can afford it, so I say, "Please," and then hand my menu back to the waitress.

"That's it?"

I nod, and the waitress sighs audibly before leaving us alone.

"What did you order? I didn't catch it," I say to Tiffany, trying to sound polite but secretly worrying that I will not have enough money left over for a good tip.

"Just tea," she says, and then we both look out the window at the cars in the parking lot.

When the raisin bran comes, I open the little single-serving box and pour the cereal into the bowl the diner provides free of charge. The milk comes in a miniature pitcher; I pour it over the brown flakes and sugared raisins. I push the bowl to the middle of the table and ask Tiffany if she would like to help me eat the cereal. "Are you sure?" she says, and when I nod, she picks up her spoon and we eat.

When we get the bill, it is for $4.59. I hand our waitress the two twenties, and the woman laughs, shakes her head, and says, "Change?" When I say, "No, thank you"—thinking Nikki would want me to overtip—the waitress says to Tiffany, "Honey, I had him all wrong. You two come back real soon. Okay?" And I can tell the woman is satisfied with her tip because she sort of skips her way to the register.

Tiffany doesn't say anything on the walk home, so I don't either. When we get to her house, I tell her I had a great time. "Thanks," I say, and then offer a handshake, just so Tiffany will not get the wrong idea.

She looks at my hand and then up at me, but she doesn't shake. For a second I think she is going to start crying again, but instead she says, "Remember when I said you could fuck me?"

I nod slowly because I wish I did not remember it so vividly.

"I don't want you to fuck me, Pat. Okay?"

"Okay," I say.

She walks around her parents' house, and then I am alone again.

When I arrive home, my mom excitedly asks me what we had for dinner, and when I tell her raisin bran, she laughs and says, "Really, what did you have?" I ignore her, go to my room, and lock the door.

Lying down on my bed, I pick up the picture of Nikki and tell her all about my date and how I gave the waitress a nice tip and how sad Tiffany seems and how much I can't wait for apart time to end so Nikki and I can share raisin bran at some diner and walk through the cool early September air—and then I am crying again.

I bury my face and sob into my pillow so my parents will not hear.

Sing and Spell and Chant

I get up at 4:30 a.m. and start lifting so I will be done with my workout by kickoff, and when I finally come up from the basement, the house smells like crabby snacks, three-meats pizza, and buffalo wings. "Smells good," I say to my mom while I put on my trash bag, and then I'm out the door for a ten-mile run.

I am shocked to see that Tiffany is jogging up and down the block, because she did not run behind me yesterday, and also, I am running in the a.m., which is not my regular time to run.

I jog toward Knight's Park, and when I look over my shoulder, I see she's following me again. "How did you know that I would be running early?" I say, but she keeps her head down and only follows silently.

We run our ten miles, and when I return to my house, Tiffany runs on without saying anything, as if we had never even eaten raisin bran together at the diner and nothing has changed.

I see my brother's silver BMW parked in front of my parents' house, so I sneak in the back door, run up the stairs, and jump into the shower. When I finish showering, I put on my Hank Baskett jersey—which my mother has laundered, getting the makeup off the numbers—and then follow the sound of the pregame show to the family room, ready to root on the Birds.

My best friend, Ronnie, is seated next to my brother, which surprises me. Both of them are wearing green away jerseys with the number 18 and the name Stallworth on the back—Ronnie's is a cheap replica jersey with iron-on numbers, but Jake's is authentic. Dad is in his chair, wearing his number 5 McNabb replica jersey.

When I say, "Go Birds!" my brother stands, turns to face me, puts both hands in the air, and says "Ahhhhhhhhhhhhh!" until Ronnie and my dad also stand, face me, raise their hands in the air, and say "Ahhhhhhhhhhhhhhh!" When I raise my hands in the air and say "Ahhhhhhhhhhhhh!" all four of us do the chant, rapidly spelling the letters with our arms and bodies—"E!-A!-G!-L!-E!-S! EAGLES!"—shooting out two arms and a leg to make an E, touching our fingertips high above our heads to make an A, and so forth.

When we finish, my brother makes his way around the couch, puts an arm around my shoulders, and starts to sing the fight song, which I remember and sing with him. "Fly, Eagles, fly! On the road to victory!" I'm so happy to be singing with my brother I do not even get mad at him for putting his arm around me. We walk around the couch as we sing, "Fight, Eagles, fight! Score a touchdown, one, two, three!" I look at my dad, and he does not look away, but only starts singing with more enthusiasm. Ronnie throws his arm around me, and then I am in between my brother and my best friend. "Hit 'em low. Hit 'em high. And watch our Eagles fly!" I see that my mom has come in to watch, and she has her hand over her mouth again like she does whenever she is about to laugh or cry—her eyes look happy, so I know she is laughing under her hands. "Fly, Eagles, fly! On the road to victory!" And then Ronnie and Jake remove their arms from my neck so they can make the letters again with their bodies. "E!-A!-G!-L!-E!-S! EAGLES!" We're all red-faced, and my father is breathing heavy, but everyone is so happy, and for the first time I really feel like I am home.

My mom sets up the food on TV trays, and the game begins. "I'm not supposed to drink," I say when Mom distributes the bottles of Budweiser, but my father says, "You can drink beer during Eagles games." Mom shrugs and smiles as she hands me a cold beer. I ask my brother and Ronnie why they aren't also wearing Baskett jerseys, since Baskett is the man, and they tell me the Eagles were able to trade for Donté Stallworth, and that *Donté Stallworth* is now the man. Because I am wearing my Baskett jersey, I insist that Baskett is the man, to which my father blows air through his teeth, and my cocky brother says, "We'll see soon," which is a weird thing for him to say, considering he was the one who gave me the Baskett jersey in the first place and just two weeks ago assured me that Baskett was really the man.

My mother watches the game nervously, like she always does, because she knows that if the Eagles lose, my father will be in a bad mood for an entire week and will yell at her a lot. Ronnie and Jake trade facts about different players and check the screens on their cell phones for updates on other games and players, because they both play fantasy football, which is a computer game that gives you points for picking players who score touchdowns and gain yardage. And I glance over at my father from time to time, making sure he sees me cheering, because I know he is only willing to sit in the same room with his mentally deranged son as long as I am rooting for the Birds with everything I got. I have to admit that it feels good to sit in the same room with my father, even though he hates me and I still have not forgiven him a hundred percent for kicking me in the attic and punching me in the face.

The Houston Texans score first, and Dad starts cursing pretty loudly, so much that my mother leaves the room, saying she will bring us new beers, and Ronnie stares at the television, pretending he has not heard what my father has said, which is, "Play some fucking defense, you piece-of-shit overpaid secondary! This is the Texans, not the Dallas Cowgirls. The fucking Texans! Jesus fucking Christ!"

"Relax, Dad," Jake says. "We got this."

Mom distributes the beers, and Dad sips quietly for a while, but when McNabb throws an interception, my father starts pointing his finger at the television and cursing even louder, saying things about McNabb that would make my friend Danny go wild, because Danny says only black people can use the n-word.

Luckily, Donté Stallworth is indeed the man, because when McNabb starts throwing to him, the Eagles build a lead and Dad stops cursing and starts to smile again.

At halftime, Jake talks my dad into joining us outside for a catch, and then the four of us are throwing a football around on our street. One of our neighbors comes out with his son, and we let them join in. The kid is only maybe ten, and he cannot really reach us from his yard, but since he is wearing a green jersey, we throw it to him again and again. He drops every pass, but we cheer for him anyway; the kid smiles wildly, and his dad nods appreciatively at us whenever one of us catches his eye.

Jake and I are the farthest apart, and we send each other long passes down the street and often have to run even farther to catch the throws. Neither of us drops a single pass, because we are excellent athletes.

My dad mostly just stands around sipping his beer, but we throw him some easy balls, which he catches with one hand and then tosses the football underhand to Ronnie, who is standing closest to him. Ronnie has a weak arm, but neither Jake nor I point this out, because he is our friend and we are all wearing green and the sun is shining and the Eagles are winning and we are so full of good hot food and ice-cold beer it doesn't really matter that Ronnie's athletic ability is not equal to ours.

When Mom announces that halftime is almost over, Jake runs over to the little kid; my brother puts his hands in the air and yells "Ahhhhhhhhhhhhh!" until the kid's dad does the same thing. The little guy catches on after only a second, puts his hands in the air, yells "Ahhhhhhhhhh!" and then we all do the Eagles chant—spelling the letters out with our arms and legs—before running back into our respective family rooms.

Donté Stallworth continues to be the man in the second half, gaining almost 150 yards and a TD, while Baskett does not even get a decent ball thrown to him and fails to record a single catch. I'm not all that upset about this, because a funny thing happens at the end of the game.

When the Eagles win 24–10, we all stand to sing the Eagles fight song together like we always do whenever the Birds win a regular season game. My brother throws his arms around Ronnie and me and says, "Come on, Dad." My dad is a little drunk from all the beer and so happy about the Eagles victory—and the fact that McNabb threw for more than 300 yards—that he lines up with us and throws his arm around my shoulders, which shocks me at first, not because I don't like being touched, but because my father has not put his arm around me in many years. The weight and warmth of his arm makes me feel good, and as we sing the fight song and do the chant afterward, I catch my mother looking at us from the kitchen, where she is washing dishes. She smiles at me even though she is crying again, and I wonder why as I sing and spell and chant.

Jake asks Ronnie if he needs a ride home, and my best friend says, "No, thanks. Hank Baskett is walking me home."

"I am?" I say, because Hank Baskett is the name Ronnie and Jake called me all throughout the game—so I know he really means me.

"Yep," he says, and we grab the football on the way out.

When we get to Knight's Park, we throw the football back and forth, standing only twenty feet away from each other because Ronnie has a weak arm, and after a few catches my best friend asks me what I think about Tiffany.

"Nothing," I say. "I don't think anything about her at all. Why?"

"Veronica told me that Tiffany follows you when you run. True?"

I catch a wobbly pass, say, "Yeah. It's sort of weird. She knows my schedule and everything," and throw a perfect spiral just over Ronnie's right shoulder so he can catch it on the run.

He doesn't turn.

He doesn't run.

The ball goes over his head.

Ronnie retrieves the ball, jogs back into his range, and says, "Tiffany is a little odd. Do you understand what I mean by *odd*, Pat?"

I catch his even more wobbly pass just before it reaches my right kneecap, and say, "I guess." I understand that Tiffany is different from most girls, but I also understand what it is like to be separated from your spouse, which is something Ronnie does not understand. So I ask, "Odd how? Odd like me?"

His face drops, and then he says, "No. I didn't mean . . . It's just that Tiffany is seeing a therapist—"

"So am I."

"I know, but—"

"So seeing a therapist makes me odd?"

"No. Just listen to me for a second. I'm trying to be your friend. Okay?"

I look down at the grass as Ronnie walks over to me. I don't really want to hear Ronnie talk his way out of this one, because Ronnie is the only friend I have, now that I am out of the bad place, and we have had such a great day, and the Eagles have won, and my father put his arm around me, and—

"I know Tiffany and you went out to dinner, which is great. You both could probably use a friend who understands loss."

I don't like the way he collectively uses the word "loss," as if I have lost Nikki—as in forever—because I am still riding out apart time and I have not lost her yet. But I don't say anything, and let him continue.

"Listen," Ronnie says. "I want to tell you why Tiffany was fired from her job."

"That's none of my business."

"It is if you are going to have dinners with her. Listen, you need to know that . . ."

Ronnie tells me what he believes is the story of how Tiffany lost her job, but the way he tells it proves he is biased. He tells it just like Dr. Timbers would, stating what he would call "facts," with no regard for what was going on in Tiffany's head. He tells me what coworkers wrote in their reports, he tells me what her boss told her parents and what the therapist has since said to Veronica—who is Tiffany's designated support buddy and therefore has weekly phone conversations with Tiffany's therapist—but he never once tells me what Tiffany thinks or what is going on in her heart: the awful feelings, the conflicting impulses, the needs, the desperation, everything that makes her different from Ronnie and Veronica, who have each other and their daughter, Emily, and a good income and a house and everything else that keeps people from calling them "odd." What amazes me is that Ronnie is telling me all this in a friendly manner, as if he is trying to save me from Tiffany's ways, as if he knows more about these sorts of things than I do, as if I had not spent the last few months in a mental institution. He does not understand Tiffany, and he sure as hell doesn't understand me, but I do not hold it against Ronnie, because I am practicing being kind rather than right, so Nikki will be able to love me again when apart time is over.

"So I'm not telling you to be mean or to gossip about her—just protect yourself, okay?" Ronnie says, and I nod. "Well, I better be getting home to Veronica. Maybe I'll drop in this week for a lifting session? Cool?"

I nod again and watch him jog away from me, the bouncy steps suggesting that he thinks his mission is accomplished. It is obvious he was only allowed to watch the game because Veronica wanted him to talk to me about Tiffany, probably because Veronica thought I might take advantage of her nymphomaniac sister, which makes me very mad, and before I know it, I'm ringing the Websters' doorbell.

"Hello?" Tiffany's mom says to me when the door opens. She is older-looking, with gray hair and a heavy sweater-coat, even though it is only September and she is inside.

"May I speak with Tiffany?"

"You're Ronnie's friend, right? Pat Peoples?"

I only nod, because I know Mrs. Webster knows who I am.

"Do you mind if I ask what you want with our daughter?"

"Who's there?" I hear Tiffany's father call from the other room.

"It's just Ronnie's friend, Pat Peoples!" Mrs. Webster yells. To me she says, "So what do you want with our Tiffany?"

I look down at the football in my hand and say, "I want to have a catch. It's a beautiful afternoon. Maybe she would like to get some fresh air in the park?"

"Just a catch?" Mrs. Webster says.

I hold up my wedding ring to prove I do not want to have sex with her daughter, and say, "Listen, I'm married. I just want to be Tiffany's friend, okay?"

Mrs. Webster looks a little surprised by my answer, which is odd because I was sure that was the answer she wanted to hear. But after a moment she says, "Go around back and knock on the door."

So I knock on the back door, but no one answers.

I knock three more times and then leave.

I'm halfway through the park when I hear a swishy sound behind me. When I turn around, Tiffany is speed walking toward me, wearing a pink tracksuit made from a material that swishes when one pant leg rubs against the other. When she is about five feet away, I throw her a light, girly pass, but she steps aside and the football falls to the ground.

"What do you want?" she says.

"Want to have a catch?"

"I hate football. I told you this, no?"

Since she doesn't want to have a catch, I decide I'll just ask her my question: "Why do you follow me when I run?"

"Honestly?"

"Yeah," I say.

She squints her eyes and makes her face look mean. "I'm scouting you."

"What?"

"I said I'm scouting you."

"Why?"

"To see if you are fit enough."

"Fit enough for what?"

But instead of answering my question, she says, "I'm also scouting your work ethic, your endurance, the way you deal with mental strain, your ability to persevere when you are unsure of what is happening around you, and—"

"Why?"

"I can't tell you yet," she says.

"Why not?"

"Because I haven't finished scouting you."

When she walks away, I follow her past the pond, over the footbridge, and out of the park. But neither of us speaks again.

She leads me to Haddon Avenue, and we walk by the new stores and swanky restaurants, passing lots of other pedestrians, kids on skateboards, and men who raise their fists in the air and say, "Go Eagles!" when they see my Hank Baskett jersey.

Tiffany turns off Haddon Avenue and weaves through residential blocks until we are in front of my parents' house, where she stops, looks at me, and—after almost an hour of silence—says, "Did your team win?"

I nod. "Twenty-four to ten."

"Lucky you," Tiffany says, and then walks away.

The Best Therapist in the Entire World

The Monday morning after the Eagles beat the Texans, a funny thing happens. I'm doing some initial stretching in the basement, when my father comes down for the first time since I have been home.

"Pat?" he says.

I stop stretching, stand up, and face him. He's on the last step, stopped as if he is afraid to set a foot down on my territory.

"Dad?"

"You certainly got a lot of equipment down here."

I don't say anything, because I know he is probably mad at my mother for buying me a gym.

"There's pretty good Eagles coverage in the papers today," he says, and then extends the sports sections of the *Courier-Post* and *The Philadelphia Inquirer* to me. "I got up early and finished reading both so that you could keep up with the team. By your comments yesterday during the game, I could tell you don't know all of the players, and I thought maybe you'd like to follow along this season now that you're home and—well, I'll just leave them on the top step from now on."

I'm too shocked to speak or move, because my father has taken the sports pages with him to work ever since Jake and I were little kids. Jake used to fight with Dad all the time about this, asking him to at least bring home the sports sections after work so we could read the articles after we finished our homework. But Dad always left with the papers before we were out of bed, and he never brought the sports sections home for us ever, saying he forgot or lost them at work. Jake finally subscribed himself when he got his first job stocking shelves at the local Big Foods, and this was when we started reading the daily sports pages together every morning before school. He was twelve; I was thirteen.

I do three hundred sit-ups on the Stomach Master 6000 before I allow myself to pick up the paper from the bottom step. As my stomach muscles crunch and burn, I worry that my father is only playing a mean trick on me and that the papers will be the entertainment or food sections, but when I finish the sit-ups and make my way to the steps, I see that Dad really did leave me the sports sections of both papers.

When it is time for me to take my a.m. pills, I find my mom in the kitchen cooking eggs. My plate is set at the breakfast bar, and my five morning pills are laid out in a line on a napkin.

"Look," I say, and hold up what my father gave me.

"Sports pages, eh?" Mom says over the sound of frying eggs.

"Yeah." I sit down and pop all five pills into my mouth, trying to decide how many I will swallow today. "But why?"

Mom scrapes the eggs from the pan and onto my plate with

her spatula. She smiles and says, "Your father is trying, Pat. But I wouldn't ask too many questions if I were you. Take what he gives you and be happy—that's what we do, right?"

She smiles at me hopefully, and right then I decide to swallow all five pills, so I take a sip of water and do just that.

Every day that week, I hear the basement door open and close, and when I check the top step, I find the sports sections, which I read from cover to cover while I eat breakfast with Mom.

The big news is the upcoming Giants game, which everyone thinks will be the key to winning the NFC East, especially since the Giants have already lost to the Indianapolis Colts in game one. A loss will put them at 0–2 and the Eagles at 2–0. The game is being hyped as a big one, and I have a ticket, thanks to Jake, which makes me really excited.

Each night, I wait for my dad to come home from work, hoping he might want to talk about the upcoming game with me—so I can use the current players' names and prove to him that I am a real fan again—but he always takes his dinner into his study and locks the door. A few times I actually go to his study and raise a fist to knock, but I chicken out every night. Mom says, "Give him time."

Sitting in the brown recliner, I talk about my dad with Dr. Cliff during my Friday appointment. I tell him how Dad is leaving me the sports sections now, and how I know this is a huge deal for Dad, but I wish he would talk to me more. Cliff listens, but says little about my father. Instead he keeps bringing up Tiffany, which is sort of annoying because she has only been following me when I run, and that's about it.

"Your mother says you are going to the beach with Tiffany tomorrow," Cliff says, and then smiles like men sometimes do when they are talking about women and sex.

"I'm going with Ronnie and Veronica and baby Emily too. The whole point is to take Emily to the beach because she did not get to go much this summer and it will be cold soon. Little kids love the beach, Cliff."

"Are you excited about going?"

"Sure. I guess. I mean, I'll have to get up super early to get a good workout in and finish when we come home, but—"

"What about seeing Tiffany in a bathing suit?"

I blink several times before I grasp what he has said to me.

"You said before that she has a nice body," Cliff adds. "Are you looking forward to seeing it? Maybe she will wear a bikini. What do you think?"

I feel mad for a second—because my therapist is sort of being disrespectful—but then I realize Cliff is testing my morals again, making sure I am fit to be out of the mental institution, so I smile, nod, and say, "Cliff, I'm married, remember?"

He nods back wisely and winks, making me feel like I passed the test.

We talk a little more about how I made it through a whole week without having an episode, which is evidence that the drugs are working, according to Cliff—because he doesn't know I spit at least half of the pills into the toilet—and when it is time for me to go, Cliff says, "I just have one more thing to say to you."

"What?"

He shocks me by jumping to his feet, throwing both hands in the air, and yelling "Ahhhhhhhhhhhhhh!"

So I jump to my feet, throw both hands in the air, and yell "Ahhhhhhhhhhh!" too.

"E!-A!-G!-L!-E!-S! EAGLES!" we chant in unison, spelling the letters with our arms and legs, and suddenly I am so happy.

Cliff predicts a 21–14 Eagles victory as he walks me out of his office, and after I agree with his prognosis, we enter the waiting room and my mother says, "Were you two just doing the Eagles chant?"

Cliff raises his eyebrows and shrugs his shoulders at my mother, but when he turns to walk back into his office, he begins whistling "Fly, Eagles, Fly," at which point I know that I am seeing the best therapist in the entire world.

On the drive home, my mother asks me if Cliff and I talked about anything other than Eagles football during the therapy session, and instead of answering her question, I say, "Do you think that Dad will start talking to me at night if the Eagles beat the Giants?"

Mom frowns, grips the steering wheel a little harder. "The sad reality is he might, Pat. He really might," she says, and I start to get my hopes up.

Tiffany's Head Floating over the Waves

When Ronnie picks me up in his minivan—which has three rows of seats—Tiffany is already buckled in next to Emily's car seat, so I climb into the very back, carrying the football and the bag my mother packed me, which contains a towel, a change of clothes, and a bagged lunch, even though I told Mom that Ronnie was bringing hoagies from the local deli.

Of course my mother feels the need to stand on the front porch and wave, as if I were five years old. Veronica, who is riding in the front passenger's seat, leans over Ronnie and yells to my mother. "Thanks for the wine and flowers!" My mother takes this as an invitation to walk to the minivan and have a conversation.

"How do you like the outfit I bought for Pat?" my mom says when she reaches Ronnie's window. She ducks down and takes a long look at Tiffany, but Tiffany has already turned her head away from my mother and is looking out the window at the house across the street.

The outfit I am wearing is ridiculous: a bright orange polo shirt, bright green swimming shorts, and flip-flops. I did not want to wear any of this, but I knew Veronica was likely to make a fuss if I wore one of my cutoff T-shirts and a pair of workout shorts. Since Veronica and my mother have pretty much the same taste, I allowed my mother to dress me—plus, it makes Mom really happy.

"He looks great, Mrs. Peoples," Veronica says, and Ronnie nods in agreement.

"Hello, Tiffany," my mother says, sticking her head into the car a little more, but Tiffany ignores her.

"Tiffany?" Veronica says, but Tiffany continues to stare out the window.

"Have you met Emily yet?" Ronnie asks, and then he is out of the car and Emily is unbuckled from her car seat and placed in my mother's arms. Mom's voice gets all funny as she talks to Emily, and standing next to Mom, Veronica and Ronnie are all smiles.

This goes on for a few minutes, until Tiffany turns her head and says, "I thought we were going to the beach today."

"Sorry, Mrs. Peoples," Veronica says. "My sister can be a little blunt sometimes, but we probably should get going so we can have lunch on the beach."

My mother quickly nods and says, "Have a good time, Pat," as Ronnie buckles Emily back into her car seat. Again I feel like I am five.

On the way to the shore, Ronnie and Veronica talk to Tiffany and me the same way they talk to Emily—as if they are not really expecting a response, saying things that really don't need to be said at all. "Can't wait to get on the beach." "We're going to have such a good time." "What should we do first—swim, walk the beach, or throw the football?" "Such a nice day." "Are you guys having fun?" "Can't wait to eat those hoagies!"

After twenty minutes of non-talk, Tiffany says, "Can we please have some quiet time?" and we ride the rest of the way listening to the yelling noises Emily makes—what her parents claim is singing.

We drive through Ocean City and over a bridge to a beach I do not know. "Little less crowded down here," Ronnie explains.

When we park, Emily is put into what looks like a cross between a stroller and a 4x4 vehicle, which Veronica pushes. Tiffany carries the umbrella. Ronnie and I carry the cooler, each of us grabbing a handle. We take a wooden walkway over a sand dune covered with sea oats and find that we have the beach all to ourselves.

Not another person anywhere to be seen.

After a brief discussion about whether the tide is coming in or out, Veronica picks a dry patch and tries to spread out the blanket while Ronnie begins digging the umbrella spike into the sand. But there is a breeze, and Veronica has some trouble, as the wind keeps folding the blanket over.

If it were anyone but Veronica, I would grab a corner and help, but I do not want to get yelled at, so I wait for instructions before I do anything. Tiffany does the same, but Veronica fails to ask for help.

Maybe some sand gets kicked up or something, because Emily starts screaming and rubbing her eyes.

"Nice," Tiffany says.

Veronica immediately attends to Emily, telling her to blink, demonstrating what to do, but Emily only screams even louder.

"I can't take a crying baby right now," Tiffany adds. "Make her stop crying. Veronica, would you please make her—"

"Remember what Dr. Lily said? What did we talk about this morning?" Veronica says over her shoulder, shooting Tiffany a serious look before turning her attention back to Emily.

"So now we're talking about my therapist in front of Pat? You fucking bitch," Tiffany says, shaking her head, and then she is walking away from us quickly.

"Christ," Veronica says. "Ronnie, can you handle Emily?"

Ronnie nods solemnly, and then Veronica is running after Tiffany, saying, "Tiff? Come back. Come on. I'm sorry. I'm really sorry."

Ronnie flushes Emily's eyes with bottled water, and after ten minutes or so, she stops crying. We get the blanket spread out under the shade of the umbrella, weighting the corners down with the cooler, our flip-flops and sandals, and Emily's super stroller—but Veronica and Tiffany do not come back.

After every inch of Emily's skin is coated with sunscreen, Ronnie and I play with her down at the water's edge. She likes running after the waves as they recede. She likes digging in the sand, and we have to watch to make sure she does not eat the sand, which seems weird to me, because why would anyone want to eat sand? Ronnie carries Emily out into the ocean, and we all float over the waves for a time.

I ask if we should be worried about Veronica and Tiffany, and Ronnie says, "No. They're just having a *therapy* session somewhere on the beach. They'll be back soon."

I don't like the way he emphasizes the word "therapy," as if therapy were some sort of ridiculous idea, but I don't say anything.

After we dry off, we all lie down on the blanket—Ronnie and Emily in the shade, and me in the sun. I doze off pretty quickly.

When I open my eyes, Ronnie's face is next to mine; he's sleeping. I feel a tap on my shoulder, and when I roll over, I see that Emily has walked around the blanket. She smiles at me and says, "Pap."

"Let Daddy sleep," I whisper, and then pick her up and carry her down to the water.

For a while we sit and dig a small hole in the wet sand with our hands, but then Emily stands and chases the foam of a receding wave, laughing and pointing.

"Want to go swimming?" I ask her, and she nods once, so I scoop her up into my arms and begin to wade out into the water.

The surf has picked up some and the waves have a lot more height, so I quickly walk past the breakers to where the water is up to my chest. Emily and I begin to float over the swells. As the waves grow in size, I have to jump and kick really hard to keep both of our heads above water, but Emily loves it and begins squealing and laughing and clapping her hands every time we float up. This goes on for a good ten minutes, and I am so happy; I kiss her chubby cheeks over and over. Something about Emily makes me want to float over waves with her for the rest of my life, and I decide that when apart time is done, I will make a daughter with Nikki ASAP, because nothing has made me even close to this happy since apart time began.

The swells get even bigger. I lift Emily up and put her on my shoulders so she will not have her face splashed by the waves, and her squeals seem to suggest that she likes being so high in the air.

We float up.

We float down.

We are so happy.

We are so, so happy.

But then I hear someone screaming.

"Pat! Pat! Paaaaaaat!"

I turn and see that Veronica is running very quickly down the beach, with Tiffany trailing far behind. I worry that maybe something is wrong, so I start to make my way in.

The waves are pretty big now, and I have to take Emily down from my shoulders and hold her against my chest to ensure her safety, but soon we are able to negotiate our way back to Veronica, who is now running into the surf.

When I get closer, Veronica seems to be very upset. Emily starts to scream and reach for her mother.

"What the hell are you doing?" Veronica says to me when I hand Emily over to her.

"I'm just swimming with Emily," I say.

Veronica's screaming must have woken up Ronnie, because he has run down to meet us. "What happened?"

"You let *Pat* take Emily out into the ocean?" Veronica says, and by the way she says my name, it's obvious she does not want Emily to be left alone with me, because she thinks I am going to hurt Emily somehow, which is unfair—especially since Emily only started crying when she heard Veronica screaming, so really *Veronica* was the one who upset her own daughter.

"What did you do to her?" Ronnie says to me.

"Nothing," I say. "We were only swimming."

"What were *you* doing?" Veronica says to Ronnie.

"I must of fallen asleep, and—"

"Jesus Christ, Ronnie. You left Emily alone with *him*?"

The way Veronica says "him," Emily crying, Ronnie accusing me of doing something awful to his daughter, the sun burning my bare chest and back, Tiffany watching now—suddenly I feel as though I might explode. I definitely feel an episode coming on, so before I blow up, I do the only thing I can think of: I start running down the beach away from Veronica and Ronnie and Emily and the crying and the accusations. I run as fast as I can, and suddenly I realize that now *I* am crying, probably because I was only swimming with Emily and it felt so right and I was trying to be good and thought I *was* being good and I let my best friend down and Veronica screamed at me and it's not fair because I have been trying so hard and how long can this fucking movie last and how much more do I need to improve myself and—

Tiffany passes me.

She runs by me like a blur.

Suddenly, only one thing matters: I need to pass her.

I start running faster and catch up to her, but she picks up her speed and we run side by side for a time until I find that gear women do not have, and I blow by her and maintain my man speed for a minute or so before I slow down and allow her to catch up with me. We jog side by side on the beach for a long time, neither of us saying a word.

What feels like an hour passes before we turn around, and what feels like another hour passes before we see Ronnie and Veronica's umbrella, but before we reach them, Tiffany veers into the ocean.

I follow her—running directly into the waves—and the salt water feels so cool on my skin after a long run. Soon we are in too deep to stand, and Tiffany's head is floating over the waves, which have calmed down considerably. Her face is a little tan and her hair hangs dark and wet and natural and I see freckles on her nose that were not there earlier that morning—so I swim over to her.

A wave lifts me up, and when I come down over the other side, I am surprised that our faces are very close. For a second Tiffany reminds me so much of Nikki, I worry we might accidentally kiss, but Tiffany swims a few feet away from me before this happens, and I am thankful.

Her toes come up out of the water, and she begins to float, facing the horizon.

I lean back, stare at the line where sky meets water, allow my toes to rise, and float next to Tiffany for a long time, neither of us saying anything.

When we walk back to the blanket, Emily is sleeping with a fist in her mouth, and Veronica and Ronnie are lying down, holding hands in the shade. When we stand over them, they squint and smile at us like nothing bad had happened earlier.

"How was your run?" Ronnie asks.

"We want to go home now," Tiffany says.

"Why?" Ronnie says, sitting up. "We haven't even eaten our lunch. Pat, you really want to go home?"

Veronica says nothing.

I look up at the sky. No clouds at all. Nothing but blue. "Yeah, I do," I tell him, and then we are in the minivan driving back to Collingswood.

A Hive Full of Green Bees

"Ahhhhhhhhh!"

I sit up, my heart pounding. When my eyes focus, I see my dad standing at my bedside with his hands above his head; he's wearing his number 5 McNabb jersey.

"Ahhhhhhhhhhhhh!" he continues to scream, until I get out of bed, raise my hands, and say "Ahhhhhhhhhh!"

We do the chant, spelling the letters with our arms and legs. "E!-A!-G!-L!-E!-S! EAGLES!" When we finish, instead of saying good morning or anything else, my father simply jogs out of my room.

I look at the clock, and it reads 5:59 a.m. The game starts at one o'clock. I promised to join Jake's tailgate party by ten, which gives me two hours to lift and an hour to run—so I lift, and Tiffany is outside at 8:00 a.m. just like she said she would be.

We do a short run—maybe only six or seven miles.

After a shower, I put on my Baskett jersey and ask my mom for a ride to the PATCO station, but she says, "Your driver is waiting for you outside." Mom kisses me on the cheek and hands me some money. "Have fun, and don't let your brother drink too much."

Outside, I see Dad in his sedan; the engine is running. I get into the car and say, "Dad, are you going to the game?"

"I wish I could," he says, and then we back out of the driveway.

The truth is that my father is still serving a self-imposed ban and is therefore not allowed to attend Eagles games. In the early eighties, Dad got into a fight with a Dallas Cowboys fan who dared to sit in the 700 Level, which were the cheap seats at the Vet, where the die-hard Eagles fans sat.

The story I heard from my since-deceased uncle was this:

When the Cowboys scored a touchdown, this Dallas fan jumped up and began cheering real loudly, so people started throwing beers and hot dogs at him. The only problem was that my dad was sitting in the row in front of this Dallas fan, so the beer and mustard and food rained down on Dad too.

Apparently, Dad lost it, attacked the Dallas fan, and beat him within an inch of his life. My father was actually arrested, convicted of aggravated assault, and incarcerated for three months. If my uncle hadn't made the mortgage payments, we would have lost the house. Dad did lose his season ticket and has not been to an Eagles game since.

Jake says we could get Dad in, since no one actually checks IDs at the gate, but Dad won't go back, saying, "As long as they let the opposing fans in our house, I can't trust myself."

This is sort of funny, because twenty-five years after Dad beat the hell out of that Dallas fan, he is just a fat old man who is not likely to beat up another fat old man, let alone a rowdy Dallas fan with the guts to wear a Cowboys jersey to an Eagles game.

Although my father did hit me pretty hard in the attic just a few weeks ago—so maybe he *is* wise to stay away from the games.

We drive over the hospital-green Walt Whitman Bridge, and he talks about how this just might be an important day in Eagles history, especially since the Giants won both games last year. "Revenge!" he keeps yelling indiscriminately. He also tells me I have to cheer real loudly so Eli Manning—who I know (from reading the sports pages) is the Giants' QB—will not be able to talk or hear during the huddles. "Scream your goddamn lungs out, because you're the twelfth man!" Dad says. The way he talks at me—never really pausing long enough for me to say anything—makes him sound crazy, I know, even though most people think I am the crazy person in the family.

When we are stopped, waiting in line to pay the bridge toll, Dad quits his Eagles rant long enough to say, "It's good that you are going to the games with Jake again. Your brother's missed you a lot. You do realize that, right? You need to make time for family no matter what happens in your life, because Jake and your mother need you."

This is a pretty ironic thing for him to say, especially since he has hardly said anything to me since I have been home and never really spends any time with me or my mother or Jake at all, but I am glad my father is finally talking to me. All the time I have ever spent with Jake or him has always revolved around sports—mostly Eagles—and I know this is all he can really afford emotionally, so I take it, and say, "I wish you were going to the game, Dad."

"Me too," he says, and then hands the toll collector a five.

After taking the first off-ramp, he deposits me about ten blocks away from the new stadium so he can turn around and avoid traffic. "You're on your own coming home," he says as I get out. "I'm not driving back into this zoo."

I thank him for the ride, and just before I shut the door, he raises his hands in the car and yells "Ahhhhhhhhh!" so I raise my hands and yell "Ahhhhhhhh!" A group of men drinking beers out of a nearby car trunk hear us, so they raise their hands and yell "Ahhhhhhhhhh!" Men united by a team, we all do the Eagles chant together. My chest feels so warm, and I remember how much fun it is to be in South Philly on game day.

As I walk toward the west Lincoln Financial Field parking lot—following the directions my brother gave me on the phone the night before—so many people are wearing Eagles jerseys. Everywhere green. People are grilling, drinking beer from plastic cups, throwing footballs, listening to the WIP 610 pregame show on AM radio, and as I walk past, they all high-five me, throw me footballs, and yell, "Go Birds!" just because I am wearing an Eagles jersey. I see young boys with their fathers. Old guys with their grown sons. Men yelling and singing and smiling as if they were boys again. And I realize I have missed this a lot.

Even though I do not want to, I look for the Vet and only find a parking lot. There's a new Phillies ballpark too, called Citizens Bank Park. By the entrance ripples a huge banner of some new player named Ryan Howard. All of this seems to suggest that Jake and Dad weren't lying when they said the Vet was demolished. I try not to think about the dates they mentioned, and I focus on enjoying the game and spending time with my brother.

I find the right parking lot and begin to look for the green tent with the black Eagles flag flying from the top. The parking lot is full—tents and grills and parties everywhere—but after ten minutes or so, I spot my brother.

Jake's in his number 99 Jerome Brown memorial jersey. (Jerome Brown was the two-time Pro Bowler defensive tackle who was killed in a car crash back in 1992.) My brother is drinking beer from a green cup, standing next to our friend Scott, who is manning the grill. Jake looks happy, and for a second I simply enjoy watching him smile as he throws an arm around Scott, whom I haven't seen since the last time I was in South Philly. Jake's face is red, and he looks a little drunk already, but he has always been a happy drunk, so I do not worry. Like my father, nothing makes Jake happier than Eagles game day.

When Jake sees me, he yells, "Hank Baskett's tailgating with us!" and then runs over to give me a high five and a chest bump.

"What's up, dude?" Scott says to me as we too exchange high fives. The big smile on his face suggests that he is happy to see me. "Man, you really *are* huge. What have you been lifting—cars?" I smile proudly as he punches my arm, like guys do when they are buddies. "It's been years—I mean, um—*how many months has it been*?" He and my brother exchange a glance that I do not miss, but before I can say anything, Scott yells, "Hey, all you fat-asses in the tent! I wanna introduce you to my boy—Jake's brother, Pat."

The tent is the size of a small house. I walk through the slit on one side, and a huge flat-screen television is set up on milk crates stacked two by four. Five really fat guys are seated in folding chairs, watching the pregame show—all of them in Eagles jerseys. Scott rattles off the names. After he says mine, the men nod and wave and then go back to watching the pregame show. All of them have handheld personal organizers, and their eyes are rapidly moving back and forth between the small screens in their hands and the large screen at the far side of the tent. Almost all have earpieces in, which I guess are connected to cellular phones.

As we exit the tent, Scott says, "Don't mind them. They're all trying to get last-minute info. They'll be a little more friendly after they've placed their bets."

"Who are they?" I ask.

"Guys from my work. I'm a computer tech now for Digital Cross Health. We do websites for family doctors."

"How are they watching television out here in the parking lot?" I ask.

My brother waves me around to the back of the tent, points to a small engine in a square of metal, and says, "Gas-powered generator." He points to the top of the tent, where a small gray plate is perched, and says, "Satellite dish."

"What do they do with all this gear when they go into the game?" I ask.

"Oh," Scott says with a laugh. "They don't have tickets."

Jake pours a Yuengling Lager into a plastic cup and hands it to me, and I notice three coolers loaded with beer cans and bottles, probably four or five cases. I know the plastic cup is to keep away the police, who can arrest you for having an open beer can in your hand but not for holding a plastic cup. The bag of empties just outside the tent suggests that Jake and Scott are way ahead of me.

As Scott finishes grilling breakfast—thick sausages and eggs scrambled in a pan he has placed over the gas flames—he does not ask me many questions about what I have been up to, which I appreciate. I'm sure my brother has already told Scott all about my time in the bad place and my separation from Nikki, but I still appreciate Scott's allowing me to reenter the world of Eagles football without an interrogation.

Scott tells me about his life, and it turns out that while I was in the bad place, he married someone named Willow, and they actually now have three-year-old twins named Tami and Jeri-Lyn. Scott shows me the picture he keeps in his wallet, and the girls are dressed alike in little pink ballerina outfits—tutus, tights—their hands stretched up over silver tiaras, pointing toward heaven. "My tiny dancers. We live on the Pennsylvania side now. Havertown," Scott says as he loads a half dozen sausages onto the top rack of the barbecue, where they will keep warm while the next batch cooks. I think about Emily and me floating over the waves only the day before, and again I promise myself I'll get busy making my own daughter just as soon as apart time is over.

I try not to do the math in my head, but I can't help it. If he has twins who are three years old and he was married sometime *after* I last saw him—but *before* his wife got pregnant—it must mean that I have not seen Scott for at least four years. Now maybe he knocked up his girlfriend and then married her, but of course, I can't ask that. Since his daughters are three, the math indicates he and I have not talked for at least three or four years.

My last memory of Scott is at the Vet. I had sold my season ticket to Scott's brother Chris a season or two before, but Chris often went away on business conferences and allowed me to buy my seat back for the few home games played when he was out of town. I came up from Baltimore to see the Eagles play Dallas; I don't remember who won or what the score was. But I remember sitting in between Scott and Jake—up in the 700 Level—when Dallas scored a rushing touchdown. Some clown behind us stood up and began cheering as he unzipped his jacket, revealing a throwback Tony Dorsett jersey. Everyone in our section started booing and throwing food at this Dallas fan, who smiled and smiled.

Jake was so drunk he could hardly stand, but he charged after this guy, climbing up over three rows of people. The sober Dallas fan shoved Jake away easily, but when Jake fell back into the arms of drunken Eagles fans, a cry went up, and the Tony Dorsett jersey was forcibly removed from the visiting fan's back and ripped into many pieces before security arrived and threw out a dozen people.

Jake was not thrown out of the game.

Scott and I were able to get Jake up and away from the mayhem, and when security arrived, we were in the men's room splashing water onto Jake's face, trying to sober him up.

In my mind, this happened last year, maybe eleven months ago. But I know if I bring up this incident now as we are grilling in front of the Linc, I will be told that the memory occurred more than three or even four years ago, so I do not bring it up, even though I want to, because I know Jake's and Scott's responses will help me figure out what the rest of the world believes about time. And also, *not knowing* what the rest of the world believes happened between then and now is terrifying. It's better not to think too much about this.

"Drink some beers," Jake says to me. "Smile. It's game day!"

So I start drinking, even though the little orange bottles that my pills come in have stickers forbidding me to drink alcohol.

After the fat guys in the tent are fed, we eat off paper plates, and then Scott, Jake, and I begin throwing the football around.

In the parking lot people are everywhere, not just tailgating, but roaming. Guys selling stolen or homemade T-shirts, moms parading around little girls in cheerleading outfits who will do a cheer if you donate a dollar to their local cheerleading booster club, crazy bums willing to tell you off-color jokes for free food and beer, strippers in short pants and satin jackets handing out free passes to the local gentlemen's clubs, packs of little kids in pads and helmets collecting money for their peewee football teams, college kids handing out free samples of new sodas or sports drinks or candy or junk food, and of course the seventy thousand other drunken Eagles fans just like us. Basically, it's a green football carnival.

By the time we decide to have a catch, I've had two or three beers, and I'd be willing to bet Jake and Scott have each had at least ten, so our passes are not all that accurate. We hit parked cars, knock over a few tables of food, beam one or two guys in the back, but no one cares, because we are Eagles fans in Eagles jerseys who are ready and willing to cheer on the Birds. Every so often, other men will jump in front of one of us and intercept a pass or two, but they always give back the ball with a laugh and a smile.

I like throwing the football with Jake and Scott because it makes me feel like a boy, and when I was a boy, I was the person Nikki fell in love with.

But then something bad happens.

Jake sees him first, points, and says, "Hey, look at the asshole." I turn my head and see a big man in a Giants jersey, maybe forty yards away from our tent. He is wearing a red, white, and blue hard hat, and the worst part is that he has a little boy with him who is also wearing a Giants jersey. The guy walks over to a group of Eagles fans who give him a hard time at first but eventually hand him a beer.

Suddenly my brother is walking toward this Giants fan, so Scott and I follow. My brother starts chanting as he walks, "Ass—hole! Ass—hole! Ass—hole!" With every syllable, he throws his index finger at the hard hat. Scott is doing the same thing, and before I know it, we are surrounded by twenty or so men in Eagles jerseys who are also chanting and pointing. I have to admit it feels sort of thrilling to be part of this mob—united in our hatred of the opposing team's fans.

When we reach the Giants fan, his friends—all Eagles fans—laugh, and their faces seem to say, "We told you this would happen." But instead of acting remorseful, the Giants fan puts his hands up in the air, as if he has just performed a magic trick or something; he smiles widely and nods his head like he is enjoying being called an asshole. He even puts his hand to his ear, as if to say, "I can't hear you." The kid with him, who has the same pale skin coloring and flat nose—probably his son—looks terrified. The little guy's jersey hangs down to his knees, and as the "ass—hole" chant intensifies, the kid holds on to his father's leg and tries to hide behind the big man's thigh.

My brother transitions the crowd into a "Giants suck" chant, and more Eagles fans come to join in. We now are at least fifty strong. And this is when the little kid breaks into tears, sobbing. When we Eagles fans see that the kid is really upset, the mob chuckles and respectfully disperses.

Jake and Scott are laughing as we walk back to our tent, but I don't feel so great. I wish we did not make that little kid cry. I know the Giants fan was stupid to wear a Giants jersey to an Eagles game, and it is really his own fault that his son was made to cry, but I also know that what we did was unkind, and this is the sort of behavior Nikki hates, what I am trying—

I feel his hands explode through my back, and I stumble forward and almost fall down. When I turn around, I see the big Giants fan. He is no longer wearing his hard hat; his son is not with him.

"You like making little kids cry?" he says to me.

I'm too shocked to speak. There were at least fifty men chanting, but he has singled out me. *Why?* I wasn't even chanting. I wasn't even pointing. I want to tell him this, but my mouth won't work, so I just stand there shaking my head.

"If you don't want a problem, don't wear a Giants jersey to an Eagles game," Scott says.

"It's just bad parenting to bring your son down here dressed like that," Jake adds.

The mob quickly forms again. A circle of green uniforms surrounds us now, and I think this Giants fan must be crazy. One of his friends has come to talk him down. The friend's a small man with long hair and a mustache—and he's wearing an Eagles shirt. "Come on, Steve. Let's go. They didn't mean anything. It was just a joke."

"What the fuck is your problem?" Steve says, and then shoves me again, his hands exploding through my chest.

At this point the Eagles fans begin chanting, "Ass—hole! Ass—hole! Ass—hole!"

Steve is staring into my eyes, gritting his teeth so the tendons in his neck bulge like ropes. He also lifts weights. His arms look even bigger than mine, and he is taller than me by an inch or two.

I look to Jake for help, and I can see that he looks a little worried himself.

Jake steps in front of me, puts his hands up to suggest that he means no harm, but before he can say anything, the Giants fan grabs my brother's Jerome Brown memorial jersey and throws Jake to the ground.

I see him hit the concrete—my brother's hands skidding along the blacktop—and then blood is dripping from his fingers and Jake's eyes look dazed and scared.

My brother is hurt.

My brother is hurt.

MY BROTHER IS HURT.

I explode.

The bad feeling in my stomach rockets up through my chest

and into my hands—and before I can stop myself, I'm moving forward like a Mack truck. I catch Steve's cheek with a left, and then my right connects with the south side of his chin, lifting him off the ground. I watch him float through the air as if he were allowing his body to fall backward into a pool. His back hits the concrete, his feet and hands twitch once, and then he's not moving, the crowd is silent, and I begin to feel so awful—so guilty.

Someone yells, "Call an ambulance!"

Another yells, "Tell 'em to bring a blue-and-red body bag!"

"I'm sorry," I whisper, because I find it hard to speak. "I'm so sorry."

And then I am running again.

I weave through the crowds of people, across streets, around cars, and through horns blaring and cursing drivers screaming at me. I feel a bubbly feeling in my midsection, and then I am puking my guts out onto the sidewalk—eggs, sausage, beer—and so many people are yelling at me, calling me a drunk, saying that I'm an asshole; and then I'm running again as fast as I can, down the street away from the stadiums.

When I feel as though I am going to throw up again, I stop and realize I'm alone—no more Eagles fans anywhere. A chain-link fence, beyond it a warehouse that looks abandoned.

I vomit again.

On the sidewalk, outside of the puddle I am making, pieces of broken glass glint and sparkle in the sun.

I cry.

I feel awful.

I realize that I have once again failed to be kind; that I lost control in a big way; that I seriously injured another person, and therefore I'm never going to get Nikki back now. Apart time is going to last forever because my wife is a pacifist who would never want me to hit anyone under any circumstance, and both God and Jesus were obviously rooting for me to turn the other cheek, so I know I really shouldn't have hit that Giants fan, and now I'm crying again because I'm such a fucking waste—such a fucking non-person.

I walk another half block, my chest heaving wildly, and then I stop.

"Dear God," I pray. "Please don't send me back to the bad place. *Please!*"

I look up at the sky.

I see a cloud passing just under the sun.

The top is all electric white.

I remind myself.

Don't give up, I think. Not just yet.

"Pat! Pat! Wait up!"

I look back toward the stadiums, and my brother is running toward me. Over the next minute or so, Jake gets bigger and bigger, and then he is right in front of me, bent over, huffing and puffing.

"I'm sorry," I say. "I'm so, so sorry."

"For *what*?" Jake laughs, pulls out his cell phone, dials a number, and holds the small phone up to his ear.

"I found him," Jake says into the phone. "Yeah, tell him."

Jake hands me the phone. I put it up to my ear.

"Is this Rocky Balboa?"

I recognize the voice as Scott's.

"Listen, the asshole you knocked out—well, he woke up and is super pissed. Better not come back to the tent."

"Is he okay?" I ask.

"You should be more worried about yourself."

"Why?"

"We played dumb when the cops showed up, and no one was able to identify you or your brother—but ever since five-o left, the big guy's been searching the parking lot, looking for you. Whatever you do, don't come back here, because this Giants fan's hell-bent on revenge."

I hand the phone back to Jake, feeling somewhat relieved to know I did not seriously hurt Steve, but also feeling numb—because I lost control again. Plus, I'm a little afraid of the Giants fan.

"So, are we going home now?" I ask Jake when he finishes talking to Scott.

"Home? Are you kiddin' me?" he says, and we start walking back toward the Linc.

When I don't say anything for a long time, my brother asks if I'm okay.

I'm not okay, but I don't say so.

"Listen, that asshole attacked you and threw me to the ground. You only defended your family," Jake says. "You should be proud. You were the *hero*."

Even though I was defending my brother, even though I did not seriously hurt the Giants fan, I don't feel proud at all. I feel guilty. I should be locked up again in the bad place. I feel as though Dr. Timbers was right about me—that I don't belong in the real world, because I am uncontrollable and dangerous. But of course I do not say this to Jake, mostly because he has never been locked up and doesn't understand what it feels like to lose control, and he only wants to watch the football game now, and none of this means anything to him, because he has never been married and he has never lost someone like Nikki and he is not trying to improve his life at all, because he doesn't ever feel the war that goes on in my chest every single fucking day—the chemical explosions that light up my skull like the Fourth of July and the awful needs and impulses and . . .

Outside the Linc, masses form thick lines, and with hundreds of other fans, we wait to be frisked. I don't remember being frisked at the Vet. I wonder when it became necessary to frisk people at NFL games, but I do not ask Jake, because he is now singing "Fly, Eagles, Fly" with hundreds of other drunken Eagles fans.

After we are frisked, we climb the steps and have our tickets scanned, and then we are inside of Lincoln Financial Field. People everywhere—it's like a hive full of green bees, and the buzz is deafening. We often have to turn sideways just to squeeze between people as we walk the concourse to get to our section. I follow Jake, worrying about getting separated, because I would be lost for sure.

We hit the men's room, and Jake gets everyone inside to sing the Eagles fight song again. The lines for the urinals are long, and I am amazed that no one pees in the sinks, because at the Vet—at least up in the 700 Level—all sinks were used as extra urinals.

When we finally get to our seats, we are in the end zone, only twenty or so rows up from the field.

"How did you get such good tickets?" I ask Jake.

"I know a guy," he replies, and smiles proudly.

Scott is already seated, and he congratulates me on my fight, saying, "You knocked that fucking Giants fan *out cold*!" which makes me feel awful again.

Jake and Scott high-five just about everyone in the section, and as the other fans call Scott and my brother by name, it becomes obvious that they are quite popular here.

When the beer man comes around, Scott buys us a round, and

I am amazed to find a cup holder in the seat in front of me. You would never see such a luxury item at the Vet.

Just before the Eagles' players are announced, clips from the Rocky movies are shown on the huge screens at each end of the field—Rocky running by the old Navy Yard, Rocky punching sides of beef in the meat locker, Rocky running up the steps of the art museum—and Jake and Scott keep saying, "That's you. That's you," until I worry that someone will hear them, understand that I just fought the Giants fan in the parking lot, and tell the police to take me back to the bad place.

When the Eagles' starting lineup is announced, fireworks explode and cheerleaders kick and everyone is standing and Jake keeps on pounding my back with his hand and strangers are high-fiving me, and suddenly I stop thinking about my fight in the parking lot. I begin to think about my dad watching the game in our family room—my mother serving him buffalo wings and pizza and beers, hoping the Eagles win just so her husband will be in a good mood for a week. I again wonder if my dad will start talking to me at night if the Eagles pull out a victory today, and suddenly it's kickoff and I am cheering as if my life depends on the outcome of the game.

The Giants score first, but the Eagles answer with a touchdown of their own, after which the whole stadium sings the fight song—punctuated by the Eagles chant—with deafening pride.

Late in the first quarter, Hank Baskett gets his first catch of his NFL career—a twenty-five-yarder. Everyone in our section high-fives me and pats me on the back because I am wearing my official Hank Baskett jersey, and I smile at my brother because he gave me such a great present.

The game is all Eagles after that, and at the start of the fourth quarter the Eagles are up 24–7. Jake and Scott are so happy, and I am beginning to imagine the conversation I am going to have with my father when I get home—how proud he will be of my yelling whenever Eli Manning was trying to call a play.

But then the Giants score seventeen unanswered points in the fourth quarter, and the Philadelphia fans are shocked.

In overtime, Plaxico Burress goes up and over Sheldon Brown in the end zone, and the Giants leave Philadelphia with a win.

It is awful to watch.

Outside of the Linc, Scott says, "Better not come back to the tent. That asshole will be there waiting, for sure."

So we say goodbye to Scott and follow the masses to the subway entrance.

Jake has tokens. We go through the turnstiles, descend underground, and push our way onto an already packed subway car. People yell, "No room!" but Jake mashes his body in between the other bodies and then pulls me in too. My brother's chest is against my back; strangers are smashed against my arms. The doors finally close, and my nose is almost touching the glass window.

The smell of beer resurfacing through everyone's sweat glands is pungent.

I don't like being this close to so many strangers, but I don't say anything, and soon we are at City Hall.

After we exit the train, we spin another turnstile, climb up into center city, and begin walking down Market Street, past the old department stores and the new hotels and The Gallery.

"You wanna see my apartment?" Jake asks when we get to the Eighth and Market PATCO stop, which is where I can hop a train over the Ben Franklin Bridge to Collingswood.

I do want to see Jake's apartment, but I am tired and anxious to get home so I can do a little lifting before bed. I ask if I might see it some other time.

"Sure," he says. "It's good to have you back, brother. You were a true Eagles fan today."

I nod.

"Tell Dad the Birds will bounce back next week against San Fran."

I nod again.

My brother surprises me by giving me a two-armed hug and saying, "I love you, bro. Thanks for getting my back in the parking lot."

I tell him that I love him too, and then he is walking down Market Street singing "Fly, Eagles, Fly" at the top of his lungs.

I descend underground, insert the five my mother gave me into the change machine, buy a ticket, stick it into the turnstile, descend more stairs, hit the waiting platform, and begin to think about that little kid in the Giants jersey. How hard did he cry when he realized his father had been knocked out? Did the kid even get to see the game? A few other men in Eagles jerseys are sitting on the chrome benches. Each nods sympathetically at me when they see my Hank Baskett jersey. One man at the far end of the platform yells, "Goddamn fucking Birds!" and then kicks a metal trash can. Another man standing next to me shakes his head and whispers, "Goddamn fucking Birds."

When the train comes, I choose to stand just inside the doors, and as the train slides across the dusk sky, over the Delaware River, across the Ben Franklin Bridge, I look at the city skyline, and—again—I start to think about that kid crying. I feel so awful when I think about that little kid.

I get off the train at Collingswood, walk across the open-air platform and down the steps, stick my card into the turnstile machine, and then jog home.

My mother is sitting in the family room, sipping tea. "How's Dad?" I ask.

She shakes her head and points at the TV.

The screen is cracked so that it looks like a spiderweb. "What happened?"

"Your father smashed the screen with the reading lamp."

"Because the Eagles lost?"

"No, actually. He did it when the Giants tied the game at the end of the fourth quarter. Your father had to watch the Eagles blow the game on the bedroom television," Mom says. "How's your brother?"

"Fine," I say. "Where's Dad?"

"In his office."

"Oh."

"I'm sorry your team lost," Mom says, just to be nice, I know.

"It's okay," I answer, and then go down into the basement, where I lift weights for hours and try to forget about that little Giants fan crying, but I still can't get the kid out of my mind.

For whatever reason I fall asleep on the rug that covers part of the basement floor. In my dreams the fight happens again and again, only instead of the Giants fan bringing a kid to the game, the Giants fan brings Nikki, and she too is wearing a Giants jersey. Every time I knock the big guy out, Nikki pushes through the crowd, cradles Steve's head in her hands, kisses his forehead, and then looks up at me.

Just before I run away, she says, "You're an animal, Pat. And I will never love you again."

I cry through my dreams and try not to hit the Giants fan every time the memory flashes through my mind, but I can't control my dream self any more than I could control my awake self after seeing the blood on Jake's hands.

I wake up to the sound of the basement door being closed, and I see the light streaming in through the small windows over the washer and dryer. I walk up the steps, and I cannot believe the sports pages are there.

I am very upset about the dream I had, but I realize it was only a dream, and despite everything that has happened, my father is still leaving me the sports pages after one of the worst Eagles losses in history.

So I take a deep breath. I allow myself to feel hopeful again and start my exercise routine.

Sister Sailor-Mouth

I'm at the Crystal Lake Diner with Tiffany; we're in the same booth as last time, eating our single-serving box of raisin bran, drinking hot tea. We did not say anything on the walk here; we did not say anything when we were waiting for our server to bring the milk, bowl, and box. I'm starting to understand that we have the type of friendship that does not require many words.

As I watch her spoon the brown flakes and sugared raisins into her pink lips, I try to decide whether I want to tell her about what happened at the Eagles game.

For two days now I have been thinking about that little kid crying, hiding behind his father's leg, and I feel so guilty about hitting the big Giants fan. I did not tell my mom, because the news would have upset her. My father has not talked to me since the Eagles lost to the Giants, and I don't see Dr. Cliff until Friday. Plus, I'm starting to think Tiffany is the only one who might understand, since she seems to have a similar problem and is always exploding, like on the beach when Veronica slipped and mentioned Tiffany's therapist in front of me.

I look at Tiffany, who is sitting slouched, both elbows on the table. She's wearing a black shirt that makes her hair look even blacker. She has on too much makeup, as usual. She looks sad. She looks angry. She looks different from everyone else I know—she cannot put on that happy face others wear when they know they are being watched. She doesn't put on a face for me, which makes me trust her somehow.

Suddenly Tiffany looks up, stares into my eyes. "You're not eating."

"I'm sorry," I say, and look down at the gold sparkles in the table's plastic coating.

"People will think I'm a hog if they see me eating while you watch."

So I dip my spoon into the bowl, drip milk onto the sparkly table, and shovel a small mound of milk-soaked raisin bran into my mouth.

I chew.

I swallow.

Tiffany nods and then looks out the window again.

"Something bad happened at the Eagles game," I say, and then wish I hadn't.

"I don't want to hear about football." Tiffany sighs. "I hate football."

"This really isn't about football."

She continues to stare out the window.

I look and confirm that there are only parked cars outside, nothing of interest. And then I am talking: "I hit a man so hard—lifting him up off the ground even—I thought I maybe killed him."

She looks at me. Tiffany squints and sort of smiles, like she might even laugh. "Well, did you?"

"Did I what?"

"Kill the man."

"No. No, I didn't. I knocked him out, but he eventually woke up."

"*Should you* have killed him?" Tiffany asks.

"I don't know." I am amazed by her question. "I mean, no! Of course not."

"Then why did you hit him so hard?"

"He threw my brother down to the concrete, and my mind just exploded. It was like I left my body and my body was doing something I did not want to do. And I haven't really talked about this with anyone and I was hoping you might want to listen to me so that I could—"

"Why did the man throw your brother to the ground?"

I tell her the whole story—start to finish—letting her know I can't get the big guy's son out of my mind. I'm still seeing the little guy hiding behind his father's leg; I'm seeing the little guy crying, sobbing, so obviously afraid. I also tell her about my dream—the one where Nikki comforts the Giants fan.

When I finish the story, Tiffany says, "So?"

"So?"

"So I don't get why you're *so* upset?"

For a second I think she might be kidding me, but Tiffany's face does not crack.

"I'm upset because I know Nikki will be mad at me when I tell her what happened. I am upset because I disappointed myself, and apart time will surely be extended now because God will want to protect Nikki until I learn to control myself better, and like Jesus, Nikki is a pacifist, which is the reason she did not like me going to the rowdy Eagles games in the first place, and I don't want to be sent back to the bad place, and God, I miss Nikki so much, it hurts so bad and—"

"Fuck Nikki," Tiffany says, and then slips another spoonful of raisin bran into her mouth.

I stare at her.

She chews nonchalantly.

She swallows.

"Excuse me?" I say.

"The Giants fan sounds like a total prick, as do your brother and your friend Scott. You didn't start the fight. You only defended yourself. And if Nikki can't deal with that, if Nikki won't support you when you are feeling down, then I say *fuck her*."

"Don't you ever talk about my wife like that," I say, hearing the sharp anger in my voice.

Tiffany rolls her eyes at me.

"I won't allow any of my friends to talk about my wife like that."

"Your wife, huh?" Tiffany says.

"Yes. My wife, Nikki."

"You mean your wife, *Nikki*, who abandoned you while you were recovering in a mental institution. Why isn't your wife, *Nikki*, sitting here with you right now, Pat? Think about it. Why are you eating fucking raisin bran with me? All you ever think about is pleasing *Nikki*, and yet your precious *Nikki* doesn't seem to think about you at all. Where is she? What's Nikki doing right now? Do you really believe she's thinking about *you*?"

I'm too shocked to speak.

"Fuck Nikki, Pat. Fuck her! FUCK NIKKI!" Tiffany slaps her palms against the table, making the bowl of raisin bran jump. "Forget her. She's gone. Don't you see that?"

Our server comes over to the table. She puts her hands on her hips. She presses her lips together. She looks at me. She looks at Tiffany. "Hey, sister sailor-mouth," the server says.

When I look around, the other customers are looking at my foulmouthed friend.

"This isn't a bar, okay?"

Tiffany looks at the server; she shakes her head. "You know what? Fuck you too," Tiffany says, and then she is striding across the diner and out the door.

"I'm just doin' my job," says the server. "Jeez!"

"I'm sorry," I say, and hand the server all the money I have—the twenty-dollar bill my mother gave me when I said I wanted to take Tiffany out for raisin bran. I asked for two twenties, but Mom said I couldn't give the server forty dollars when the meal only costs five, even after I told Mom about overtipping, which I learned from Nikki, as you already know.

The waitress says, "Thanks, pal. But you better go after your girlfriend."

"She's not my girlfriend," I say. "She's just a friend."

"Whatever."

Tiffany is not outside of the diner.

I look down the street and see her running away from me.

When I catch up to her, I ask what's wrong.

She doesn't answer; she keeps running.

At a quick pace, we jog side by side back into Collingswood, all the way to her parents' house, and then Tiffany runs around to the back door without saying goodbye.

The Implied Ending

That night I try to read *The Bell Jar* by Sylvia Plath. Nikki used to talk about how important Plath's novel is, saying, "Every young woman should be forced to read *The Bell Jar*." I had Mom check it out of the library, mostly because I want to understand women so I can relate to Nikki's feelings and whatnot.

The cover of the book looks pretty girly, with a dried rose hung upside down, suspended over the title.

Plath mentions the Rosenbergs' execution on the first page, at which point I know I'm in for a depressing read, because as a former history teacher, I understand just how depressing the Red Scare was, and McCarthyism too. Soon after making a reference to the Rosenbergs, the narrator starts talking about cadavers and seeing a severed head while eating breakfast.

The main character, Esther, has a good internship at a New York City magazine, but she is depressed. She uses fake names with the men she meets. Esther sort of has a boyfriend named Buddy, but he treats her horribly and makes her feel as though she should have babies and be a housewife rather than become a writer, which is what she wants to be.

Eventually Esther breaks down and is given electroshock therapy, tries to kill herself by taking too many sleeping pills, and is sent to a bad place like the one I was in.

Esther refers to a black man who serves food in her bad place as "the Negro." This makes me think about Danny and how mad the book would make my black friend, especially because Esther was white and Danny says only black people can use controversial racial terms such as "Negro."

At first, even though it is really depressing, this book excites me because it deals with mental health, a topic I am very interested in learning about. Also, I want to see how Esther gets better, how she will eventually find her silver lining and get on with her life. I am sure Nikki assigns this book so that depressed teenage girls will see there's hope if you just hold on long enough.

So I read on.

Esther loses her virginity, hemorrhages during the process, and almost bleeds to death—like Catherine in *A Farewell to Arms*—and I do wonder why women are always hemorrhaging in American literature. But Esther lives, only to find that her friend Joan has hung herself. Esther attends the funeral, and the book ends just as she steps into a room full of therapists who will decide if Esther is healthy enough to leave her bad place.

We do not get to see what happens to Esther, whether she gets better, and that made me very mad, especially after reading all night.

As the sun begins to shine through my bedroom window, I read the biographical sketch at the back of the book and find out that the whole "novel" is basically the story of Sylvia Plath's life and that the author eventually stuck her head in an oven, killing herself just like Hemingway—only without the gun—which I understand is the implied ending of the book, since everyone knows the novel is really Sylvia Plath's memoir.

I actually rip the book in half and throw the two halves at my bedroom wall.

Basement.

Stomach Master 6000.

Five hundred crunches.

Why would Nikki make teenagers read such a depressing novel?

Weight bench.

Bench press.

One-hundred-thirty-pound reps.

Why do people read books like *The Bell Jar*?

Why?

Why?

Why?

I'm surprised when Tiffany shows up the next day for our sunset run. I don't know what to say to her, so I say nothing—like usual.

We run.

We run again the next day too, but we don't discuss the comments Tiffany made about my wife.

An Acceptable Form of Coping

In the cloud room, I pick the black recliner because I am feeling a little depressed. For a few minutes I don't say anything. I am worried that Cliff will send me back to the bad place if I tell him the truth, but I feel so guilty sitting there—and then I'm talking at Cliff, spilling everything in a wild slur of sentences: the big Giants fan, the little Giants fan, my fistfight, the Eagles' loss to the Giants, my father smashing the television screen, his bringing me the sports pages but refusing to speak with me, my dream about Nikki wearing a Giants jersey, Tiffany saying "Fuck Nikki" but still wanting to run with me every day; and then Nikki teaching Sylvia Plath to defenseless teenagers, my ripping *The Bell Jar* in half, and Sylvia Plath sticking her head in an oven. "An oven?" I say. "Why would anyone stick their head in *an oven*?"

The release is powerful, and I realize now that somewhere in the middle of my rant I had begun crying. When I finish speaking, I cover my face, because Cliff is my therapist, yes, but he is also a man and an Eagles fan and maybe a friend too.

I start sobbing behind my hands.

All is quiet in the cloud room for a few minutes, and then Cliff finally speaks, saying, "I hate Giants fans. So arrogant, always wanting to talk about L.T., who was nothing but a dirty rotten cokehead. Two Super Bowls, yes, but XXV and XXI were some time ago—more than fifteen years have passed. And we were there just two years ago, right? Even if we did lose."

I am surprised.

I was sure Cliff was going to yell at me for hitting the Giants fan, that he would again threaten to send me back to the bad place, and his bringing up Lawrence Taylor seems so random that I lower my hands and see that Cliff is standing, although he is so small his head is not much higher than mine, even though I am sitting down. Also, I sort of think he just implied that the Eagles were in the Super Bowl two years ago, which would make me very upset because I have absolutely no memory of this, so I try to forget what Cliff said about our team being in the big game.

"Don't you hate Giants fans?" he says to me. "Don't you just hate 'em? Come on now, tell the truth."

"Yeah, I do," I say. "A lot. So do my brother and father."

"Why would this man wear a Giants jersey to an Eagles game?"

"I don't know."

"Did he *not* think he would be mocked?"

I don't know what to say.

"Every year I see these stupid Dallas and Giants and Redskins fans come into our house wearing their colors, and every year these same fans get manhandled by drunken Eagles fans. When will they learn?"

I am too shocked to speak.

Does this mean Cliff is a season-ticket holder? I wonder, but do not ask.

"Not only were you defending your brother, but you were defending your team too! Right?"

I realize that I am nodding.

Cliff sits down. He pulls the lever, his footrest comes up, and I stare at the well-worn soles of his penny loafers.

"When I am sitting in this chair, I am your therapist. When I am not in this chair, I am a fellow Eagles fan. Understand?"

I nod.

"Violence is not an acceptable solution. You did not have to hit that Giants fan."

I nod again. "I didn't *want* to hit him."

"But you did."

I look down at my hands. My fingers are all squirmy.

"What alternatives did you have?" he says.

"Alternatives?"

"What else could you have done, *besides* hitting the Giants fan?"

"I didn't have time to think. He was pushing me, and he threw my brother down—"

"What if he had been Kenny G?"

I close my eyes, hum a single note, and silently count to ten, blanking my mind.

"Yes, the humming. Why not try that when you feel as though you are going to hit someone? Where did you learn that technique?"

I'm a little mad at Cliff for bringing up Kenny G, which seems like a dirty trick, especially since he knows Mr. G is my biggest nemesis, but I remember that Cliff did not yell at me when I told him the truth, and I am thankful for that, so I say, "Nikki used to hum a single note whenever I offended her. She said she learned it in yoga class. And whenever she hummed, it would catch me off guard. I would get really freaked out, because it is strange to sit next to someone who is humming a single note with her eyes closed—and Nikki would keep humming that single note for such a long time. When she finally stopped, I would be grateful, and I also would be more aware of her displeasure and more receptive to her feelings, which is something I did not appreciate until recently."

"So that's why you hum every time someone brings up Kenny—"

I close my eyes, hum a single note, and silently count to ten, blanking my mind.

When I finish, Cliff says, "It allows you to express your displeasure in a unique way, disarming those around you. Very interesting tactic. Why not use this in other areas of your life? What if you had closed your eyes and hummed when the Giants fan pushed you?"

I hadn't thought of that.

"Do you think he would have continued to push you if you had closed your eyes and hummed?"

Probably not, I think. The Giants fan would have thought I was crazy, which is exactly what I thought about Nikki when she first used the tactic on me.

Cliff smiles and nods at me when he reads my face.

We talk a little about Tiffany. He says it seems as though Tiffany has romantic feelings for me, and he claims she is most likely jealous of my love for Nikki, which I think is silly, especially since Tiffany never even talks to me and is always so aloof when we are together. Plus Tiffany is so beautiful, and I have not aged well at all.

"She's just a weird woman," I say in response.

"Aren't they all?" Cliff replies, and we laugh some because women truly are hard to figure out sometimes.

"What about my dream? Me seeing Nikki in a Giants jersey? What do you think that means?"

"What do *you* think it means?" Cliff asks, and when I shrug, he changes the subject.

Cliff says Sylvia Plath's work is very depressing to read, and that his own daughter had recently suffered through *The Bell Jar* because she is taking an American literature course at Eastern High School.

"And you didn't complain to administration?" I asked.

"About what?"

"About your daughter being forced to read such depressing stories."

"No. Of course not. Why would I?"

"Because the novel teaches kids to be pessimistic. No hope at the end, no silver lining. Teenagers should be taught that—"

"Life is hard, Pat, and children have to be told how hard life can be."

"Why?"

"So they will be sympathetic to others. So they will understand that some people have it harder than they do and that a trip through this world can be a wildly different experience, depending on what chemicals are raging through one's mind."

I had not thought about this explanation, that reading books like *The Bell Jar* helped others understand what it was like to be Esther Greenwood. And I realize now that I have a lot of sympathy for Esther, and if she were a real person in my life, I would have tried to help her, only because I knew her thoughts well enough to understand she was not simply deranged, but suffering because her world had been so cruel to her and because she was depressed, due to the wild chemicals in her mind.

"So you're not mad at me?" I ask when I see Cliff look at his watch, which signifies our session is almost over.

"No. Not at all."

"Really?" I ask, because I know Cliff is probably going to write all my recent failures down in a file as soon as I leave. That he probably thinks he has failed as my therapist—at least for this week.

Cliff stands, smiles at me, and then looks out the bay window at the sparrow washing in the stone birdbath.

"Before you leave, Pat, I want to say something very important to you. This is a matter of life and death. Are you listening to me? Because I really want you to remember this. Okay?"

I start to worry because Cliff sounds so serious, but I swallow, nod, and say, "Okay."

Cliff turns.

Cliff faces me.

His face looks grave, and for a second, I am very nervous.

But then Cliff throws his hands up in the air and yells "Ahhhhhhhhh!"

I laugh because Cliff has tricked me with his funny joke. I immediately stand, throw my hands up in the air, and yell "Ahhhhhhhhh!"

"E!-A!-G!-L!-E!-S! EAGLES!" we chant in unison, throwing

Balanced Very Carefully, As If the Whole Thing Might Topple When the Heater Vents Begin to Blow Later This Fall

From the basement, I hear my dad say, "It goes right here, on this table." Three sets of footsteps are moving across the family-room floor, and soon I hear something heavy being set down. After fifteen minutes or so, the sounds of college football explode through the floor above—big bands playing, drums galore, fight songs being sung—and I realize my father has replaced the family-room television. I hear the deliverymen's footsteps exit, and then Dad increases the volume so I can hear every play call the commentators make, even though I am in the basement and the basement door is shut. I don't follow college football, so I don't really know the players or the teams being discussed.

I do some curls and simply listen, secretly hoping Dad will

our arms and legs out in an effort to represent each letter with our bodies, and I have to say—as stupid as it may sound—chanting with Cliff makes me feel a whole lot better. And judging by the smile on his little brown face, he knows the value of what he is doing for me.

come down into the basement, tell me about the new television, and ask me to watch the game with him. But he doesn't.

Suddenly, maybe a half hour after the deliverymen leave, the volume is turned down, and I hear Mom ask, "What the hell is this?"

"It's a high-definition television with surround sound," my father replies.

"No, *that* is a movie screen, and—"

"Jeanie—"

"Don't you 'Jeanie' me."

"I work hard for our money, and I won't have you telling me how to spend it!"

"Patrick, it's ridiculous. It doesn't even fit on the end table. How much did you pay for that?"

"Never mind."

"You smashed the old television just so you could buy a bigger one, didn't you?"

"Jesus Christ, Jeanie. Will you please stop bitching at me for once?"

"We're on a budget. We agreed—"

"Oh. Okay. We're on a budget."

"We agreed that—"

"We have money to feed Pat. We have money to buy Pat a new wardrobe. We have money to buy Pat a home gym. We have money for Pat's medications. Well then, the way I see it, we have money for a new fucking television set too."

I hear my mother's footsteps exit the family room. Just before my father turns up the game again, I hear her stomp up the steps to her bedroom, where I know she will cry because my father has cursed at her again.

And it's my fault their money is stretched.

I feel awful.

I do sit-ups on the Stomach Master 6000 until it is time to run with Tiffany.

When I finally go upstairs, I see that Dad's television set is one of those new flat-screen models they advertised when we watched the Eagles play Houston, and it is literally almost the size of our dining-room table. It's huge; only the center third rests on the end table, making it look as if it is balanced very carefully, as if the whole thing might topple when the heater vents begin to blow later this fall. Even still, while I do feel bad about Mom, I have to admit that the picture quality is excellent and the speakers set up on stands behind the couch fill the house with sound, making it seem as though the college football game is being played *in* our family room—and I start to look forward to watching the Eagles on the new set, thinking the players will almost appear life-size.

I stand behind the couch for a second, admiring my father's new television, hoping he will acknowledge my presence. I even say, "Dad, did you get a new television?"

But he doesn't answer me.

He is mad at my mom for questioning his purchase, so now he will sulk. He will not talk to anyone for the rest of the day, I know from experience, so I leave the house and find Tiffany jogging up and down the street.

Tiffany and I run together, but we do not talk.

When I return home, Tiffany keeps jogging without even saying goodbye, and as I jog up the driveway to the back door, Mother's car is gone.

The "Pat" Box

By 11:00 p.m. my mother has not returned home, and I start to worry because every night at 10:45 p.m. I'm supposed to take pills that help me sleep. It isn't like Mom to foul up my medication schedule.

I knock on my parents' bedroom door. When no one answers, I push the door open. My father is sleeping with the small bedroom television on. The blue glow makes his skin look alien—he sort of looks like a big fish in a lit aquarium, only without gills, scales, and fins. I walk over to my dad and shake his shoulder lightly. "Dad?" I shake him a little harder. "Dad?"

"Whaddya want?" he says without opening his eyes. He is lying on his side, and the left side of his mouth is smashed into the pillow.

"Mom's not home yet. I'm worried."

He doesn't say anything.

"Where is she?"

Still, he does not say anything.

"I'm worried about Mom. Do you think we should call the police?"

I wait for a reply, but only hear my father snoring softly.

After turning off the television, I leave my parents' bedroom and go downstairs to the kitchen.

I tell myself if Dad isn't worried, I shouldn't be either. But I know it isn't like Mom to leave me alone without telling me where she will be, especially without talking to me about my medications.

I open the kitchen cabinet and take out the eight bottles of pills that all have my name printed on the labels. So many long, depressing drug names are on the labels as well, but I only know the pills by their colors, so I open all the lids and look for what I need.

Two white-and-reds for sleeping, and also a green one with a yellow stripe, but I do not know what the green one with a yellow stripe does. Maybe antianxiety? I take all three pills because I want to sleep, and also, I know that is what Mom would want me to do. Maybe Mom is testing me. Since my father talked down to her earlier today, I really want to please Mom even more than on regular days, although I am not sure why.

I lie in bed wondering where Mom could be. I want to call her cell phone, but I don't know the number. Maybe she had a car accident? Maybe she had a stroke or a heart attack? But then I think a police officer or a hospital doctor would have called us by now if any of those things had happened, because she would certainly have her credit cards and license on her. Maybe she got lost while driving? But then she would have used her cell phone to call home and would have told us she was running late. Maybe she got sick of Dad and me and ran away? I think about this and realize that excluding the times when she teases me about Tiffany being "my friend," I haven't seen my mother laugh or smile in a very long time—in fact, if I really think about it, I often see Mom crying or looking like she is about to cry. Maybe she got sick of keeping track of my pills? Maybe I forgot to flush one morning and Mom found some of my pills in the toilet and is now mad at me for hiding pills under my tongue? Maybe I have failed to appreciate Mom just like I failed to appreciate Nikki, and now God is taking Mom away from me too? Maybe Mom is never coming home again and—

Just as I start to feel seriously anxious, as if I might need to bang the heel of my hand against my forehead, I hear a car pull into the driveway.

When I look out the window, I see Mom's red sedan.

I run down the stairs.

I'm out the door before she even reaches the back porch.

"Mom?" I say.

"Is-jus-me," she says through the shadows in the driveway.

"Where were you?"

"Out." When she enters into the white circle cast from the outside light, she looks like she might fall backward, so I run down the steps and give her a hand, bracing her shoulders with my arm. Her head is sort of wobbly, but she manages to look me in the eyes; she squints and says, "Nikki-sa-fool t'ave let *you* getta-way."

Her mentioning Nikki makes me feel even more anxious, especially what she said about my getting away, because I have not gotten away and would be more than willing to go back to Nikki now or whenever, and it was me who was the fool, never appreciating Nikki for what she was—all of which Mother knows so well. But I can smell the alcohol on her breath; I hear her slurring her words, and I realize it's probably just the alcohol talking nonsense. Mom does not usually drink, but tonight she is obviously drunk, and this also makes me worry.

I help her into the house and sit her down on the couch in the family room. Within minutes she's passed out cold.

It would be a bad idea to put my drunk mother in bed with my sulking father, so I put an arm under her shoulders and another arm under her knees, lift her up, and carry her to my bedroom. Mom is small and light, so it is not hard for me to carry her up the stairs. I get her into my bed, take off her shoes, throw the comforter over her body, and then go to get a glass of water from the kitchen.

Back upstairs, I find a bottle of Tylenol and tap out two white pills.

I pick my mother's head up, get her into a seated position, shake her lightly until she opens her eyes, and tell her to take the pills along with the glass of water. At first she says, "Jus lemme sleep," but I know from college days just how much this pre-bed water and headache medicine can reduce the morning hangover. Finally my mother takes the pills, drinks half a glass of water, and is back asleep in no time at all.

I watch her rest for a few minutes, and I think she still looks pretty, that I really do love my mom. I wonder where she went to drink—with whom she drank and what she drank—but really I am only happy that she is home safe. I try not to think about her downing drinks at some depressing bar, with middle-aged men all around. I try not to think about Mom bad-mouthing my father to one of her girlfriends and then driving home drunk. But it's all I can think about: how my mother is being driven to drink—how *I'm* driving my mother to drink, and my father isn't helping much either.

After grabbing my framed picture of Nikki, I climb the stairs to the attic, set Nikki up next to my pillow, and get into my sleeping bag. I leave the lights on so I can fall asleep looking at Nikki's freckled nose, which is exactly what I do.

When I open my eyes, Kenny G is standing over me, his legs bridging my body, a foot on either side of my chest; the sexy synthesizer chords are softly lighting the darkness.

The last time Mr. G visited my parents' attic flashes through my head—my father kicking and punching me, my father threatening to send me back to the bad place—so I close my eyes, hum a single note, and silently count to ten, blanking my mind.

But Kenny G is undaunted.

The soprano sax enters Mr. G's lips once more and "Songbird" takes flight. I keep my eyes closed, hum a single note, and silently count to ten, blanking my mind, but he continues to blow his horn. The little white scar above my right eyebrow starts to burn and itch as the melody flutters toward climax. Desperately, I want to pound the heel of my hand against my forehead, but instead I keep my eyes closed, hum a single note, and silently count to ten, blanking my mind.

Just when Kenny G's smooth jazz seems unconquerable—

Seven, eight, nine, ten.

Suddenly silence.

When I open my eyes, I see Nikki's still face, her freckled nose—I kiss the glass, feeling so relieved that Kenny G has stopped playing. I exit my sleeping bag, look all around the attic—moving a few dusty boxes and other items, searching behind hanging rows of out-of-season clothes—and Mr. G is gone. "I've defeated him," I whisper. "He didn't make me punch my forehead, and—"

I see a box marked "Pat" and begin to experience that bad feeling I sometimes get just before something unpleasant is about to happen. It feels as though I have to go to the bathroom very badly, even though I know I don't.

The box is at the far end of the attic. It was hidden under a braided rug I moved when I was searching for Kenny G. I have to navigate my way back through the mess I made during my search, but soon I reach the box. I flip open the flaps at the top, and my Collingswood High School soccer jacket is on top. I take it out of the box and hold the dusty thing up. The jacket looks so small. I'd rip the yellow leather sleeves off if I tried it on now, I think, and then set the relic down on another nearby box. When I next look into the "Pat" box, I am shocked and scared into rearranging the attic so it looks exactly how it was before I began searching for Mr. G.

When the attic is restored, I lie in my sleeping bag, feeling as if I am in a dream. Several times during the night I get up, move the braided rug, and look in the "Pat" box again, just to make sure I had not hallucinated before. Every time, the contents condemn Mom and make me feel betrayed.

Mom's Handwriting Emerges

The sun bursts through the attic window and lands on my face, warming it, until I open my eyes and greet the day with a squint. After a kiss, I return Nikki to my bedroom dresser and find my mother still asleep in my bed. I notice that the glass of water I left her is now empty, and I am glad to have left it there, even if I am mad at Mom now.

As I descend the staircase, I smell something burning.

When I reach the kitchen, my father is standing in front of the stove. He is wearing Mom's red apron.

"Dad?"

When he turns around, he has a spatula in one hand and a pink oven mitt on the other. Behind him, meat hisses—a thick river of smoke flies up into the exhaust fan.

"What are you doing?"

"Cooking."

"Cooking what?"

"Steak."

"Why?"

"I'm hungry."

"Are you frying it?"

"I'm cooking it Cajun style. Blackened."

"Maybe you should turn the burner down?" I suggest, but he returns to his cooking, continuing to flip the sizzling cut over and over, so I go down into the basement to begin my workout.

The fire alarm goes off for fifteen minutes or so.

When I return to the kitchen two hours later, the pan he used is blackened and still on the now greasy stove; a plate and utensils are in the sink. Dad is watching ESPN on his new television, and his surround sound speaker system seems to shake the house. The clock on the microwave reads 8:17 a.m. My mother has forgotten my meds again, so I take out my eight bottles, remove all the caps, and search for the right colors. Soon I have a half dozen pills lined up on the counter, and I confirm that the colors are what I take every morning. I swallow all of my pills, thinking maybe my mother is testing me again, and even though I am technically mad at her, I am also now very worried about Mom, so I climb the steps to my room and see that she is still sleeping.

Downstairs, I stand behind the couch and say, "Dad?"

But he ignores me, so I return to my basement gym and continue my workout, listening to the ESPN commentators recap the college games and forecast the upcoming NFL action. Their voices arrive crisply through the floorboards above. I know from reading the paper that the Eagles are favored to win over San Francisco, which makes me excited to watch the game with my father, who will be in a great mood if the Eagles are victorious, and therefore he will also be more likely to speak with me.

Midmorning, Mom descends, which is a relief, because I was

starting to worry that she was really sick. I am riding the bike, and—after finding the "Pat" box last night—I just continue pedaling when Mom says, "Pat?" I do not face Mom, but using my peripheral vision, I see that she is showered, her hair is done, her makeup is applied, and she is wearing a pretty summer dress. Mom also smells really nice—lavender. "Did you take your pills last night?" she asks.

I nod once.

"What about this morning?"

I nod again.

"Dr. Patel told me I should have allowed you to take control over your meds when you first came home, that this was a step toward independence. But I was being a mom when you did not need me to be a mom. So congratulations, Pat."

"Congratulations" is a strange thing for her to say, especially since I have not won a prize or anything, but I am really only thinking about what happened last night, why Mom came home drunk. So I ask her, "Where were you last night? Did you go out with friends?"

Using the corner of my eye again, I see her look down at the old brown rug beneath us. "I appreciate your putting me to bed last night. The water and the Tylenol helped. It was a bit of a role reversal, eh? Well, I appreciate it. Thanks, Pat."

I realize she has not answered my question, but I don't know what to say, so I say nothing.

"Your father has been a bear lately, and I'm simply tired of it. So I'm making some demands, and things are going to change a little around here. Both of my men are going to start taking care of themselves a little more. You need to get on with your life, and I'm sick and tired of the way your father treats me."

Suddenly I forget all about the "Pat" box and face my mother as I continue pedaling. "Are you mad at me? Did I do something wrong?"

"I'm not mad at you, Pat. I *am* mad at your father. He and I had a long talk yesterday when you were running. Things might be a little rough around here for a few weeks, but I think we'll all be better for it in the long run."

A wild thought leaps into my head and terrifies me. "You're not leaving us, Mom, are you?"

"No. I'm not," Mom says, looking me in the eyes, which makes me believe her one hundred percent. "I would never leave you, Pat. But I *am* going out today because I'm done with Eagles football. You two are on your own for food."

"Where are you going?" I ask, pedaling faster now.

"Out," Mom says, and then kisses the little white scar on my sweaty forehead before she leaves.

I am so nervous about what Mom has told me that I do not eat anything all day, but simply drink my water and do my routine. Because the Eagles are playing at 4:15, I get in a full workout. The whole time, I secretly hope my father will come down into the basement and ask me to watch the 1:00 NFL game with him, but he doesn't.

Midafternoon I climb up out of the basement and stand behind the couch for a second.

"Dad?" I say. "Dad?"

He ignores me and keeps watching the 1:00 game, and I don't even look to see who is playing, because I am so nervous about what Mom told me. I put on my trash bag and hope Tiffany is outside, because I could really use someone to talk to. But after I stretch for fifteen minutes, Tiffany doesn't show, so I run alone, thinking it funny that when I want to run alone, Tiffany is always there, but today she is not.

I am very hungry, and the pain in my stomach increases as I run, which I relish because it means I am losing weight, and well, I feel as though I might have put on some extra fat in the past week, especially after drinking beer with Jake last weekend. This reminds me that I have not spoken with Jake since the Eagles lost to the Giants, and I wonder if he is coming over today to watch the game with Dad and me. Since the pain has sharpened, I decide to run farther than usual, pushing myself. Also, I am sort of afraid to go home, now that my mother has left me alone with my father for the day, and I am not sure what she meant by "changes" anyway. I keep wishing Tiffany was running with me so I might talk to her and tell her how I feel, which is a strange desire since she usually never says much in response, and the last time I tried to talk to her about my problems, she started cursing very loudly in a public place and said some really awful things about Nikki. Still, I am starting to feel as though Tiffany is my best friend, which is sort of strange and scary.

At the end of my run, I jog down my street, and Jake's silver BMW is nowhere to be seen. Maybe he took the train in from Philadelphia, I think. I am hoping not to be left alone with my father for the game, but somehow I know this is exactly what is going to happen.

When I enter the house, my dad is still alone on the couch, wearing his McNabb jersey now and watching the end of the 1:00 game. A small collection of beer bottles stand at his feet like bowling pins.

"Is Jake coming over?" I ask my father, but he ignores me again.

Upstairs, I shower and put on my Hank Baskett jersey.

When I reach the family room, the Eagles game is just coming on, so I sit down at the end of the couch my father is not occupying.

"What the hell is that noise?" Dad says, and then turns down the volume.

I realize my stomach is making crazy gurgling noises, but I say, "I don't know," and Dad turns up the volume again.

Just as I had hoped, the new television is an experience. The players warming up on the field look life-size, and the sound quality makes me feel as though I am in San Francisco, sitting on the fifty-yard line. Realizing that my brother is not going to make it by kickoff, when a commercial comes on, I jump to my feet and yell "Ahhhhhhhhh!" but Dad only looks at me like he wants to hit me in the face again. So I sit down and do not say anything else.

The announcers state that Donté Stallworth was a late scratch, so I start to hope Baskett will get a few more balls thrown his way, since the Eagles' number one receiver is out of action.

The Eagles set up a nice drive and score on their first possession with a shovel pass to Westbrook, at which point my father's emotions morph. He reaches across the couch and repetitively claps his hand against my thigh, saying over and over again, "Touchdown Eagles! Touchdown Eagles!" I start to feel hopeful for my dad, but when the Eagles kick off, he resumes his negative ways and says, "Don't celebrate too much. Remember what happened last week." And it is almost as if he is talking to himself, reminding himself not to be overly hopeful.

The defense holds strong, and tight end L. J. Smith scores a touchdown with only a few minutes left in the first quarter, making it 13–0. Even though the Eagles have blown big leads before, it seems safe to say the Birds are the superior team today. My thoughts are confirmed after Akers hits the extra point and my father jumps up and starts singing "Fly, Eagles, Fly." So I jump up and sing with him, and we both do the chant at the end, spelling the letters with our arms and legs: "E!-A!-G!-L!-E!-S! EAGLES!"

Between quarters, my father asks me if I am hungry, and when I say yes, he orders us a pizza and brings me a Bud from the refrigerator. With the Eagles up 14–0, he is all smiles, and as we sip our beer, he says, "Now all we need is your boy Baskett to get a catch or two."

As if my father's words were a prayer answered, McNabb's first completion in the second quarter is to Baskett for eight yards. Dad and I cheer so loudly for the undrafted rookie.

The pizza arrives during halftime, and the Eagles are up 24–3. "If only Jake were here," my father says. "Then this day would be perfect."

My dad and I have been so happy that I've forgotten Jake is not with us. "Where is Jake?" I ask, but Dad ignores the question.

In the third quarter the San Francisco running back fumbles on the Eagles' one-yard line and defensive tackle Mike Patterson picks up the ball and runs toward the opposite end zone. Dad and I are out of our seats, cheering on the three-hundred-pound lineman as he runs the whole length of the field, and then the Eagles are up 31–3.

San Francisco scores a few touchdowns late in the second half, but it doesn't matter, because the game is basically out of reach, and the Eagles win 38–24. At the conclusion of the game, my father and I sing "Fly, Eagles, Fly" and do the chant one last time, celebrating the Eagles' victory, and then Dad simply turns off the television and returns to his study without even saying goodbye to me.

The house is so quiet.

Maybe a dozen or so beer bottles on the floor, the pizza box is still on the coffee table, and I know the sink is stacked full of dishes and the pan in which Dad cooked his breakfast steak. Since I am practicing being kind, I figure I should at least clean up the family room so Mom won't have to do it. I carry the Bud bottles out to the recycle bucket by the garage and throw away the pizza box in the outside garbage can. Back inside, a few used napkins are on the floor, and when I reach down to pick up the mess, I spot a crumpled ball of paper under the coffee table.

I pick up the ball, uncrumple it, and realize it is not one but two pieces of paper. Mom's handwriting emerges. I flatten the papers out on the coffee table.

Patrick,

I need to tell you I will no longer allow you to disregard the decisions we make together, nor will I allow you to talk down to me any longer—especially in front of others. I have met a new friend who has encouraged me to assert myself more forcefully in an effort to gain your respect. Know that I am doing this to save our marriage.

Your options:

1. *Return the monstrous television you purchased, and everything will go back to normal.*
2. *Keep the monstrous television, and you must agree to the following demands:*
    - A. *You must eat dinner at the table with Pat and me five nights a week.*

B. You must go on a half-hour walk with either Pat or me five nights a week.
C. You must have a daily conversation with Pat, during which you ask him at least five questions and listen to his replies, which you will report to me nightly.
D. You must do one recreational activity a week with Pat and me, such as eating at a restaurant, seeing a movie, going to the mall, shooting baskets in the backyard, etc.

Failure to complete either option 1 or 2 will force me to go on strike. I will no longer clean your house, buy or cook your food, launder your clothes, or share your bed. Until you declare which option you wish to take, consider your wife on strike.

With best intentions,
Jeanie

It does not seem like Mom to be so forceful with Dad, and I do wonder if her "new friend" coached her through the writing of the two-page letter. It is very hard for me to picture Dad returning his new television, especially after watching the Eagles win on the new set. His purchase will be considered good luck for sure, and Dad will want to watch next week's Eagles game on the same television so he will not jinx the Birds, which is understandable. But the demands Mom made—especially the one where Dad has to talk to me every night—also seem incredibly improbable, although I do think it would be nice to eat dinner together as a family and maybe even go out to a restaurant, but not to the movies, since I am now only willing to watch the movie of my own life.

Suddenly I need to speak with my brother, but I do not know his phone number. I find the address book in the cabinet above the stove and place a call to Jake's apartment. A woman picks up on the third ring; her voice is beautiful.

"Hello?" she says.

I know it is not my brother on the other end, but I still say, "Jake?"

"Who is this?"

"It's Pat Peoples. I'm looking for my brother, Jake. Who are you?"

I hear the woman cover the phone with her hand, and then my brother's voice comes through loud and clear: "Did you see that ninety-eight-yard fumble return? Did you see Patterson run?"

I want to ask about the woman who answered my brother's phone, but I am a little afraid of finding out who she is. Maybe I should already know, but forget somehow. So I simply say, "Yeah, I saw it."

"Frickin' awesome, dude. I didn't know a defensive tackle could run that far."

"Why didn't you come over and watch the game with Dad and me?"

"Truthfully?"

"Yes."

"I can't lie to my brother. Mom called me this morning and told me not to come, so I went to a bar with Scott. She called Ronnie too. I know because Ronnie called me to make sure everything was okay. I told him not to worry."

"Why?"

"Should he be worried?"

"No, why did Mom tell you and Ronnie not to come over?"

"She said it would give you a chance to be alone with Dad. She said it would force Dad to talk to you. So did he?"

"A little."

"Well, that's good, right?"

"I found a note from Mom to Dad."

"What?"

"I found a note from Mom to Dad."

"Okay. What did it say?"

"I'll just read it to you."

"Go ahead."

I read him the note.

"Shit. Go Mom."

"You know he won't be taking the television back now, right?"

"Not after the Birds won today."

"Yeah, and I'm worried that Dad won't be able to meet the demands."

"Well, he probably won't, but maybe he'll at least try, right? And trying would be good for him—and Mom."

Jake changes the subject by mentioning Baskett's catch in the second quarter, which turned out to be his only catch of the game. My brother doesn't want to talk about our parents anymore. He says, "Baskett's coming along. He's an undrafted rookie, and he's getting catches. That's huge." But it doesn't feel huge to me. Jake says he's looking forward to seeing me next Monday night, when the Eagles will play the Green Bay Packers. He asks me to have lunch in the city before we tailgate with Scott and the fat men, and then we hang up.

It's getting late, and my mother is still not home.

I begin to worry about her, and so I do all the dishes by hand. For a good fifteen minutes—with steel wool—I scrub the pan my father burned. And then I vacuum the family room. Dad had splattered some pizza sauce on the couch, so I find some cleaning spray in the hall cabinet and do my best to remove the stain—dabbing lightly and then wiping a little harder in a circular motion, just like it says on the side of the bottle. My mom comes home as I am on my knees cleaning the couch.

"Did your father tell you to clean up his mess?" Mom asks.

"No," I say.

"Did he tell you about the letter I wrote him?"

"No—but I found it."

"Well, then you know. I don't want you to do any cleaning, Pat. We're going to let this place rot until your father gets the message."

I want to tell her I found the "Pat" box in the attic, how hungry I was today, that I really don't want to live in a filthy house, and I need to take one thing at a time—finding the end of apart time first and foremost—but Mom looks so determined and almost proud. So I agree to help her make the house filthy. She says we will be eating takeout, and when my father is not home, everything will be as it was before she wrote the note, but when my father *is* home, we will be slovenly. I tell Mom that while she is on strike, she can sleep in my bed, because I want to sleep in the attic anyway. When she says she'll sleep on the couch, I insist she take my bed, and she thanks me.

"Mom?" I say when she turns to leave.

She faces me.

"Does Jake have a girlfriend?" I ask.

"Why?"

"I called him today, and a woman answered the phone."

"Maybe he *does* have a girlfriend," she says, and then walks away.

The indifference Mom shows regarding Jake's love life makes me feel as though I am forgetting something. If Jake had a girlfriend Mom did not know about, she would have asked me a million questions. Her lack of interest suggests that Mom is keeping another secret from me, maybe something larger than what I found in the "Pat" box. Mom must be protecting me, I think, but I still want to know from what.

The Asian Invasion

After a relatively short workout and an even shorter—and silent—run with Tiffany, I hop a train to Philadelphia. Following Jake's directions, I walk down Market Street toward the river, turn right on Second Street, and follow the road to his building.

When I reach the address, I am surprised to find that Jake lives in a high-rise that overlooks the Delaware River. I have to give my name to the doorman and tell him who I am visiting before he will let me in the building. He's just an old man in a funny costume, who says "Go Eagles" when he sees my Baskett jersey, but my brother having a doorman *is* sort of impressive, regardless of the man's uniform.

Another old man wears a different sort of funny costume in the elevator—he even has on one of those brimless monkey hats—and this man takes me to the tenth floor after I tell him my brother's name.

The elevator doors open, and I walk down a blue hallway on a thick red carpet. When I find number 1021, I knock three times.

"What's up, Baskett?" my brother says after he opens the door. He's in his Jerome Brown memorial jersey because it's game day again. "Come on in."

There is a huge bay window in the living room, and I can see the Ben Franklin Bridge, the Camden Aquarium, and tiny boats floating on the Delaware. It's a beautiful view. I immediately notice that my brother has a flat-screen television thin enough to hang on the wall like a picture—and it is even bigger than Dad's television. But strangest of all, my brother has a baby grand piano in his living room. "What's this?" I ask.

"Check it out," Jake says. He sits down on the piano bench, lifts the cover off the keys, and then actually starts playing. I am amazed that he can play "Fly, Eagles, Fly." His version isn't very fancy, just a simple chord progression, but it's definitely the Eagles' fight song. When he begins to sing, I sing along with him. When he finishes, we do the chant and then Jake tells me he has been taking lessons for the past three years. He even plays me another song, which is very unlike "Fly, Eagles, Fly." This next song is familiar—surprisingly gentle, like a kitten walking through high grass—and it seems so unlike Jake to create something this beautiful. I actually feel my eyes moistening as my brother plays with his eyes shut, moving his torso back and forth with the sway of the piece, which also looks funny because he is wearing an Eagles jersey. He makes a couple of mistakes, but I don't even care, because he is trying very hard to play the piece correctly for me and that's what counts, right?

When he finishes, I clap loudly and then ask him what he was playing.

"*Pathétique*. Piano Sonata number 8. Beethoven. That was part of the second movement. Adagio cantabile," Jake says. "Did you like it?"

"Very much." Truthfully, I am amazed. "When did you learn to play?"

"When Caitlin moved in with me, she brought her piano, and she's sort of been teaching me all about music ever since."

I start to feel dizzy because I have never heard mention of this Caitlin, and I think my brother just told me she lives here with him, which would mean my brother is in a serious relationship I know nothing about. This does not seem right. Brothers should know about each other's lovers. Finally I manage to say, "Caitlin?"

My brother takes me into his bedroom, and there's a big wooden poster bed with two matching armoires that look like guards facing each other. He picks up a framed black-and-white photo from the bed stand and hands it to me. In the photo, Jake's cheek is smashed against a beautiful woman's. She has short blond hair, cut almost like a man's, and she is very delicate-looking, but pretty. She is in a white dress; Jake is in a tuxedo. "That's Caitlin," Jake says. "She plays with the Philadelphia Orchestra sometimes and does a lot of recording in New York City too. She's a classical pianist."

"Why have I not heard about Caitlin before?"

Jake takes the portrait from my hands and stands it up on the dresser. We walk back into the living room and sit down on his leather couch. "I knew you were upset about Nikki, so I didn't want to tell you that I was . . . well . . . happily married."

Married? The word hits me like a giant wave, and suddenly I am slick with sweat.

"Mom actually tried to get you out of that place in Baltimore for the Mass, but it was when you were first admitted and they wouldn't let you out. Mom didn't want me to tell you about Caitlin yet, so I didn't at first, but you're my brother, and now that you're home, I wanted you to know about my life, and Caitlin's the best part. I've told her all about you and—if you want—you can meet her today. I had her go out this morning while I broke the news to you. I can call her now, and we can have lunch before we go down to the Linc. So, *do you want to meet my wife?*"

The next thing I know, I'm at a little swanky café off South Street, sitting across from a beautiful woman who holds my brother's hand under the table and smiles at me unceasingly. Jake and Caitlin carry the conversation, and it feels a lot like when I am with Veronica and Ronnie. Jake answers most of the questions Caitlin asks me, because I do not say much at all. No mention is made of Nikki or my time at the bad place or just how bizarre it is that Caitlin has been married to my brother for years, yet I had never met her. When the waiter comes, I say I'm not hungry, because I don't have very much money on me—only the ten bucks my mother gave me for the subway, since I already spent five bucks on the PATCO ticket. But my brother orders for all of us and says he is treating, which is nice of him. We eat fancy ham sandwiches with some sort of sun-dried tomato paste, and when I finish, I ask Caitlin if the ceremony was a nice one.

"What ceremony?" she says, and I catch her looking at the little white scar above my right eyebrow.

"Your wedding ceremony."

"Oh," she says, and then looks lovingly at my brother. "Yes. It was really nice. We had the Mass at St. Patrick's Cathedral in New York City and then a small reception at the New York Palace."

"How long have you been married?"

My brother shoots his wife a look that I do not miss.

"A while now," she says, which makes me feel crazy because everyone present knows that I do not remember the last couple of years—and because she is a woman, Caitlin knows exactly how long she has been married to Jake. It is obvious she is trying to protect me by being vague. This makes me feel awful, even though I realize Caitlin is trying to be kind.

My brother pays the bill, and we walk Caitlin back to their apartment building. Jake kisses his wife by the entrance door, and his love for her is so obvious. But then Caitlin kisses *me* right on the cheek, and with her face only a few inches from mine, she says, "I'm glad I finally got to meet you, Pat. I hope we'll become good friends." I nod because I don't know what else to say, and then Caitlin says, "Go Baker!"

"It's Baskett, dummy," Jake says, and Caitlin blushes before they kiss again.

Jake hails a taxi and tells the driver, "City Hall."

In the taxi I tell my brother I don't have any money to pay for the taxi ride, but he says I never have to pay for anything when I am with him, which is a nice thing to say, but his saying it makes me feel sort of strange.

Underneath City Hall, we buy subway tokens, spin a turnstile, and then wait for the southbound Orange Line.

Even though it is only 1:30 p.m. and kickoff is not for seven hours yet, even though it is a Monday, a day when most people have to work, many men in Eagles jerseys are already waiting on the platform. This makes me realize that Jake is not working today—it makes me realize I do not even know what Jake does for a living, which really starts to freak me out. I think hard and remember that my brother was a business major in college, but I cannot remember where he works, so I ask him.

"I'm an options trader," he says.

"What's that?"

"I play the stock market."

"Oh," I say. "So who do you work for?"

"Myself."

"What do you mean?"

"I work for myself and do all my business online. I'm self-employed."

"Which is why you could take off early to hang out with me."

"That's the best part about being self-employed."

I am very impressed with Jake's ability to support himself and his wife by playing the stock market, but he doesn't want to talk about his work. He thinks I'm not smart enough to understand what he does; Jake doesn't even try to explain his work to me.

"So what did you think of Caitlin?" he asks me.

But the train comes, and we join the herd of boarding Eagles fans before I can answer.

"What did you think of Caitlin?" he asks again after we find seats and the train starts moving.

"She's great," I say, avoiding eye contact with my brother.

"You're mad at me for not telling you about Caitlin right away."

"No, I'm not." I want to tell him all about Tiffany following me when I run; finding the "Pat" box; how Mom is still on strike and dirty dishes are in the sink and Dad turned his white shirts pink when he did the wash; how my therapist Cliff says I need to stay neutral and not get involved in my parents' marital problems but only focus on improving my own mental health but how can I do that when Dad and Mom are sleeping in separate rooms and Dad is always telling me to clean the house and Mom is telling me to leave it filthy—and I was having a hard time keeping it together before I found out my brother plays the piano and trades stocks and is living with a beautiful musician and I have missed his gala wedding and therefore will never see my brother marry, which is something I very much wanted to see, because I love my brother. But instead of saying any of this, I say, "Jake, I'm sort of worried about seeing that Giants fan again."

"Is that why you've been so quiet today?" my brother asks, as if he has forgotten all about what happened before the last home game. "I doubt a Giants fan will show up at the Green Bay game, but we're going to set up in a different parking lot anyway, just in case any of the asshole's friends are looking for us. I got your back. Don't worry. The fat guys are setting up the tent in the lot behind the Wachovia Center. No worries at all."

When we arrive at Broad and Pattison, we exit the subway car and climb back up into the afternoon. I follow my brother through the thin crowds of diehards who—like us—have begun tailgating seven hours before kickoff, on a Monday no less. We walk past the Wachovia Center, and when the fat men's green tent comes into view, I can't believe what I see.

The fat men are outside of the tent with Scott, and they are yelling at someone hidden by their collective girth. A huge school bus painted green—it's running, and the driver is inching toward our tent. On the hood of the bus is a portrait of Brian Dawkins's bust, and the likeness is incredible. (Dawkins is a regular Pro Bowler who plays free safety for the Birds.) As we get closer, I make out the words THE ASIAN INVASION along the side of the bus, which is full of brown-faced men. This early in the afternoon, parking spaces are plentiful, so I wonder what the argument is about.

Soon I recognize the voice, which argues, "The Asian Invasion has been parked in this very spot for every home game since the Linc was opened. It's good luck for the Eagles. We are Eagles fans, just like you. Superstition or not, our parking the Asian Invasion bus in this very spot *is crucial* if you want the Birds to win tonight."

"We're not moving our tent," Scott says. "No fucking way. You should have gotten here earlier." The fat men reiterate Scott's sentiment, and things are getting heated.

I see Cliff before he sees me. "Move the tent," I say to our friends.

Scott and the fat men turn to face me; they look surprised by my command, almost bewildered, as if I have betrayed them.

My brother and Scott exchange a glance, and then Scott asks, "Hank Baskett—destroyer of Giants fans—says, 'Move the tent'?"

"Hank Baskett says, 'Move the tent,'" I say.

Scott turns and faces Cliff, who is shocked to see me. Scott says, "Hank Baskett says, 'Move the tent.' So we move the tent."

The fat guys groan, but they begin to break down our tailgate party, and soon it is moved three parking spaces over, along with Scott's van, at which time the Asian Invasion bus pulls forward and parks. Fifty or so Indian men exit—each one of them wearing a green number 20 Dawkins jersey. They are like a small army, and soon, several barbecues are going and the smell of curry is all around us.

Cliff played it cool and did not say hello to me, which I realize was his way of saying, "It's your call, Pat." He simply faded away into the other Dawkins jerseys, so I would not have to explain our relationship, which was kind of him.

When we have our tent resituated, when the fat men are inside watching television, Scott says, "Hey, Baskett. Why did you let the dot heads have our parking spot?"

"None of them have a dot on their head," I say.

"Did you know that little guy?" Jake asks me.

"Which little guy, me?"

We turn around, and Cliff is standing there with a sizzling platter of vegetables and meat cubes skewered on sticks of wood.

"Indian kabobs. Quite delicious. For allowing us to park the Asian Invasion bus in its usual spot."

When Cliff lifts the platter up, we each grab an Indian kabob, and the meat is spicy, but delicious, as are the vegetables.

"And the men in the tent—would they also like one?"

"Hey, fat-asses," Scott yells. "Food."

The fat men come out and partake. Soon everyone is nodding and complimenting Cliff on his delicious food.

"Sorry for the trouble," Cliff says so nicely.

He's been so kind—even after hearing Scott call him a dot head—that I can't help claiming Cliff as a friend, so I say, "Cliff, this is my brother, Jake, my friend Scott, and . . ." I forget the fat men's names, so I just say, "Friends of Scott."

"Shit," Scott says. "You should have just told us you were friends with Baskett here and we wouldn't have given you any trouble. You want a beer?"

"Sure," Cliff says, putting the empty tray down on the concrete.

Scott hands everyone a green plastic cup, we all pour bottles of Yuengling Lager, and then I am drinking beers with my therapist. I am afraid Cliff will yell at me for drinking when I am on medications, but he doesn't.

"How do you guys know each other?" one of the fat guys says, and then I realize that by "you guys," he means Cliff and me.

I am so happy to be drinking beers with Cliff that I say, "He's my therapist," before I can remind myself to lie.

"And we are friends too," Cliff quickly adds, which surprises me but makes me feel pretty good, especially since no one says anything about my needing a therapist.

"What are your boys doing?" Jake asks Cliff.

I turn around and see ten or so men rolling out huge sheets of Astroturf.

"They are rolling out the Kubb fields."

"What?" everyone says.

"Come on, I'll show you."

And this is how we came to play what Cliff calls the Swedish Viking game while tailgating before Monday Night Football.

"Why do a bunch of Indians play a Swedish Viking game?" one of the fat men asks.

"Because it's fun," Cliff replies, so cool.

The Indian men are quick to share their food and are also so knowledgeable regarding Eagles football. They explain Kubb, which is a game where you throw wooden batons to knock down your opponent's kubbs, which are wooden blocks set up on opposite baselines. The knocked-down kubbs get tossed to the opponents' field and set up where they land. To be truthful, I am still not exactly sure how it all works, but I know the game ends when you clean the opponents' field of kubbs and knock down the kubb king, which is the tallest block of wood, set up in the center of the Astroturf.

Cliff surprises me by asking if he can be my partner. All afternoon he tells me which blocks to aim for, and we win many games in between bouts of eating Indian kabobs and drinking our Yuengling Lager and the Asian Invasion's India Pale Ale out of green plastic cups. Jake, Scott, and the fat men assimilate into the Asian Invasion tailgate party very nicely—we have Indians in our tent, they have white guys on their Kubb fields—and I think all it really takes for different people to get along is a common rooting interest and a few beers.

Every so often one of the Indian men yells "Ahhhhhhhh!" and when we all do the chant, we are fifty or so men strong, and our "E!-A!-G!-L!-E!-S! EAGLES!" is deafening.

Cliff is deadly with his wooden batons. He mostly carries our team as we play Kubb against various groupings of men, but we end up winning the money tournament, in which I did not even know we were playing until we won. One of Cliff's boys hands me fifty dollars. Cliff explains that Jake paid my entry fee, so I try to give my brother my winnings, but Jake will not let me. Finally, I decide to buy rounds of beer inside the Linc, and I stop arguing with my brother over money.

After the sun sets, when it is just about time to go into Lincoln Financial Field, I ask Cliff if I can talk to him alone, and when we walk away from the Asian Invasion, I say, "Is this okay?"

"This?" he replies, and the glassy look in his eyes suggests he is a little drunk.

"The two of us hanging out like boys. What my friend Danny would call 'representing.'"

"Why not?"

"Well, because you are my therapist."

Cliff smiles, holds up a little brown finger, and says, "What did I tell you? When I am not in the leather recliner . . ."

"You're a fellow Eagles fan."

"Damn right," he says, and then claps me on the back.

After the game I catch a ride back to Jersey on the Asian Invasion bus, and the Indian men and I sing "Fly, Eagles, Fly" over and over again because the Eagles have beaten the Packers 31–9 on national television. When Cliff's friends drop me off in front of my house, it's after midnight, but the funny driver, who is named Ashwini, hits the horn on the Asian Invasion bus—a special recording of all fifty members screaming "E!-A!-G!-L!-E!-S! EAGLES!" I worry that maybe they have woken up everyone in my neighborhood, but I can't help laughing as the green bus pulls away.

My father is still awake, sitting on the family-room couch watching ESPN. When he sees me, he doesn't say hello, but loudly begins to sing, "Fly, Eagles, fly. On the road to victory . . ." So I sing the song one more time with my father, and when we finish the chant at the end, my dad continues to hum the fight song as he marches off to bed without so much as asking me a single question about my day, which has been extraordinary to say the least, even if Hank Baskett only had two catches for twenty seven yards and has yet to find the end zone. I think about cleaning up my father's empty beer bottles, but I remember what my mother told me about keeping the house filthy while she is on strike.

Downstairs, I hit the weights and try not to think about missing Jake's wedding, which still has me down some, even if the Birds did win. I need to work off the beer and the Indian kabobs, so I lift for many hours.

Weathering the Relative Squalor

When I ask to see Jake's wedding pictures, my mother plays dumb. "What wedding pictures?" she asks. But when I tell her I have met Caitlin—that we had lunch together and I have already accepted my sister-in-law's existence as fact—my mother looks relieved and says, "Well then, I guess I can hang up the wedding photos again."

She leaves me sitting in the living room by the fireplace. When she returns, she hands me a heavy photo album bound in white leather and begins to stand large frames up on the mantel—pictures of Jake and Caitlin previously hidden for my benefit. As I flip through the pages of my brother's wedding album, Mom also hangs up a few portraits of Jake and Caitlin on the walls. "It was a beautiful day, Pat. We all wished you were there."

The massive cathedral and the plush reception hall suggest that Caitlin's family must have what Danny calls "mad cheddar," so I ask what Caitlin's father does for a living.

"For years he was a violinist for the New York Philharmonic, but now he teaches at Juilliard. Music theory. Whatever that means." Mom has finished hanging the framed pictures, and she sits next to me on the couch. "Caitlin's parents are nice people, but they're not really *our* kind of people, which became painfully obvious during the reception. How do I look in the pictures?"

In the photos, my mother wears a chocolate brown dress and a bloodred sash over naked shoulders. Her lipstick matches the sash perfectly, but it looks as if she has on too much eye makeup, making her look sort of like a raccoon. On the plus side, her hair is in what Nikki used to call "a classic updo" and looks pretty good, so I tell Mom she photographs well, which makes her smile.

Tension occupies my father's face; he does not look comfortable in any of the pictures, so I ask if he approves of Caitlin.

"She's from a different world as far as your father's concerned, and he did not enjoy interacting with her parents—*at all*—but he's happy for Jake, in his own non-expressive way," Mom says. "He understands that Caitlin makes your brother happy."

This gets me thinking about how strange my father was at my own wedding, refusing to speak to anyone unless he was spoken to first and then answering everyone with monosyllabic responses. I remember being mad at my father during the rehearsal dinner because he would not even look at Nikki, let alone interact with her family. I remember my mother and brother telling me that Dad did not deal well with change, but their explanation meant nothing to me until the next day.

Halfway through the Mass, the priest asked the congregation if they would hold Nikki and me up in their prayers, and as instructed, we turned to face the response. I instinctively looked toward my parents, curious to see if my father would say the words "we will" like he was supposed to, chanting along with everyone else, and this is when I saw him wiping his eyes with a tissue and biting down on his lower lip. His whole body was trembling slightly, as if he were an old man. It was the strangest sight, my father crying during a wedding that had seemed to make him so annoyed. The very man who never showed any emotions other than anger was crying. I kept staring at my father, and when it became obvious that I was not going to turn back toward the priest, Jake—who was my best man—had to give me a little nudge to break the spell.

Sitting on the couch with my mother, I ask her, "When were Caitlin and Jake married?"

My mother looks at me strangely. She doesn't want to mention the date.

"I know it happened when I was in the bad place, and I also know that I was in the bad place for years. I've accepted that much."

"Are you sure you really want to know the date?"

"I can handle it, Mom."

She looks at me for a second, trying to decide what to do, and then says, "The summer of 2004. August seventh. They've been married for just over two years now."

"Who paid for the wedding photos?"

My mother laughs. "Are you kidding me? Your father and I never could have afforded that fancy sort of wedding album. Caitlin's parents were very generous, putting together the album for us and allowing us to blow up whatever photos we wanted and—"

"Did they give you the negatives?"

"Why would they give us—"

She must see the look on my face, because Mom stops speaking immediately.

"Then how did you replace the photos after that burglar came and stole all the framed photos in the house?"

Mother is thinking how best to answer as I wait for her response; she begins chewing on the inside of her cheek the way she sometimes does when she is anxious. After a second, she calmly says, "I called up Caitlin's mother, told her about the burglary, and she had copies made that very week."

"Then how do you explain these?" I say just before pulling framed wedding pictures of Nikki and me out from behind the pillow at the far end of the love seat. When my mother says nothing, I stand and return my wedding picture to its rightful place on the mantel. Then on the wall by the front window I rehang the picture of my immediate family gathered around Nikki in her wedding dress—her white train spilling out across the grass toward the camera. "I found the 'Pat' box, Mom. If you really hate Nikki so much, just tell me, and I'll hang the pictures up in the attic, where I sleep."

Mom doesn't say anything.

"Do you hate Nikki? And if so, why?"

My mother will not look at me. She's running her hands through her hair.

"Why did you lie to me? What else have you lied about?"

"I'm sorry, Pat. But I lied to . . ."

Mom does not tell me why she lied; instead she starts to cry again.

For a very long time, I look out the window and stare at the neighbors' house across the street. Part of me wants to comfort my mother—to sit down next to her and throw an arm over her shoulders, especially since I know my father has not talked to her in more than a week and is happily eating takeout three times a day, doing his own laundry, and weathering the relative squalor. I have caught Mom cleaning here and there, and I know she is a little upset about her plan not working out like she hoped it would. But I am also mad at my mother for lying to me, and even though I am practicing being kind rather than right, I can't find it in me to comfort her right now.

Finally I leave Mom crying on the couch. I change, and when I go outside for a run, Tiffany is waiting.

As If He Were Yoda and I Were Luke Skywalker Training on the Dagobah System

When we finish discussing our Kubb tournament victory and Mrs. Patel's extraordinary ability to render an exact likeness of Brian Dawkins's bust on the hood of a school bus, I pick the black recliner and tell Cliff I am a little depressed.

"What's wrong?" he says, pulling the lever and raising his footrest.

"Terrell Owens."

Cliff nods, as if he were expecting me to bring up the wide receiver's name.

I did not want to talk about this earlier, but it was reported that Terrell Owens (or T.O.) tried to kill himself on September 26. News reports stated that T.O. overdosed on a pain medication. Later, after T.O. was released from the hospital, he said he did not try to kill himself, and then everyone began to think he was crazy.

I remember T.O. as a young 49er, but Owens was not on the 49ers' roster when I watched the Eagles play in San Francisco a few weeks ago. What I learned from reading the sports pages was that T.O. had played for the Eagles when I was in the bad place, and he had helped the Birds get to Super Bowl XXXIX, which I do not remember at all. (Maybe this is good, since the Eagles lost, but not remembering still makes me feel crazy.) T.O. apparently held out for more money the next year, said bad things about Eagles QB Donovan McNabb, was suspended for the second half of the season, and then was actually cut from the team, so he signed with the very team Eagles fans hate most—the Cowboys. And because of this, everyone in Philadelphia currently hates T.O. more than just about anyone else on the planet.

"T.O.? Don't worry about him," Cliff says. "Dawkins is going to hit him so hard that Owens will be afraid to catch any balls at the Linc."

"I'm not worried about T.O. making catches and scoring touchdowns."

Cliff looks at me for a second, as if he does not know how to respond, and then says, "Tell me what worries you."

"My father refers to T.O. as a psychopathic pill popper. And on the phone this week, Jake also made jokes about T.O. taking pills, calling Owens a nutter."

"Why does this bother you?"

"Well, the reports I read in the sports pages claimed that T.O. was possibly battling depression."

"Yes."

"Well," I say, "that would suggest maybe he needs therapy."

"And?"

"If Terrell Owens is really depressed or mentally unstable, why do the people I love use it as an excuse to talk badly about him?"

Cliff takes a deep breath. "Hmmm."

"Doesn't my dad understand that I'm a psychopathic pill popper too?"

"As your therapist, I can confirm that you are clearly not psychopathic, Pat."

"But I'm on all sorts of pills."

"And yet you are not abusing your medications."

I can see what Cliff means, but he doesn't really understand how I feel—which is a mix of very complicated and hard-to-convey emotions, I realize—so I drop the subject.

When the Dallas Cowboys come to Philadelphia, the fat men's tent and the Asian Invasion bus are combined to create a super party that again features a Kubb tournament on Astroturf, satellite television, Indian kabobs, and much beer. But I cannot concentrate on the fun, because all around me is hatred.

The first things I notice are the homemade T-shirts other tailgaters are buying and selling and wearing. So many different slogans and images. One has a cartoon of a small boy urinating on the Dallas star, and the caption reads DALLAS SUCKS. T.O. SWALLOWS . . . PILLS. Another shirt has a large prescription bottle with the universal skull-and-crossbones poison symbol on the label and TERRELL OWENS written underneath. Yet another version features the pill bottle on the front and a gun on the back, under which the caption reads T.O., IF AT FIRST YOU DON'T SUCCEED, BUY A GUN. A nearby tailgater has nailed T.O.'s old Eagles jersey to a ten-foot cross, which is also covered with orange prescription bottles that look exactly like mine. People are burning their old T.O. jerseys in the parking lot; human-size dolls in T.O. jerseys are strung up so people can hit them with bats. And even though

I do not like any Dallas Cowboy, I feel sort of bad for Terrell Owens because maybe he really is a sad guy who is having trouble with his mind. Who knows, maybe he really did try to kill himself? And yet everyone mocks him, as if his mental health is a joke—or maybe they want to push him over the edge and would like nothing more than to see T.O. dead.

Because of my poor throws, Cliff and I get knocked out of the Kubb tournament early, losing the five bucks my brother fronted me, and this is when Cliff asks me to help him move some India Pale Ale out of the Asian Invasion bus. When we are inside of the bus, he closes the door and says, "What's wrong?"

"Nothing," I say.

"You weren't even looking to see where your batons landed, you were so distracted during the Kubb games."

I say nothing.

"What's wrong?"

"You're not in your leather seat."

Cliff sits down, pats the bus seat, and says, "Pleather will have to do today."

I sit down in the seat across from Cliff and say, "I just feel bad for T.O. That's all."

"He's getting millions of dollars to endure this type of criticism. And he thrives on it. He brings it on himself with those touchdown dances and the hoopla. And these people don't really want T.O. to die; they just don't want him to perform well today. It's all in good fun."

Now, I know what Cliff means, but it doesn't seem like good fun to me. And regardless of whether T.O. is a millionaire or not, I'm not sure T-shirts encouraging *anyone* to shoot himself in the head should be condoned by my therapist. But I don't say anything.

Back outside the bus I see that Jake and Ashwini are in the final game of the Kubb tournament, so I try to cheer for them and block out the hatred that surrounds me.

Inside the Linc, all throughout the first half, the crowd sings, "O.D.—O.D., O.D., O.D.—O.D.—O.D." Jake explains that the crowd used to sing, "T.O.—T.O., T.O., T.O.—T.O. –T.O." back when Owens was an Eagle. I watch Owens on the sideline, and even though he doesn't have many catches yet, he seems to be dancing to the rhythm of the crowd's O.D. song, and I wonder if he is really so immune to seventy thousand people mocking his near overdose or if he really feels differently inside. Again I can't help feeling bad for the guy. I wonder what I would do if seventy thousand people mocked my forgetting the last few years of my life.

By halftime Hank Baskett has two catches for twenty-five yards, but the Eagles are losing 21–17.

All throughout the second half, Lincoln Financial Field is alive; we Eagles fans know that first place in the NFC East is at stake.

With just under eight minutes to go in the third, everything changes.

McNabb throws a long one down the left side of the field. Everyone in my section stands to see what will happen. Number 84 catches the ball in Dallas territory, puts a move on the defender, takes off for the end zone, and then I am in the air. Under me are Scott and Jake. I'm riding high on their shoulders. Everyone in our section is high-fiving me because Hank Baskett has finally scored his first NFL touchdown—an eighty-seven-yarder—and of course I am wearing my Baskett jersey. The Eagles are winning, and I am so happy that I forget all about T.O. and start to think about my dad watching at home on his huge television, and I wonder if maybe the TV cameras caught me when I was riding high on Jake's and Scott's shoulders. Maybe Dad saw a life-size me celebrating on his flat screen, and maybe he is even proud.

A series of tense moments get our hearts beating at the end of the fourth quarter, when Dallas is driving, down 31–24. A score will send the game into OT. But Lito Sheppard intercepts Bledsoe and returns the pick for a TD, and the whole stadium sings the Eagles fight song and chants the letters, and the day is ours.

When the clock ticks down, I look for T.O. and see him sprint off the field and into the locker room without even shaking the hand of one single Eagle. I still feel bad for him.

Jake and Scott and I exit the Linc and run into the Asian Invasion—which is easy to spot from far away because it consists of fifty Indian men, usually clumped together, all in Brian Dawkins jerseys. "Just look for fifty number 20's," they always say. Cliff and I run up to each other and high-five and scream and yell, and then all fifty Indian men start chanting, "Baskett, Baskett, Baskett!" And I am so happy; I pick little Cliff up and hoist him onto my shoulders and carry him back to the Asian Invasion bus as if he were Yoda and I were Luke Skywalker training on the Dagobah System in the middle section of *The Empire Strikes Back*, which is—as I told you before—one of my all-time favorite movies. "E!-A!-G!-L!-E!-S! EAGLES!" we chant so many times as we navigate the crowds and find our way back to our spot behind the Wachovia Center, where the fat men are waiting with ice-cold celebration beers. I keep hugging Jake and high-fiving Cliff and chest bumping the fat men and singing with the Indians. I am so happy. I am so impossibly happy.

When the Asian Invasion drops me off in front of my house,

it's late, so I ask Ashwini not to blow the Eagles chant horn and he reluctantly agrees—although when the bus rounds the corner at the end of my street, I hear fifty Indian men chant, "E!-A!-G!-L!-E!-S! EAGLES!" I can't help smiling as I enter my parents' home.

I am ready for Dad. After such a big win—a win that puts the Eagles in first place—surely Dad will want to talk to me. But when I enter the family room, no one is there. No beer bottles on the floor, no dishes in the sink. In fact, the whole house looks spotless.

"Dad? Mom?" I say, but no one answers. I saw both of their cars in the driveway when I came home, so I am very confused. I begin to climb the steps, and the house is deadly quiet. I check my bedroom, and my bed's made and the room is empty. So I knock on my parents' bedroom door, but no one answers. I push the door open and immediately wish I hadn't.

"Your father and I made up after the Eagles victory," Mom says with a funny smile. "He aims to be a changed man."

The sheet is pulled up to their necks, but somehow I know my parents are naked underneath the covers.

"Your boy Baskett healed the family," my father says. "He was a god out there on the field today. And with the Eagles in first place, I thought, Why not make up with Jeanie?"

Still, I cannot speak.

"Pat, maybe you'd like to go for a run?" my mom suggests. "Maybe just a little half-hour run?"

I close their bedroom door.

While I change into a tracksuit, I think I hear my parents' bed squeak, and the house seems to shake a little too. So I slip on my sneakers and run down the stairs and out the front door. I sprint across the park, run around to the back of the Websters' house, and knock on Tiffany's door. When she answers, she's in some sort of nightgown and her face looks confused.

"Pat? What are you—"

"My parents are having sex," I explain. "Right now."

Her eyes widen. She smiles and then laughs. "Just let me get changed," she says, and then shuts the door.

We walk for hours—all around Collingswood. At first I ramble on and on about T.O., Baskett, my parents, Jake, the Asian Invasion, my wedding pictures, my mother's ultimatum actually working—everything—but Tiffany does not say anything in response. When I run out of words, we simply walk and walk and walk, and finally we are in front of the Websters' house and it is time to say good night. I stick my hand out and say, "Thanks for listening." When it is clear that Tiffany's not going to shake, I start to walk away.

"Turn around, bright eyes," Tiffany says, which is a very weird thing for her to say, because my eyes are brown and very dull, but of course I turn around. "I'm going to give you something that will confuse you, and maybe even make you mad. I don't want you to open it until you are in a very relaxed mood. Tonight is out of the question. Wait a few days, and when you are feeling happy, open this letter." She pulls a white business envelope out of her jacket pocket and hands it to me. "Put it away in your pocket," she says, and I do as I am told, mostly because Tiffany looks so deathly serious. "I will not be running with you until you give me your answer. I will leave you alone to think. Regardless of what you decide, you cannot tell anyone about what is inside of that envelope. *Understand?* If you tell anyone—even your therapist—I'll know by looking in your eyes, and I will never speak to you again. It's best if you simply follow my directions."

My heart is pounding. What is Tiffany talking about? All I want to do is open the envelope now.

"You have to wait at least forty-eight hours before you open that. Make sure you are in a good mood when you read the letter. Think about it, and then give me your answer. Remember, Pat, I can be a very valuable friend to you, but you do not want me as an enemy."

I remember the story Ronnie told me about how Tiffany lost her job, and I begin to feel very afraid.

I Will Have to Require a First-Place Victory

"Question number one," my father says. "How many touchdowns will McNabb throw against the Saints?"

I can hardly believe I am actually eating a sit-down meal with my father. Mom smiles at me as she winds spaghetti around her fork. She even shoots me a wink. Now don't get me wrong, I am happy that Mom's plan has worked out, and I am delighted to be eating a meal with my father, having a conversation even—and I am especially happy to see my parents playing with love again—but I *also* know my father, and I worry that a single Eagles loss will turn Dad back into a grump. I worry for Mom, but decide to ride out the moment.

"Ten touchdowns," I tell my father.

Dad smiles, pops a small sausage into his mouth, chews enthusiastically, and then tells my mother, "Pat says ten touchdowns."

"Maybe eleven," I add, just to be optimistic.

"Question number two. How many touchdowns will undrafted rookie sensation Hank Baskett catch?"

Now, I fully realize that Baskett has only caught one TD in the first five games, but I also know my family is being overly optimistic tonight, so I say, "Seven."

"Seven?" Dad says, but smiling.

"Seven."

"He says seven, Jeanie. Seven!" To me Dad says, "Question number three. In what quarter will quarterback Drew Brees finally suffer a concussion because he has been sacked so many times by the Eagles' superior defense?"

"Um. That's a tough one. *The third quarter?*"

"That is incorrect," my father says, shaking his head in mock disappointment. "First quarter is the correct answer. Question four. When are you going to bring home that broad you're always running with? When are you going to introduce your girlfriend to your father?"

When Dad finishes asking question four, he slurps a load of spaghetti into his mouth and then begins chewing. When I fail to respond, he encourages me with his left hand, tracing invisible circles with his index finger.

"Did you see that Pat found his wedding pictures and put them back up in the living room?" Mom says, and her voice sort of quivers.

"Jake told me you were over Nikki," Dad says. "He said you were into this Tiffany broad. No?"

"May I be excused?" I ask my mother, because my little scar is itching, and I feel as though I might explode if I don't start banging my fist against my forehead.

When my mother nods, I see sympathy in her eyes, which I appreciate.

I lift for a few hours, until I no longer feel the need to punch myself.

In the new reflector vest my mother has recently bought for me, I run through the night.

I was going to open Tiffany's letter this evening because I was so excited about having dinner with my father, but now I know I am most definitely not in a good mood, so opening the letter would be a violation of the rules Tiffany clearly laid out for me two nights ago. I almost opened the letter last night, when I was in an excellent mood, but it hadn't been forty-eight hours.

As I run, I try to think about Nikki and the end of apart time, which always makes me feel better. I pretend that God has made a bet with me and if I run fast enough, He will bring Nikki back, so I begin sprinting the last two miles of my run. Soon I'm running so fast, it's amazing—faster than any human being has ever run before. In my mind I hear God tell me I have to do the last mile in under four minutes, which I know is almost impossible, but for Nikki I try. I run even faster, and when I am a block away, I hear God counting down from ten in my mind. "Five—four—three—two—" And when my right foot lands on the first concrete square of my parents' sidewalk, God says "One," which means I ran fast enough—that I made it home before God said "Zero." I am so happy. I am so impossibly happy!

My parents' bedroom door is closed when I go upstairs, so I shower and then slip under my comforter. I pull Tiffany's envelope from under the mattress of my bed. I take a deep breath. I open the letter. As I read the several typed pages, my mind explodes with conflicting emotions and awful needs.

Pat,

Read this letter start to finish! Do not make any decisions until you have read the entire letter! Do not read this letter unless you are alone! Do not show this letter to anyone! When you have finished reading this letter, burn it—immediately!

Do you ever feel like you're living in a powder keg and giving off sparks?

Well, there was nothing I could do to bring my Tommy back, and the inability to accept his death kept me ill for two whole years—but then you came into my life. Why? At first I thought, God is sending me a new man, a replacement for my Tommy, which made me mad, because Tommy is irreplaceable (no offense). But when I listened to the way you talked about Nikki, I realized God had sent you to me so I might help you find the end of apart time. This was to be my mission. And so I have been working on it.

"What?" I can hear you saying right now. "How can my friend Tiffany end apart time?"

Well, this is the part that might make you mad.

Are you ready, Pat? Brace yourself.

I've been talking to your Nikki on the phone—regularly. Every night for the past two weeks. I got the phone number from Veronica, who—through Ronnie's conversations with your mom—has been providing Nikki with information about you ever since you were permanently assigned to that neural health facility in Baltimore. It turns out that your family banned Nikki from obtaining information about you, which they could do because Nikki divorced you soon after you were permanently admitted. I know this bit of news has most likely upset you terribly. Sorry, but it's best just to state things plainly at this point. Don't you think?

Okay, this next part is bad too. Nikki was able to divorce you because you committed a crime, which you do not remember. (I am not going to tell you what that crime was, because you have probably blocked it from your memory intentionally; most likely, you are not yet mentally ready to deal with this very frightening reality. My therapist Dr. Lily and I theorize that you will remember committing this crime when you are mentally and emotionally ready.) Nikki was granted a divorce and all your assets, and in exchange, someone else dropped all charges against you. Of course, the deal also sent you to the bad place indefinitely for "rehabilitation." You agreed to all of the above at the time and were deemed to be "of sound mind" by your therapist Dr. Timbers, but soon after being put away for good, you "lost" your memory and your marbles as well.

I am not telling you all of this to be mean—quite the contrary. Remember, God put me in charge of helping you end apart time. It turns out Nikki has wanted to communicate with you very much. She misses you. This is not to say she wants to marry you all over again. I want to be clear about this. She still remembers what you did—the crime you committed. And she is a little afraid of you as well, as she fears you might be mad at her and want to retaliate. But she was married to you for years and she wants to see you well, and maybe even become friends again. I have reported your desire to reconcile with Nikki. To be honest, your desire is much stronger than hers. But you never know what might happen if you begin to communicate again.

Two problems: One. After you committed that crime, Nikki took out a restraining order against you, so technically it is illegal for you to contact her. Two. Your parents—on your behalf, and probably in retaliation—took out a restraining order against Nikki, claiming any contact she made could jeopardize your mental health. So it is also illegal for her to contact you. Even still, Nikki would like to communicate with you, if only to smooth over what happened. Her guilt is glaring. She walked away with all your assets, and you had to spend years in a mental institution, right?

So. Coming to the point. I am offering myself as a liaison. The two of you can communicate through me, and there will be no trouble. You will be able to write Nikki letters—one every two weeks. I will read these letters to Nikki over the phone. She will be able to dictate her responses to me, again over the phone, which I will type up on my laptop, print out, and present to you.

Pat, we are friends, and I value our friendship very much. That having been said, you must appreciate that what I am offering puts me in a very precarious position. If you decide to take me up on my offer, I would be putting myself at risk legally, and also I would be jeopardizing our friendship. I need to inform you that I will not be your liaison for free, but am offering you a trade.

What do I want?

Remember when I said I was scouting you?

Well, I want to win this year's Dance Away Depression competition, and I need a strong man to do it. "What is Dance Away Depression?" I hear you asking. Well—it is an annual competition organized by the Philadelphia Psychiatric Association that allows women diagnosed with clinical depression to transform their despair into movement. The sole focus is supposed to be diminishing depression through use of the body, but judges award a wreath of flowers to the second-best dance routine and a golden trophy to the first-place dance routine. Dancing solo, I have won that fucking wreath two years straight, and this year I want to win the golden trophy. This is where you figure in, Pat. God sent me the strongest man I have ever met in my entire life; tell me this isn't divine intervention. Only a man with your muscles could perform the type of lifts I have in mind—award-winning lifts, Pat. The competition will be held at the Plaza Hotel in center city, on a Saturday night—November 11th. Which gives us just under a month to practice. I know the routine already, but you'll be starting from scratch, and we both will have to practice the lifts. This will take a lot of time.

I told Nikki about my conditions, and she wants to encourage you to be my dance partner. She says you need to broaden your interests, and that she had always wanted to take dance lessons with you. So it is more than okay with her; she encourages you to do this.

Also, I'm afraid I will have to require a first-place victory in exchange for being your liaison. Lucky for you, the routine I have choreographed is first-rate. But in order to win, you will have to immerse yourself in dance. Below are the non-negotiable conditions.

Should you decide to be my dance partner, you will:

1. *Give up Eagles football for the duration of our training. No going to games. No watching games on television. No discussing Eagles football with anyone. No reading the sports pages. You may not even wear your beloved Baskett jersey.*
2. *End your weight training by two o'clock each afternoon, at which point we will go for a five-mile run, after which we will rehearse from 4:15 p.m. to 11:00 p.m. on weekdays. On weekends we will rehearse from 1:00 p.m. to 10:00 p.m. No exceptions.*
3. *Make sure at least 15 of your friends and relatives attend the dance recital, because the judges are often swayed by applause.*
4. *Do whatever I say without asking any questions.*
5. *Assure I win the competition.*
6. *MOST IMPORTANTLY: Tell no one about our arrangement. You can tell people you are training for a dance competition,*

but you cannot tell anyone about my demands and my contacting Nikki on your behalf—never ever.

Should you meet all six demands, I will act as a liaison between Nikki and you; I will attempt to end apart time, and then who knows what will happen between you and your ex-wife. If you fail to meet my demands, I am afraid you might never talk to Nikki again. She says this is your only shot.

Contact me within 24 hours with your decision. Reread my list of demands, memorize each, and then burn this letter.

Remember, if you want me to be your liaison, tell no one I am in contact with Nikki.

With best intentions,
Tiffany

I reread the letter over and over all night. Parts I do not want to believe are true—especially the parts about my committing a crime and Nikki divorcing me, which are ideas that make me feel like smashing my fist against my forehead. What type of crime would put me in such a situation, and who would drop charges when I checked myself into a neural health facility? I can understand Nikki's divorcing me because I was a bad husband, especially because, well, I *was* a bad husband. But I have a hard time believing I actually committed a crime that could result in such drastic legal measures. And yet Tiffany's letter seems to explain so much—my mother's taking down my wedding pictures, all the awful things Jake and Dad said about Nikki. If I am really divorced, everything my family has done to keep Nikki out of my memory would have been for my protection, especially since they are not optimistic enough to realize that I am not dead and therefore still have at least a shot at getting Nikki back, which I don't have to tell you is the silver lining to the letter.

Of course, I cannot be sure about anything, since I have no memory of the past few years. Maybe Tiffany made up the story just to get me to perform in her dance competition. This is possible. I certainly would not have volunteered to be her partner, even if I am practicing being kind now. I realize that Tiffany's letter might be a trick, but the possibility of communicating with Nikki is too good to chance—as it may be my *last* opportunity. Also, Tiffany's mentioning God's will seems to suggest that she understands what apart time is all about. It makes sense that Nikki would want me to take dancing lessons. She always wanted me to dance with her, but I never did. The thought of dancing with Nikki in the future is enough to make me accept that I will be missing the three Eagles games before the bye week, including the home game against Jacksonville. I think about how angry this will make my father, Jake, and maybe even Cliff, but then I think about the possibility of finally living out the happy ending to my movie—getting Nikki back—and the choice is obvious.

When the sun comes up, I open the window in the downstairs bathroom, burn the letter over the toilet, and flush the charred remains. Next, I run across Knight's Park, jog around the Websters' house, and knock on Tiffany's door. She answers in a red silk nightgown, squinting at me. "Well?"

"When do we start training?" I ask.

"Are you ready to commit fully? Ready to give up everything—even Eagles football?"

I nod eagerly. "Only I can't miss my therapy sessions on Fridays, because some judge will send me back to the bad place if I do, and then we won't be able to win the competition."

"I'll be outside your house tomorrow at two o'clock," Tiffany says, and then shuts the door.

* * *

The first floor of Tiffany's in-law suite is a dance studio. All four walls are completely covered by full-length mirrors, and three have railings like you see ballerinas using. The floor is hardwood, like a pro-basketball court, only without any painted lines and with a lighter varnish. The ceiling is high, maybe thirty feet tall, and a spiral staircase in the corner leads to Tiffany's apartment.

"I had this built when Tommy died," Tiffany says. "I used the insurance money. Do you like my studio?"

I nod.

"Good, because it's going to be home for the next month. Did you bring your photograph?"

I open the bag that Tiffany instructed me to bring and pull out my framed picture of Nikki; I show it to Tiffany, and then she walks over to the stereo system behind the spiral staircase. From an iron hook on the wall she removes a pair of headphones—the kind that cover your entire ears like earmuffs—and brings them to me. A very long cord is attached.

"Sit," she says. I drop to the floor and sit with my legs crossed. "I'm going to play our song, the one we are going to dance to. It's important that you feel a deep connection with this song. It needs to move you if it's going to flow through your body. I've picked this song for a reason. It's perfect for both of us, which you'll soon see. When I put the headphones on you, I want you to stare into Nikki's eyes. I want you to feel the song. Understand?"

"It's not a song played by a soprano saxophonist, is it?" I ask, because Kenny G is my nemesis, as you know.

"No," she says, and then places the headphones on my ears. My ears are enveloped in the padding. Wearing the headphones makes me feel as if I am alone in this large room, even though if I look up, Tiffany will be there. With the frame in my hands, I stare into Nikki's eyes, and soon the song begins to play.

Piano notes—slow and sad.

Two voices taking turns singing.

Pain.

I know the song.

Tiffany was right. It is the perfect song for both of us.

The song builds, the voices become more emotional, and everything inside of my chest starts to hurt.

The words express exactly what I have felt since I was released from the bad place.

And by the chorus, I am sobbing, because the woman singing seems to feel exactly what I am feeling, and her words, and her emotion, and her voice . . .

The song ends with the same sad piano notes that began the number. I look up and realize that Tiffany has been watching me cry, and I begin to feel embarrassed. I set my photo of Nikki down on the floor and cover my face with my hands. "I'm sorry. Just give me a second."

"It's good that the song makes you cry, Pat. Now we just have to transform those tears into motion. You need to cry through your dancing? Understand?"

I do not understand, but I nod anyway.

My Movie's Montage

Explaining how I learned Tiffany's routine and became an excellent dancer would be difficult—mostly because our rehearsals are long and grueling and extremely boring. We do the same little things over and over again endlessly. For example, if I had to lift a finger in the air for the routine, Tiffany would make me do it a thousand times every single day until I could do it to her liking on command. So I will spare you most of the boring details. To make things even more complicated, Tiffany has forbidden me to document our rehearsals in any thorough manner that would allow others to steal her training techniques. As she wants to open up a studio someday, she is very guarded about her methods—and her choreography too.

Luckily, as I am starting to write this part, I remember that in every one of his films, whenever Rocky needs to become a better boxer, they show clips of him doing one-arm push-ups, running on the beach, punching slabs of meat, running the stairs of the art museum, gazing at Adrian lovingly, or being yelled at by Mickey or Apollo Creed or even Paulie—all while his theme song plays, which is perhaps the greatest song in the world, "Gonna Fly Now." In the Rocky movies, it only takes a few minutes to cover weeks of training, and yet the audience still understands that a lot of preparation went into the actual development of Rocky's boxing skills, even though we only get to see a few clips of the Italian Stallion working hard.

During a therapy session, I ask Cliff what this movie technique is called. He has to call his wife, Sonja, on his cell phone, but she knows the answer and tells us that what I am trying to describe is called a montage. So that is what I am now going to create below, my movie's montage. Maybe you'll want to play "Gonna Fly Now" on your CD player, if you have a copy handy—or you could put on any song you find inspiring—and read along to the music. Music is not required, however. Okay, here it is, my montage:

In anticipation of our big performance, I'm running a little faster with Tiffany every day. We push ourselves, and when we get to the park, we sprint the last mile to her house and get really sweaty. I always beat Tiffany, because I am a man, yes, but also because I am an excellent runner.

See me pumping iron: bench press, leg lifts, sit-ups on the Stomach Master 6000, bike riding, squats, knuckle push-ups, curls—the works.

"Crawl!" Tiffany yells. So I crawl on the hardwood floor of her dance studio. "Crawl like you have no legs and you haven't eaten for two weeks and there's a single apple in the middle of the room and another man with no legs is also crawling toward the apple. You want to crawl faster, but you cannot, because you are maimed. Desperation flows out of your face like sweat! You are so afraid you will not get to the apple before the other legless man! He will not share the apple with—no, no, no. Stop! You're doing it all wrong! Jesus Christ, Pat! We only have four weeks left!"

"Jeanie," I hear my father say. He is in the kitchen eating his breakfast. I am on the basement stairs listening. "Why does Pat close his eyes and hum every time I mention the Eagles? Is he going crazy again? Should I be concerned?"

"What's this I hear about you missing the Saints game?" Jake says through the telephone when I call him back sometime after 11:00 p.m. He has called two nights in a row, and the note my mother left for me on my pillow read *Call your brother back no matter how late. IMPORTANT.* "Don't you want to see what Baskett does this week? Why are you humming?"

"When you are a dancer, you are allowed to put your hands anywhere on your partner's body, Pat. It's not sexual. So when you do this first lift, yes, your hands will be cradling my ass and crotch. Why are you pacing? Pat, it's not sexual—it's modern dance."

See me pumping iron: bench press, leg lifts, sit-ups on the Stomach Master 6000, bike riding, knuckle push-ups, curls—the works.

"I'm okay, Pat. I'm fucking fine. You're going to drop me a few times while we're learning the lifts, but it's not because you're not strong enough. You need to center your palm directly at the base of my crotch. If you need me to get more specific, I will. Here. I'll show you. Put out your hand."

"Your mother tells me you will not discuss Eagles football with your—why are you humming?" Cliff asks. "I did not mention that certain saxophonist's name. What's this all about?"

"I never thought I would say this, but maybe you should consider taking a break from your dance training and watch the game with Jake and your dad," my mother says. "You know I hate football, but you and your father seemed to be making a connection, and Jake and you are just getting back to being brotherly again. Pat, please stop humming."

"For the second lift you need to look up at me, Pat. Especially just before I go into the flip. You don't have to look at my crotch, but you have to be ready to push up so I'll get more height. If you don't give me a push when I bend my knees, I won't be able to complete the flip and will probably crack my head open on the floor."

"I know you can hear me through the humming, Pat. Look at you!" my father says. "Curled up in your bed, humming like a child. Birds lose by a field goal in New Orleans, and your boy Baskett had zero catches. Zilch. Don't think your dancing through the game didn't affect the outcome."

"You look like a retarded snake! You are supposed to crawl with your arms—not slither or wiggle or whatever the fuck you are doing down there. Here. Watch me."

• • •

In anticipation of our big performance, I'm running a little faster with Tiffany every day. We push ourselves, and when we get to the park, we sprint the last mile to her house and get really sweaty. I always beat Tiffany, because I am a man, yes, but also because I am an excellent runner.

"What's Tiffany holding over you?" Ronnie says. We are in my parents' basement. I have already spotted him as he benched one wimpy sixty-pound rep, and now he is taking a break. This is a surprise visit disguised to look like a prework lifting session. "I told you to protect yourself. I'm telling you, Pat, you don't know what that woman is capable of. My sister-in-law is capable of anything. *Anything!*"

"You're making the sun with your arms. In the center of the stage, you represent the sun. And when you make the huge circle with your arms, it has to be slow and deliberate—just like the sun. The dance is one day's worth of sun. You are going to rise and set all onstage—to the flow of our song. Understand?"

"I want you to talk to Tiffany and tell her it's important for you to watch the Eagles game with your father," Mom says. "Please stop humming, Pat. Please, just stop humming!"

"The second lift is the hardest by far, as it requires you to go from a squatting position to a standing position with me standing on your hands, which will be just above your shoulders. Do you think you're strong enough to do this, because we can do something else if you are too weak, but let's try it now and we'll just see."

• • •

"Why is this dance competition so important to you?" Cliff asks me. I look up at the sun painted on the ceiling of his office and smile. "What?" he says.

"The dancing lets me be that," I say, and point up.

Cliff's eyes follow my finger. "It lets you be the sun?"

"Yes," I say, and smile again at Cliff, because I really like being the sun, exactly what allows clouds to have a silver lining. Also, being the sun is what will provide me with the opportunity to write letters to Nikki.

"Please stop humming into the phone, Pat. I'm on your side here. I understand wanting to learn an art for a woman. Don't you remember my playing the piano for you? But the difference is that Caitlin would never ask me to miss an Eagles game, because she knows it's more than just football to me. I can hear you fucking humming through the phone, Pat, but I'm just going to keep talking, all right? You're acting crazy, you know. And if the Eagles lose tomorrow against the Buccaneers, Dad is going to think you cursed the Birds."

"Okay, you know your routine—roughly, anyway. So now I want you to watch mine. I'll say 'lift' when it's time for one of your lifts, just so you know when they're coming. But don't worry, because as long as you do your routine, I'll make sure we link up with the lifts. Okay?"

Tiffany is in tights and a T-shirt like every other day, but she transforms her face just before she pushes PLAY on the CD player. So solemn. Those sad piano notes and those two dueling voices fill the room, and Tiffany begins to dance beautifully but sadly. Her body moves so gracefully, and it is only now that I understand what she means by crying through movement. She jumps, she rolls, she spins, she runs, she slides. She yells "Lift!" and then falls to the floor dead, only to explode upward in resurrection when the music picks up again. And her dancing is one of the most beautiful things I have ever seen. I could watch her dance for the rest of my life, and strangely, watching Tiffany soar around the dance floor makes me feel like I am floating over waves with baby Emily. Tiffany is *that* good.

"Your father has stopped eating dinner with me, Pat. He's not taking walks with me either. Ever since the Eagles lost to the Buccaneers, he's back to his—Pat, please stop humming. Pat!"

In anticipation of our big performance, I'm running a little faster with Tiffany every day. We push ourselves, and when we get to the park, we sprint the last mile to her house and get really sweaty. I always beat Tiffany, because I am a man, yes, but also because I am an excellent runner.

"I don't think you understand how much this means to my sister," Veronica says, and I am shocked to see her and baby Emily in my basement gym. "Do you know that since Tommy passed, she has *never* asked her family to see her dance? In fact, for two years she's banned us from attending any of her performances. But this year she thinks she is going to perform flawlessly enough to invite her family—she's convinced, in fact—and while I am glad to see her so happy, I'm afraid to even think about what she might do if you guys screw up the performance. She's not a stable person, Pat. You do understand that, right? You do understand that your performing poorly will result in months of serious depression? So I need to ask you how are the rehearsals *really* going? Do you *truly* think you can win? *Do you?*"

• • •

Before I turn off the lights, I stare into framed-picture Nikki's eyes. I see her freckled nose, her strawberry blond hair, her full lips. I kiss her so many times. "Soon," I say. "I'm doing everything I can. I won't let you down. Remember—'Forever's gonna start tonight.'"

See me pumping iron: bench press, leg lifts, sit-ups on the Stomach Master 6000, bike riding, knuckle push-ups, curls—the works.

"The Asian Invasion will pick you up at—" Cliff nods at me and smiles. "Ah, the humming again. Your mother tells me you won't talk to anyone about Eagles football, but you aren't seriously going to miss a home game, are you?"

"The most important thing is to make the lifts look effortless, as if you are holding up air. I should appear to be floating. Understand? Good, because I need you to stop shaking during the routine, Pat. You look like you have fucking Parkinson's disease, for Christ's sake."

"How does a four-and-one team lose three games straight?" Dad yells down from the top of the basement steps. "A team that beat the Dallas Cowboys handily? A team with a first-ranked offense and more sacks than any other team in the league? You can hum all you want, Pat. But that don't change the fact that you took the good luck away from the Birds and *are ruining our season*!"

See me pumping iron: bench press, leg lifts, sit-ups on the Stomach Master 6000, bike riding, knuckle push-ups, curls—the works.

• • •

"Okay. Not bad. You got the crawling down, and one of the lifts doesn't look awful anymore. But we only have a week left. Can we do this? *Can we do this?*"

"I bought you a present," Tiffany tells me. "Go into the powder room and try it on."

In her studio's washroom, I remove a pair of yellow tights from a plastic bag. "What's this?" I call out to Tiffany.

"It's your outfit. Put it on, and we'll have a dress rehearsal."

"Where's the shirt?"

"Again," Tiffany says, even though it is 10:41 p.m. and my elbows feel as though they might explode. I am dancing on raw nerves. I am dancing on bone. "Again!"

Eleven fifty-nine p.m. "Again," Tiffany says, and then takes her place at the left side of the studio. Knowing that arguing is no use, I drop to the floor and prepare to crawl.

"This might tickle some," Tiffany says just before she slides her pink lady razor through the shaving cream coating my chest, and then she shows me how much hair is in the teacup she rinses the blade in. I am lying on a yoga mat in the middle of her dance studio. My chest is covered with some sort of green aloe shaving gel that turns white when you make foam. Being shaved by Tiffany sort of makes me feel strange, as I have never been shaved by a woman before and have never had my torso shaved at all. When she lathers me up, I close my eyes, and my fingers and toes tingle wildly.

I sort of giggle each time she shaves a line of hair off my chest.

I sort of giggle each time she shaves a line of hair off my back.

"We want those muscles to gleam like the sun onstage, right?"

"Why can't I just wear a shirt?" I say, even though—in a weird sort of way—I secretly enjoy being shaved by Tiffany.

"Does the sun wear a shirt?"

The sun does not wear yellow tights either, but I do not say so.

In anticipation of our big performance, I'm running a little faster with Tiffany every day. We push ourselves, and when we get to the park, we sprint the last mile to her house and get really sweaty. I always beat Tiffany, because I am a man, yes, but also because I am an excellent runner.

Two days before the competition, just before we are about to perform the routine for the twenty-fifth time that day—twenty-five being Tiffany's favorite number—she says, "We need to do this flawlessly."

So I try my best, and as I watch bits of our routine in the mirrors that surround us, I think, We really are dancing flawlessly! I am so excited when we finish, because I know we will win—especially since we have improved ourselves so much with sacrifice and hard training. This mini-movie will have a happy ending for sure!

But something about Tiffany's demeanor is off as we take our water break. She is not yelling at me, nor is she using the f-word, so I ask, "What's wrong?"

"How many people did you recruit to come to the competition?"

"I asked everyone I know."

"Veronica tells me your family is mad at you for abandoning the Eagles."

"Not my mom."

"I'm worried that if we don't get enough fans there to cheer for us, the judges might be swayed by another dancer's larger fan base. We might not win, and then I would not be able to act as your liaison, Pat."

"Maybe if you are not doing anything tomorrow night, you might want to bring your wife and children to my dance recital," I tell Cliff. "We've really got a good routine, and I think we can win if only we have enough audience support, and I don't think that my father or brother will be likely to show up, so—"

"After tomorrow night, you'll be done with these long rehearsals?"

"Yeah."

"So you will be able to go to the Redskins game on—"

"Hmmmmmm."

"Just tell me this, if I go to the dance recital, will you go to the Eagles game with us on Sunday? The Asian Invasion misses you, and truthfully, we sort of feel like you've cursed the Eagles by abandoning them mid-season. Poor Baskett has only caught two balls in the last three games and had zero catches last week. And the Birds have lost three straight. We miss you down at the Linc, Pat."

"I can't talk about that subject until my dance recital is over tomorrow night. I can only say that I need to recruit as many people as possible to cheer for Tiffany and me so the judges will be swayed. Let me just say that winning is really important, and Tiffany says that crowd reaction can sway the judges."

"If I come, will you talk to me about that-thing-you-are-not-allowed-to-talk-about after your performance?"

"Cliff, I can't talk about that until after the performance."

"Well then, neither can I tell you whether I will be at your performance," Cliff says.

At first I think he is bluffing, but he doesn't bring up the subject again, and by the end of our therapy session I feel as though I have blown my shot at getting Cliff to bring his wife to my recital, which makes me feel very depressed.

Hello, you've reached *Jake and Caitlin's machine. Please leave a message after the beep. Beep.*

"Jake. Sorry to call so late, but I just got done rehearsing. I know that you are mad at me because you think I jinxed those-people-who-make-me-hum-at-the-present-moment, but if you bring Caitlin to my dance recital, there's a chance I might be able to do that thing we used to do on Sundays, especially if you cheer for Tiffany and me very loudly. We need people to cheer for us, because the judges are sometimes swayed by the audience. It's really important that we win this competition. So as your brother, I'm asking you to please bring your wife to the Plaza—"

Beep.

I hang up and redial the number.

Hello, you've reached Jake and Caitlin's machine. Please leave a message after the beep. Beep.

"That's the Plaza Hotel at—"

"Hello? Is everything okay?"

It's Caitlin's voice, which makes me nervous, so I hang up, fully realizing I have blown my shot at getting Jake to come to my dance recital.

• • •

"Pat, you know I'll be there. And I'll cheer so loudly for you, but winning isn't everything," my mom says. "It's the fact that you were able to learn to dance in only a few weeks that is impressive."

"Just ask Dad, okay?"

"I will. But I don't want you to get your hopes up. A dance recital is not something he would have attended even if the Eagles *won* the last three games."

Like a Shadow on Me All of the Time

Veronica drops us off in front of the Plaza Hotel on Saturday, saying, "Break a leg," just before she pulls away. I follow Tiffany into the lobby, where four towers of water shoot out of a large fountain—at least ten feet up in the air. Real fish swim around in the pool of water, and signs read DO NOT THROW COINS INTO THE FOUNTAIN. Tiffany has been here before. She walks right past the information desk and leads me through a maze of hallways with gold wallpaper and swanky-looking light fixtures that are all large bronze fish with lightbulbs in their mouths. Finally, we find the hall where the dance recital will take place.

Red curtains frame a large stage. A huge banner hangs high above the dance floor; it reads DANCE AWAY DEPRESSION. We try to register at a desk, and it becomes obvious that we are the first contestants to show up, because the fat woman who is in charge of registration says, "Registration is not for another hour."

We sit down in the last row of seats. I look around. A huge chandelier dangles above us, and the ceiling is not just a regular ceiling, but has all sorts of plaster flowers and angels and other fancy things sticking out of it. Tiffany is nervous. She keeps cracking her knuckles. "Are you okay?" I ask.

"Please don't talk to me before the performance. It's bad luck."

So I sit there and start to get nervous myself, especially since I have a lot more riding on this competition than Tiffany does, and she is obviously rattled. I try not to think about losing my chance to send Nikki a letter, but of course this is all I can think about.

When other contestants begin to arrive, I notice that most of them look like high school students, and I think this is strange, but I do not say anything—mostly because I am not allowed to talk to Tiffany.

We register, give our music to the sound guy, who remembers Tiffany from last year, I know, because he says, "You again?" After Tiffany nods, we are backstage, changing. Thankfully, I'm able to slip into my tights before any of the other contestants make it backstage.

In the far corner, I'm minding my own business, sitting with Tiffany, when an ugly woman waddles over and says to Tiffany, "I know you dancers are pretty liberal about your bodies. But do you really expect me to allow my teenage daughter to change in front of this half-naked man?"

Tiffany is really nervous now. I know because she does not curse out this ugly woman, who reminds me of the nurses in the bad place, especially since she is so out of shape and has a poofy old-lady haircut.

"Well?" the mom says.

I see a storage closet on the other side of the room. "How about I go in there while everyone else changes?"

"Fine with me," the woman says.

Tiffany and I enter the supply closet, which is full of abandoned costumes from what must have been a children's show—all sorts of pajama-looking suits that would make me look like a lion or a tiger or a zebra if I put one on. A dusty box of percussion instruments—tambourines, triangles, cymbals, and wooden sticks you bang together—reminds me of the music room in the bad place and music relaxation class, which I attended until I was kicked out. And then I have this terrifying thought: What if one of the other contestants is dancing to a Kenny G song?

"You need to find out what songs the other dancers are performing to," I tell Tiffany.

"I told you not to talk to me before the performance."

"Just find out whether anyone is dancing to any songs played by a smooth jazz performer whose initials are K.G."

After a second she says, "Kenny—"

I close my eyes, hum a single note, and silently count to ten, blanking my mind.

"Jesus Christ," Tiffany says, but then stands and leaves the closet.

Ten minutes later she returns. "No music by that person," Tiffany says, and then sits down.

"Are you sure?"

"I said no Kenny G."

I close my eyes, hum a single note, and silently count to ten, blanking my mind.

• • •

We hear a knock, and when Tiffany opens the door, I see that many moms are backstage now. The woman who knocked tells Tiffany that all the dancers have checked in and are changed. When I leave the storage closet, I am shocked to see that Tiffany and I are the oldest contestants by at least fifteen years. We are surrounded by teenage girls.

"Don't let their innocent looks fool you," Tiffany says. "They're all little pit vipers—and extraordinarily gifted dancers."

Before the audience arrives, we are given a chance to practice on the Plaza Hotel stage. We nail our routine perfectly, but most of the other dancers also nail their impressive routines as well, which makes me worry we will not win.

Just before the competition begins, the contestants are brought out before the crowd. When Tiffany and I are announced, we take the stage, wave, and the applause is mild. The lights make it hard to see, but I spot Tiffany's parents in the front row, seated with little Emily, Ronnie, Veronica, and a middle-aged woman who I guess is Dr. Lily, Tiffany's therapist, because Tiffany told me that her therapist would be in attendance. I scan the rest of the rows quickly as we walk offstage, but I do not see my mother. No Jake. No Dad. No Cliff. I catch myself feeling sad, even though I did not really expect anyone but Mom to show up. Maybe Mom is out there somewhere, I think, and the thought makes me feel a little better.

Backstage, in my mind I admit that the other contestants received more applause than we did, which means their fan bases are larger than ours. Even though the woman who announced us is now giving a speech, saying this is a showcase and *not* a competition, I worry that Tiffany will not get the golden trophy, which would kill my chance to write Nikki letters.

We are scheduled to perform last, and as the other girls do

their numbers, the applause ranges from mild to enthusiastic, which surprises me, because during the preshow rehearsal, I thought all the routines were excellent.

But right before we are set to dance, when little Chelsea Chen concludes her ballet number, the applause is thunderous.

"What did she do out there to get such good applause?" I ask Tiffany.

"Don't talk to me before the performance," she says, and I start to feel very nervous.

The woman in charge of the recital announces our names, and the applause is a little livelier than what we received before the competition. Right before I lie down at the back of the stage, I look to see if maybe Jake or Cliff showed up late, but all I see when I look out into the audience is the hot white from the spotlights that are on me. Before I have a chance to think, the music starts.

Piano notes—slow and sad.

I begin my incredibly drawn-out crawl to center stage, using only my arms.

The male voice sings, "Turn around . . ."

Bonnie Tyler answers, "Every now and then I get a little bit lonely and you're never coming round."

At this point Tiffany runs onto the stage and leaps over me like a gazelle or some other animal that is beautifully nimble. As the two voices continue to exchange verses, Tiffany does her thing: running, jumping, tumbling, spinning, sliding—modern dance.

When the drums kick in, I stand and make a huge circle with my arms so people will know that I am the sun and I have risen. Tiffany's movements also become more fervent. When Bonnie Tyler builds up to the chorus, singing, "Together we can take it to the end of the line; your love is like a shadow on me all of the time," we go into the first lift. "I don't know what to do and I'm always in the dark." I have Tiffany up over my head; I am steady as a rock; I am performing flawlessly. "We're living in a powder keg and giving off sparks." I begin to rotate Tiffany as she lifts her legs out into a split and Bonnie Tyler sings, "I really need you tonight! Forever's gonna start tonight! Forever's gonna start tonight." We make a 360-degree rotation, and when Bonnie Tyler sings, "Once upon a time I was falling in love, but now I'm only falling apart," Tiffany rolls forward down into my arms and I lower her to the floor as if she were dead—and I, as the sun, mourn her. "Nothing I can say, a total eclipse of the heart."

When the music builds again, she explodes upward and begins to fly all around the stage so beautifully.

As the song continues, I again make huge, slow circles with my arms, representing the sun as best I can. I know the routine so well, I can think about other things while I am performing, so I begin to think that I am actually nailing this performance pretty easily and it is a shame my family and friends are not here to see me dancing so excellently. Even though we will most likely not win the audience's loudest applause—especially after Chelsea Chen obviously brought every single one of her family members to the performance—I begin to think we will win anyway. Tiffany is really good, and as she flies by me so many times, I begin to admire her in a way I had not previously. She has kicked her game up a notch for the competition and is now showing a part of herself I had not previously seen. If she was crying with her body for the last month or so, whenever we practiced in her studio, she is weeping uncontrollably with her body tonight, and you would have to be a stone not to feel what she is offering the audience.

But then Bonnie Tyler is singing, "Together we can make it to the end of the line," which means it is time for the second lift—the hardest one—so I lower myself into a squatting position and place the backs of my hands on my shoulders. As the song builds, Tiffany stands on my palms, and when Bonnie Tyler sings, "I really need you tonight," Tiffany bends her knees, so I engage my leg muscles and push upward as fast as I can, extending my arms, elevating my palms. Tiffany shoots high up into the air, does a full flip, falls into my arms, and as the chorus dies down, we gaze into each other's eyes. "Once upon a time I was falling in love, but now I'm only falling apart. Nothing I can do, a total eclipse of the heart." She falls from my arms, as if dead, and I—being the sun—set, which means I lie back on the floor and use only my arms to slowly push myself backward and out of the spotlight, which takes almost a full minute.

The music fades.

Silence.

For a second I worry that no one will clap.

But then the house explodes with applause.

When Tiffany stands, I do too. Just like we practiced so many times, I hold Tiffany's hand and take a bow, at which time the applause thickens and the audience stands.

I'm so happy, but at the same time I am sad because none of my family and friends came to support me—but then I hear the loudest Eagles chant I have ever heard in my entire life. "E!-A!-G!-L!-E!-S! EAGLES!" I look up toward the back rows, and not only do I spot Jake and Caitlin and Mom, but also Scott and the fat men and Cliff and the entire Asian Invasion. They are all wearing Eagles jerseys, and I start to laugh when they begin to chant, "Baskett! Baskett! Baskett! Baskett!"

In the front row, Ronnie is smiling at me proudly. He gives me the thumbs-up when we make eye contact. Veronica is also smiling, and so is little Emily, but Mrs. Webster is crying and smiling at the same time, which is when I realize that she thinks our dance was really beautiful—enough to make her cry.

Tiffany and I run offstage, and the high school girls congratulate us with their gaping eyes and their smiles and their chatter. "Oh, my God. That was *so* amazing!" they all say. It is easy to see that every one of them admires Tiffany because Tiffany is an excellent dancer and a talented choreographer.

Finally Tiffany faces me and says, "You were perfect!"

"No, you were perfect!" I say. "Do you think we won?"

She smiles and looks down at her feet.

"What?" I say.

"Pat, I need to tell you something."

"What?"

"There's no gold trophy."

"What?"

"There are no winners at Dance Away Depression. It's just an exhibition. I made up the part about the wreath just to motivate you."

"Oh."

"And it worked, because you were beautiful out there onstage! Thank you, and *I will* be your liaison," Tiffany says just before she kisses me on the lips and hugs me for a very long time. Her kiss tastes salty from the dancing, and it is strange to have Tiffany hugging me so passionately in front of so many teenage girls in tights—especially because I am shirtless and my torso is freshly shaved—and also I do not like to be touched by anyone except Nikki.

"So now that we are done dancing, can I talk about Eagles football again? Because I have a lot of Eagles fans out there waiting for me."

"After nailing the routine, you can do whatever you want, Pat," Tiffany whispers into my ear, and then I wait a long time for her to stop hugging me.

After I change in the storage closet, Tiffany tells me there are no more naked teenagers backstage, so I go to greet my fans. When I hop down off the stage, Mrs. Webster grabs my hands, looks into my eyes, and says, "Thank you." She keeps looking into my eyes, but the old woman doesn't say anything else, which makes me feel sort of weird.

Finally Veronica says, "What my mother means to say is that tonight meant a lot to Tiffany."

Emily points at me and says, "Pap!"

"That's right, Em," Ronnie says. "Uncle Pat."

"Pap! Pap! Pap!"

We all laugh, but then I hear fifty Indian men chanting, "Baskett! Baskett! Baskett!"

"Better go greet your rowdy fans," Ronnie says, so I walk up the aisle toward the sea of Eagles jerseys. Other audience members I don't know pat me on the back and congratulate me as I weave my way through them.

"You were so good up there!" my mother says in a way that lets me know she was surprised by my excellent dancing skills, and then she hugs me. "I'm so proud!"

I hug her back and then ask, "Is Dad here?"

"Forget Dad," Jake says. "You got sixty or so wild men waiting to take you to the most epic tailgate party of your life."

"Hope you weren't planning on getting any sleep tonight," Caitlin says to me.

"You ready to end the Pat Peoples curse?" Cliff asks me.

"What?" I say.

"The Birds haven't won since you stopped watching. Tonight we're taking drastic measures to end the curse," Scott says. "We're sleeping in the Asian Invasion bus, right outside the Wachovia parking lot. We set up the tailgate party at daybreak."

"Ashwini is driving around the block right now, waiting for us," Cliff says. "So. Are you ready?"

I am a little shaken by the news, especially since I just finished such an excellent dance routine and was hoping to simply enjoy the accomplishment for more than ten minutes. "I don't have my clothes."

But my mom pulls my Baskett jersey out of a duffel bag I hadn't noticed before and says, "You have everything you need in here."

"What about my meds?"

Cliff holds up a little plastic bag with my pills inside.

Before I can say or do anything else, the Asian Invasion begins chanting louder: "Baskett! Baskett! Baskett!" The fat men pick me up above their heads and carry me out of the auditorium, past the fountain full of fish, out of the Plaza Hotel, and onto the streets of Philadelphia. And then I am in the Asian Invasion bus, drinking a beer and singing, "Fly, Eagles, fly! On the road to victory . . ."

In South Philadelphia, we stop at Pat's for cheesesteaks—which take a long time to prepare, as there are sixty or so of us, and no one would dare go next door to Geno's Steaks, because Geno's steaks are inferior—and then we are at the Wachovia parking lot, parked just outside the gate so we will be the first vehicle admitted in the morning and therefore will be guaranteed the lucky parking spot. We drink, sing, throw a few footballs, and run around on the concrete; we roll out the Astroturf and play a few Kubb games under the streetlights, and even though I have only had two or three beers, I begin to tell everyone I love them because they came to my dance recital, and I also tell them I'm sorry for abandoning the Eagles mid-season and that it was for a good reason, but I just can't say what—and then I am on a bus seat and Cliff is waking me up, saying, "You forgot to take your night meds."

When I wake up the next morning, my head is on Jake's shoulder, and it feels good to be so close to my brother, who is still asleep. Quietly I stand and look around and realize that everyone—Scott, the fat men, Cliff, all fifty or so Asian Invasion members—is asleep on the bus. Two or three men are sleeping in every seat, with their heads on each other's shoulders. Everywhere brothers.

I tiptoe to the front of the bus, past Ashwini, who—in the driver's seat—is asleep with his mouth wide open.

Once outside, on the small patch of grass between the street and the sidewalk, I begin the same push-up and sit-up routine I used to do back in the bad place, before I had access to free weights and a stationary bike and the Stomach Master 6000.

After an hour or so, first light comes.

As I finish the last set of sit-ups, I feel as though I have burned off my cheesesteak and the beers I drank the night before, but I can't help feeling like I should go for a run, so I run a few miles, and when I return, my friends are still sleeping.

As I stand next to Ashwini and watch my boys sleep, I feel happy because I have so many friends—a whole busful.

I realize that I left the Plaza Hotel without saying goodbye to Tiffany, and I feel a little bad about that, even though she said I could do whatever I wanted after we performed so well. Also I am very eager to write my first letter to Nikki. But there is Eagles football to think about now, and I know that an Eagles victory is just about the only thing that will smooth things over with my father, so I begin to hope, and I even say a little prayer to God, who I bet was pretty impressed with my dance routine last night, so maybe He will cut me a break today. Looking at all those sleeping faces, I realizc I have missed my green-shirted brothers, and I begin to anticipate the day.

Letter #2—November 15, 2006

Dear Pat,

First, let me say it's good to hear from you. It's been a long time, which has been strange for me. I mean, when you are married to someone for years and then you don't see that person for almost as many years, it's strange, right? I don't know how to explain it, especially since our marriage ended so abruptly and scandalously. We never got a chance to talk things over—one-on-one—like civilized adults. Because of this, sometimes I think maybe it's almost as if I'm not really sure the multiple "Pat-less" years have truly transpired, but maybe it's been only a brief separation that feels like years. Like a solo car ride that takes all night but feels like a lifetime. Watching all those highway dashes flying by at seventy miles an hour, your eyes becoming lazy slits and your mind wandering over the memory of a whole lifetime—past and future, childhood memories to thoughts of your own death—until the numbers on the dashboard clock do not mean anything anymore. And then the sun comes up and you get to your destination and the ride becomes the thing that is no longer real, because that surreal feeling has vanished and time has become meaningful again.

Finally making contact with you is like arriving at the end of a long car ride and realizing I went to the wrong place—that I have ended up in the past somehow, at the port of origin instead of the dock of destination. But at least I finally get to say that to you, which is important. It probably sounds stupid, but maybe you know what I mean. The part of my life you once filled has been nothing but highway dashes since you were put away, and I am hoping this exchange of letters will help to provide closure for both of us, because soon I will drive back to the place I was before Tiffany contacted me, and we will be only memories to each other.

I can hardly believe how much you wrote. When Tiffany told me you were writing me a letter, I did not expect you to give her two hundred photocopied pages of your diary. As you can imagine, Tiffany was not able to read me all of the pages over the phone, because that would have taken hours! She did read me the introductory note and then filled me in on the rest, citing your diary often. You need to know it was a lot of work for her to read through the manuscript and pick out the parts she thought I should hear. For Tiffany's sake, please limit your next letter to five pages—should there be a next letter—as reading five pages aloud takes a long time and Tiffany is typing up what I dictate over the phone as well, which is already too much to ask of her. (She really is a phenomenally kind woman, don't you think? You are lucky to have Tiffany in your life.) Maybe it's the English teacher in me, but I feel as though a page limit is best. No offense, but let's try to be concise. Okay?

Congratulations on your dance performance. Tiffany says you performed flawlessly. I'm so proud of you! It's hard to imagine you dancing, Pat. The way that Tiffany described the performance was very impressive. I'm glad you are taking an interest in new things. That's good. I certainly wish you had danced more with me.

Things at Jefferson High School are gloriously shitty. The PTA pushed for online grade books, and now parents have access to their children's grades 24/7. You would hate working here now because of this new development. All parents have to do is log on to a computer, go to the Jefferson High School Web page, enter an ID # and a password, and they can see if their kid turned in his homework on any given day or scored poorly on a pop quiz or whatever. Of course, this means if we are behind on our grading, parents will know and the aggressive ones will call. Parent-teacher conferences have increased because of this. Every time a student misses a single homework, I'm hearing from parents. Our sports teams are losing pretty regularly too. Coach Ritchie and Coach Malone both miss you. Believe me when I say they could not fill your shoes, and the kids are worse off without Coach Peoples at the helm. The life of a teacher is still hectic and crazy—and I am glad you don't have to deal with this type of stress as you heal.

Sorry to hear about your father being aloof. I know how much that used to upset you. And I'm also sorry your Eagles are up and down—but at least they beat the Redskins last weekend, right? And season tickets with Jake, you must feel as though you died and went to heaven.

I think it's best to say I am remarried. I won't go into details unless you want me to, Pat. I'm sure this comes as a shock to you, especially after Tiffany read me the many parts of your diary that seemed to indicate you still hope to reconcile our marriage. You need to know this is not going to happen. The truth is I was planning on divorcing you before the accident, before you were checked into the neural health facility. We were not a good match. You were never home. And let's face it—our sex life was shit. I cheated on you because of this, which you may or may not remember. I am not trying to hurt you, Pat—far from it. I am not proud of my infidelity. I regret cheating on you. But our marriage was over before I began my affair. Your mind is not right, but I have been told your therapist is one of the best in South Jersey, your treatments are working, and your memory will return soon; when it does, you will remember how I hurt you, and then you will not even want to write me, let alone try to re-create what you think we once had.

I understand my blunt response to your very long and passionate letter might make you upset, and if you don't want to write me again, I will understand. But I wanted to be honest with you. What's the point if we lie now?

Yours,
Nikki

P.S.—I was very impressed with your finally reading many of the books on my American Lit. syllabus. Many students have also complained about the novels being so depressing. Try Mark Twain. Huck Finn *ends happily. You might like that one. But I'll tell you the same thing I tell my students when they complain about the depressing nature of American literature: life is not a PG feel-good movie. Real life often ends badly, like our marriage did, Pat. And literature tries to document this reality, while showing us it is still possible for people to endure nobly. It sounds like you have endured very nobly since you returned to New Jersey, and I want you to know I admire that. I hope you are able to reinvent yourself and live out the rest of your life with a quiet sense of satisfaction, which is what I have been trying to do since we parted.*

Letter #3—November 18, 2006

Dear Nikki,

As soon as I read your letter, I had my mother check out The Adventures of Huckleberry Finn *from the Collingswood Public Library. Eager to enjoy a literary book with a happy ending, I read the entire work in one sitting, which required me to forgo sleep for an evening. I don't know if Tiffany read you the parts in my diary about my black friend Danny, but this book would make him go wild, as Twain uses the n-word more than 200 times. I know this because after reading the first few chapters, I started over and kept a running tally. Every time Twain used the n-word, I made a mark on a piece of paper, and when I finished the book, there were more than 200 marks! Danny says that only black people can use the n-word, which is sort of a universal truth nowadays, so I am surprised the school board allows you to teach such a book.*

But I did like the book very much. Even though Tom Sawyer should have told Jim he was free right away, I was so happy for Jim at the end of the novel when he gained his freedom. Also, the way that

Huck and Jim stuck together through bad times reminded me of Danny and Pat getting each other's backs in the bad place. What really struck me was how Huck kept struggling with the idea that God did not want him to help Jim run away, because Jim was a slave. I realize people had different values back then, and that the church and government approved of slavery, but Huck really impressed me when he said if helping free Jim meant going to hell, he would go to hell.

When I read your letter, I cried for a long time. I know I was a bad husband, and I am not mad at you for cheating on me or leaving me or even remarrying. You deserve to be happy. And if you are married now, your getting back together with me would be a sin, because it would mean that we would be committing adultery, even though I still think of you as my wife. These thoughts make me feel dizzy, as if I am spinning out of control. These thoughts make me want to bang my fist against the little white scar above my right eyebrow, which itches every time I get confused or agitated. To use your metaphor . . . since I can remember, I have been driving on a dark highway, passing endless dashes and lines. Everything else has only been a pit stop—family, Eagles, dancing, my workouts. I have been driving toward you the whole time, only desiring one thing—our reunion. And now I finally realize I'm trying to woo a married woman, which I know is a sin. But I don't think you understand how hard I worked for this happy ending. I am very fit, and am now practicing being kind rather than right. I am not the man you were married to for all those lonely years. I am a better man. A man who will take you dancing and will give up sports entirely—coaching and Eagles—if that makes you happy. My conscience tells me that I should not continue to pursue these feelings, but your telling me to read Twain's novel made me think that maybe you were giving me a sign. Huck thought he shouldn't help Jim escape, but he followed his heart, he freed Jim, and that is what led to the happy ending. So maybe you are telling me in an indirect way that I should follow my heart? Why else would you specifically recommend The Adventures of Huckleberry Finn *to me?*

Also, our time together wasn't all bad. Maybe the end was grim, but remember the beginning? Remember college? Remember when we drove to Massachusetts in the middle of the night? It was the Friday after midterms and we were watching one of those travel shows on PBS, because we both thought we would travel back then. All our friends had gone to the rugby house for a party, but we stayed in together for a night of pizza and wine on the couch of my town house. We were watching that show about whale watching off the coast of Martha's Vineyard, and you asked me if they made wine in Martha's Vineyard. I said the New England growing season would be too short to get the proper types of grapes, but you insisted that there must be a vineyard there if the island was called Martha's Vineyard. We had this really heated fake argument—laughing and hitting each other with pillows—and then suddenly we were in my old Taurus, driving north.

I'm sure you didn't think I was really going to drive you all the way to Massachusetts without a change of clothes or toiletries, but soon we were over the Tappan Zee Bridge, and you were smiling, and I was holding your hand.

We never made it to Martha's Vineyard, but we spent a pretty wild weekend in an economy motel just outside of Cape Cod. Do you remember walking on the beach in March? Our lovemaking smelling like decades' worth other people's cigarette smoke as we enjoyed each other over and over in that motel room? Remember how when we jumped on the mattress, smoke seemed to leak out the sides? The lobster dinner we splurged for at that cheesy restaurant called Captain Bob's, where the waiters wore eye patches?

We always said we were going to return to Massachusetts, take the ferry, and see if Martha's Vineyard actually had vineyards. Why didn't we do this then? Probably because we had class on Monday morning. But I wish we had taken that ferry when we had the chance. What was the worst thing that could have happened? We would have missed class. It seems so silly now to drive all the way to Cape Cod with the intention of taking the ferry to Martha's Vineyard only to spend the weekend in an economy motel on the mainland.

What I'm trying to say is that maybe we can still take the ferry, Nikki. Maybe it's not too late.

I know this is all so complicated right now. But there must be a reason that we are in contact again. There must be a reason that I lost my memory and then was filled with a vicious need to improve myself. There must be a reason if Tiffany was able to arrange this letter exchange. All I'm asking is that you keep the possibility of a reunion open as we continue to communicate through our liaison.

My therapist Cliff says he feels as though I am poised for a breakthrough, and he feels he has stabilized my violent tendencies with medications. I know that in my writings I mentioned spitting out many of my meds when I first came home, but I am taking all my pills now and can feel my mental health stabilizing. Every day I feel as though I am getting closer to regaining my memory of our demise. And no matter what I remember—no matter what really happened between us—it will not change how I feel about you. You are living with another man, you are remarried—what could be worse? I still love you. I will always love you and am only now ready to prove *my love for you.*

I hope this note was concise enough, as I tried very hard to keep it under five pages and was successful. I miss you so much, Nikki. Every freckle on your beautiful nose.

Love,

Pat, Your Sexy Stud Muffin

(Remember that from the wedding video?)

Letter #4—November 29, 2006

Dear Pat,

Tiffany informs me you are sincere, and from what she has told me about your new personality, it seems as though you are a completely transformed man. Whether this is the result of the accident, therapy, medication, or simply sheer willpower, you are to be congratulated, because this is no small feat.

First allow me to say I recommended Huck Finn *for your reading enjoyment only. I was not trying to send you a hidden message. Based on everything you have written and what Tiffany has told me—maybe you should read* The Catcher in the Rye. *It's about a young boy named Holden who has a hard time coping with reality. Holden wants to live in a childhood world for the rest of his life, which makes him a very beautiful and interesting character, but one who has trouble finding his place in the real world. At present, it seems as though you are having a hard time dealing with reality. Part of me thrills at the changes you have made, because your letters really do present a better man. But I also worry that this worldview you have developed is fragile, and may be what kept you in the neural health facility for so many years and is keeping you in your parents' basement for so many months. At some point you are going to have to leave the basement, Pat. You are going to have to get a job and earn money again, and then you might not be able to be the person you have been for the last few months.*

Of course I remember Massachusetts. We were so young, and the memory is beautiful. I'll carry it with me forever. But we WERE CHILDREN, Pat. That was more than a decade ago. I'm not the type of woman who would sleep in an economy motel anymore. Maybe you have again become the type of man who would whisk a woman away to Martha's Vineyard. Maybe you are experiencing some sort of second childhood. I don't know. But I do know you will NOT be experiencing a second childhood with me. I am not a child, Pat. I'm a woman who loves her current husband very much. My aim when I agreed to write you was never to allow you a second chance. My goal was not to allow you to reenter my life. I only wanted to give you a chance to say goodbye—to resolve any unresolved issues. I want to be clear about this.

Nikki

Letter #5—December 3, 2006

Dear Nikki,

The night after the Tennessee Titans destroyed the Eagles on their home turf—a game in which Donovan McNabb tore his ACL, ending his season and maybe even his career—Andre Waters shot himself to death. I realize you don't care about any of this, but Waters was one of my favorite players back when I was a teenager. He was a big part of the Gang Green Defense. People called him Dirty Waters because he was fined so much for hitting too hard. And when I was a kid, Waters was a god to me. Jake says Waters probably killed himself after watching the Eagles play so poorly against the Titans, which was not a funny thing to say at all. My father is not talking to anyone, because he is upset about McNabb's injury, which will most likely ruin the Eagles' chances of making the play-offs. My new favorite player, Hank Baskett, is not getting many balls thrown to him anymore, but he actually threw *an interception during a stupid trick play during the Indy Colts' win over the Birds just this past weekend. And of course, there was also your last letter.*

So I'm thinking this is the part of my movie where things appear as if nothing is going to work out. I have to remind myself that all movie characters go through this sort of dark period before they find their happy ending.

It was hard to wait two weeks for your reply. Your letter made me very sad, and in the past twenty-four hours I have written my reply at least a hundred times.

I don't know if Tiffany read you the part of my memoir where I described my therapist's office, but he has two leather recliners—one black, one brown. My therapist lets his patients choose which seat they want to sit in just so he can see what type of mood we are in. I've been picking the black one lately.

I've read certain parts of your letters to Cliff—that's my therapist's name. He doesn't know about Tiffany's involvement, because I promised her that I would not tell anyone that she has agreed to act as our liaison. When Cliff asked how I was able to make contact with you, I refused to answer. I hope that you don't mind my reading some of your words to my therapist. It's funny. Cliff keeps hinting that I should pursue a relationship with Tiffany. And I know Tiffany is reading this letter to you, so this part will be awkward for everyone involved, but Tiffany will just have to deal with it because this is what being a liaison requires, and I already danced so well, fulfilling my end of the bargain.

Cliff says that Tiffany and I have a lot in common at this point and that you and I have very little in common, because we are in very different places. I thought he meant that you were in Maryland and I was in New Jersey, but it turns out he means that I am still fighting to regain my mental health, and you are mentally stable. I asked Cliff why he would want me to pursue a relationship with someone who is as mentally unstable as me, and he said that you were not able to support me in the way I needed to be supported, which is why our marriage failed. I got very mad at Cliff when he said that, especially since I am the one to blame, but he insisted that you allowed me to become the person I was by enabling me—never putting me in my place and allowing me to emotionally abuse you for so long. He says that Tiffany will not allow me to do this and that our friendship is based on a mutual need and a commitment to bettering ourselves through physical fitness and dance.

Tiffany and I are great friends, and I appreciate all that she is doing for me now. But she is not you. I still love you, Nikki. And you can't control or alter true love.

Mom checked out The Catcher in the Rye *from the Collingswood Public Library. I liked Holden Caulfield very much and felt a lot of sympathy for him because he really was a nice guy, always trying to do right by his sister Phoebe, yet always failing, like when he bought that record for Phoebe and broke it before he could give it to her. I also liked how he was always so worried about what the NYC ducks do in winter. Where do they go? But my favorite part was the ending, when Holden takes his sister to the carousel and she rides on the horse and tries to reach for the gold ring. Holden says, "I was sort of afraid she'd fall off the goddamn horse, but I didn't say anything or do anything. The thing with kids is, if they want to grab for the gold ring, you have to let them do it, and not say anything. If they fall off, they fall off, but it's bad if you say anything to them." When I read this, I thought about your writing that I was in my second childhood and that I would have to "leave the basement" someday. But then I thought about how my improving myself and learning how to dance with Tiffany was like reaching for the gold ring, which is you. Nikki, you are my gold ring. So maybe I will fall off the goddamn carousel, but I have to reach for you, right?*

I want to see you. I want to talk to you face-to-face. Just once. Afterward, if you never want to see me again, I can live with that. Just give me one chance to show you how much I have changed. Just one chance. One face-to-face meeting. Please.

Love,

Pat

Letter #6—December 13, 2006

Dear Pat,

I'm sorry your childhood hero committed suicide. I'm sorry McNabb was injured. And I am especially sad to hear that your father is still allowing the results of football games to govern the relationships he has with his immediate family. Your poor, poor mother.

Your decision to reveal your therapist's views regarding Tiffany made for an awkward phone conversation. It is obvious that Tiffany cares for you enough to put together this exchange of letters. I hope you will protect her legally by refraining from discussing the arrangement further with your therapist or anyone else. You do realize that by showing Cliff my letters, you have put me in a precarious legal position. I am not allowed to make contact with you by law, remember? So this will be my last letter. Sorry.

Regarding Holden Caulfield and the gold ring Phoebe reaches for at the end of the novel, please don't think of me as your golden ring. I am your ex-wife. I wish you well, but your therapist was right to say we are incompatible.

I can see clearly we are not moving toward closure, which makes me regret opening up this dialogue. My only hope is that someday—after you have stabilized your mental health—you will take comfort in the fact that I reached out to you after all that happened. I wish you well in this world, Pat.

Goodbye.
Nikki

Letter #7—December 14, 2006

Dear Nikki,

I believe in happy endings with all my heart. I've worked too hard on self-improvement to give up on my movie now. Remember where I asked you to marry me? Meet me there on Christmas Day at dusk. This is the only thing I will ever ask of you. But I feel as though you owe me this one last request. Please.

Love,
Pat

This Square in My Hand

My father refuses to go with Mom, so I put on the new suit she bought me earlier this month and accompany her to the candlelit Mass at St. Joseph's. It is a crisp night, but we walk the few blocks required, and soon we are in the very sanctuary where I was confirmed so many years ago. Rows of red and white poinsettias are lined up on the altar, and antique wrought-iron lamps stand guard at the ends of the pews, just like every other Christmas Eve. The candlelight makes the stone building look even more antiquated—almost medieval. And sitting down in the pew again reminds me of when Jake and I were just boys. We'd come to Christmas Eve Mass so excited for the next day, ready to tear into all those presents. But tonight it's just Mom and me, as Jake and Caitlin are spending Christmas Eve in New York City with Caitlin's parents, and Dad is home drinking beer.

After some announcements and Christmas hymns, the priest talks about stars and angels and mangers and donkeys and miracles, and somewhere in the story, I start praying.

Dear God, I know it would take a miracle to get Nikki to show up tomorrow at the place where we were engaged, but lucky for me, You and I both believe in miracles. As I sit here thinking about this, I wonder if You actually believe in miracles, since You are all-powerful and can do anything. So technically, Your making Nikki show up tomorrow or putting Baby Jesus inside of the Virgin Mary is no more difficult for You than, say, watching an Eagles game—which has been pretty easy since backup QB Jeff Garcia has managed to win three straight. It's sort of funny when I think about it now. If You created the world in only a week, sending Your Son down to do a mission must have been no sweat for You. But I am still glad You took the time to send Jesus to teach us all about miracles, because the possibility of miracles happening keeps a lot of people moving forward down here. I don't have to tell You that I have been working pretty hard on bettering myself since apart time began. I actually want to thank You for disrupting my life, because I would never have taken the time to improve my character if I did not get sent to the bad place, nor would I have met Cliff, or even Tiffany for that matter, and I know this journey has been for a reason. I trust that there is a divine plan in effect, and that is why I believe You will make sure Nikki shows up tomorrow. I want to thank You in advance for helping me get my wife back. I am looking forward to the years ahead, when I can treat Nikki how a woman should be treated. Also, if it is not too much trouble, please allow the Eagles to win on Christmas Day, because a win over the Cowboys will put the Eagles in first place and then my dad might be in a good mood and maybe he will even talk to Mom and me. It's strange, even with the Birds in play-off contention, Dad has been a grinch this holiday season, and it has really made Mom sad. I've caught her crying several times, but You probably already know that since You are all-knowing. I love You, God.

I cross myself just as the priest finishes the homily, and then the candles are passed out and lighted while the people sing "Silent Night." Mom is sort of leaning against me, so I throw an arm around her shoulder and give her a little squeeze. She looks up at me and smiles. "My good boy," her lips mouth, bathed in candlelight, and then we both join in with the singing.

My father is in bed asleep when we return home. Mom pours some eggnog and plugs in the lights, and we sip in the glow of the Christmas tree. Mom talks about all the ornaments Jake and I made as little kids. She keeps pointing to painted pinecones, little Popsicle-stick picture frames with our grade school photos inside, and reindeers made from clothespins and pipe cleaners. "Remember when you made this in so-and-so's class?" she keeps saying, and I nod every time, even though I don't remember making any of the ornaments. It's funny how Mom remembers everything about Jake and me, and somehow I know that Nikki will never love me as much—no matter how much I improve my character—and that's what I really truly love about my mom.

Just when we are finishing the last sips of our eggnog, the doorbell rings. "Who could that be?" Mom asks in a dramatic way, suggesting she knows exactly who it could be.

I start to get excited because I think that it might be Nikki, that Mom has arranged the best Christmas present ever. But when I answer the door, it's only Ronnie, Veronica, Tiffany, and little Emily. They all but skip into the foyer and start singing, "We wish you a Merry Christmas. We wish you a Merry Christmas. We wish you a Merry Christmas and a Happy New Year." At this point Tiffany stops singing, but Ronnie and Veronica continue to belt out the first verse, and my mother is all smiles as she listens to the good tidings they bring. Little Emily looks like an Eskimo, all bundled up, but her parents' singing makes her little round face look content. I can even see the Christmas tree lights reflected in her dark eyes. As they sing, Ronnie's family looks like a happy one, and I envy my friend.

Tiffany is looking at her feet, but she rejoins the singing when they get to the chorus again.

The song ends with Ronnie holding the last note too long, but my mother claps anyway, and then we are all seated around the Christmas tree drinking more eggnog.

"Maybe you want to give your friends their presents," Mom says.

Mom had taken me shopping many times in the past few weeks, and we picked out presents for the people who have helped me get better, because Mom says it's important to recognize the special people in your life around the holidays. Cliff loved his Eagles dartboard, and it turns out that Veronica and Tiffany both like the perfume we purchased—thank God, as I did sniff just about every bottle in the Cherry Hill Mall. Ronnie loves the official NFL leather football I picked out for him so that he can work on his throws, and little Emily hugs the stuffed eagle wearing an Eagles jersey that I picked out special for her, and she even begins to chew on the yellow beak just as soon as she finishes ripping off the paper.

For my mom's sake, I keep hoping my father might come downstairs and join the party, but he doesn't.

"And we have a present for you too," Ronnie tells me. "Come on, Em. Let's give Uncle Pat his present." He hands Emily a box, which is too heavy for her to carry, even though she is walking pretty well now, so he and Emily both carry the present over to me.

"For Pap!" Emily says, and then starts to rip off the wrapping paper.

"You want to help me?" I ask her, and she tears the rest of the paper off as everyone watches.

Once Emily finishes with the paper, I open the box and fish through the Styrofoam peanuts and find what feels like a plaque of some sort. I pull it out of the peanuts and can see it is a framed picture of Hank Baskett. He's in the end zone with a football in his hand.

"It was taken during the Dallas game," Ronnie says.

"Read what's written on the picture," says Veronica.

To Pat,
You're on the road to victory!
Hank Baskett #84

"This is the greatest present ever! How did you get Baskett to sign the picture?"

"Veronica's cousin's a barber," Ronnie explains, "and one of his customers works for the Eagles promotions department, so we were able to pull a few strings. Vinnie said that this was the first request his contact got for a Baskett autograph, and Baskett was actually pretty excited to get a specific request, since his autograph is not in such high demand."

"Thanks, Ronnie," I say, and then we give each other one-armed manly hugs.

"Merry Christmas," Ronnie says to me as he thumps my back.

"Well, I hate to break up the party, but we need to get Emily in bed before Santa comes down the chimney," Veronica says.

As they put on their coats, my mom is putting their presents into a holiday bag with fancy handles and thanking everyone for coming over, saying, "You don't know how much it means to Pat and me. You've been so good to us this year. You're good people.

All of you. Such great people." And then Mom is crying again, saying, "I'm sorry. Thanks. Merry Christmas. Don't mind me. God bless you."

Just before everyone leaves, Tiffany grabs my hand, kisses me on the cheek, and says, "Merry Christmas, Pat." When she pulls her palm away from mine, I have a square in my hand, but the look in Tiffany's eyes commands silence, so I stick the square in my pocket and say goodbye to Ronnie's family.

I help my mother clean up the wrapping paper and empty eggnog mugs, and then she catches me under the mistletoe in the hallway. She's pointing up and smiling, so I kiss her good night, and she reaches up to hug me. "I'm so glad I have you in my life right now, Pat," my mother says to me, flexing her arm muscles so hard, pulling my head down so that her shoulder juts up into my throat and it becomes a little harder to breathe.

In my room, by the light of the electric Christmas candle Mom has stuck in my window for the holiday season, I unfold the note Tiffany passed me.

Letter #8—December 24, 2006

Dear Pat,

I won't be coming on Christmas. I won't be coming ever. Move on. Start over. Tiffany and your family will help you through this. Goodbye for real this time. I will not be writing more, nor will I be taking any more calls from Tiffany, because I do not appreciate her yelling and cursing at me on your behalf. Do not try to contact me. The restraining order is still in effect.

Nikki

An Episode Seems Inevitable

I rise before dawn on Christmas morning and begin my weight-lifting routine. I am nervous about being reunited with Nikki today, so I double-time my exercises in an effort to work off my anxiety. I realize the note Tiffany gave me last night suggests that Nikki might not be interested in meeting me at that special place once dusk rolls around, but I also know that in the movies, just when the main character is about to give up, something surprising happens, which leads to the happy ending. I'm pretty sure that this is the part of my movie when something surprising will happen, so I am trusting in God, who I know will not let me down. If I have faith, if I go to that special place, something beautiful will happen when the sun sets—I can feel it.

When I hear Christmas music, I stop lifting and go upstairs. My mother is cooking eggs and bacon. Coffee is brewing. "Merry Christmas," Mom says, and gives me a little kiss on the cheek. "Don't forget your pills."

I take the orange bottles from the cabinet and twist off the lids. As I swallow my last pill, my father comes into the kitchen and throws the newspaper's plastic cover into the waste bucket. When he turns and heads for the family room, my mother says, "Merry Christmas, Patrick."

"Merry Christmas," Dad mumbles.

We eat eggs and bacon and toast together as a family, but no one says much.

In the living room we sit around the tree. Mom opens her present from Dad. It's a diamond necklace from some department store—tiny diamonds in the shape of a heart on a thin gold chain. I know for a fact that Mom has a similar necklace, because she wears it almost every day. My father probably gave her the same thing last year, but Mom acts really surprised and says, "Patrick, you shouldn't have," before she kisses my father on the lips and then hugs him. Even though Dad doesn't hug Mom back, I can tell he is happy, because he sort of smirks.

Next, we give Dad his present, which is from both Mom and me. He tears off the wrapping paper and holds up an authentic Eagles jersey, not one with iron-on decals. "Why doesn't it have any numbers or a name on it?" he asks.

"Since McNabb went down, we thought you'd want to pick a new favorite player," Mom says. "So when you do, we'll have the correct number and name sewn onto the jersey."

"Don't waste your money," Dad says, putting the jersey back into the box. "They won't win today without McNabb. They're not going to make the play-offs. I'm done watching that lousy excuse for a football team."

Mom smiles at me because I told her that Dad would say as much, even though the Eagles have been playing pretty well. But Mom and I both know Dad will be watching the Eagles play the

Cowboys later today and will pick a new favorite player late next summer—after watching one or two preseason games—at which time he will say something like, "Jeanie, where's my authentic Eagles jersey? I want to get those numbers sewn on before the season starts."

A few dozen presents are for me, all of which Mom bought and wrapped. I get a new Eagles sweatshirt, new running shoes, workout clothes, dress clothes, a few ties, a brand-new leather jacket, and a special running watch that will help me time my runs and will even calculate the calories I burn while running. And—

"Jesus Christ, Jeanie. How many presents did you buy the kid?" Dad says, but in a way that lets us know he is not really all that mad.

After we eat lunch, I shower and put on underarm deodorant, some of my father's cologne, and one of my new running outfits.

"I'm going to try out my new watch," I tell Mom.

"Caitlin and your brother will be here in an hour," Mom says. "So don't be too long."

"I won't," I say just before I exit the house.

In the garage, I change into the dress clothes I hid there earlier in the week—tweed pants, a black button-down shirt, leather loafers, and the expensive overcoat my father no longer wears. Next, I walk to the Collingswood PATCO stop and catch the 1:45 train to Philadelphia.

It begins to rain lightly.

I get off at Eighth and Market, walk through the drizzle to City Hall, and catch an Orange Line train headed north.

Not many people are on the train, and underground it does not feel like Christmas at all. But the trash-smelling steam that wafts in at every stop when the doors open, the marker graffiti on the orange seat across from me, the half-eaten hamburger lying bunless in the aisle—none of it brings me down, because I am about to be reunited with Nikki. Apart time is finally about to end.

I get off at Broad and Olney and climb the steps up into North Philly, where it is raining a little harder. Even though I remember being mugged twice near this subway stop when I was a college student, I do not worry, mostly because it's Christmas and I am a lot stronger than I used to be when I was an undergraduate. On Broad Street I see a few black people, which gets me thinking about Danny and how he always used to talk about going to live with his aunt in North Philly just as soon as he got out of the bad place—especially whenever I mentioned my graduating from La Salle University, which is apparently close to where Danny's aunt lives. I wonder if Danny ever made it out of the bad place, and the thought of him having Christmas in a mental institution makes me really sad because Danny was a good friend to me.

I stick my hands into my dad's overcoat pockets as I walk down Olney. With the rain, it is sort of cold. Soon I am seeing the blue-and-yellow flags that line the campus streets, and it makes me feel happy and sad at the same time to be back at La Salle—almost like looking at old pictures of people who have either died or with whom you have lost contact.

When I get to the library, I turn left and walk past the tennis courts, where I make a right and stroll past the security building.

Beyond the tennis courts is a walled-in hill, with so many trees you'd never believe it was in North Philly if someone had led you here blindfolded and then removed the blindfold and asked, "Where do you think you are?"

At the bottom of the hill is a Japanese teahouse, which is as picturesque as it is out of place in North Philly, although I have never been inside to have tea—because it is a private teahouse—so maybe the inside has a city feel to it; I don't know. Nikki and I used to meet on this hill, behind an old oak tree, and sit on the grass for hours. Surprisingly, not many students hung out in this spot. Maybe they did not know it was there. Maybe no one else thought it was a nice spot. But Nikki loved sitting on the grassy hill and looking down at the Japanese teahouse, feeling as though she were somewhere else in the world—somewhere other than North Philadelphia. And if it weren't for the occasional car horn or gunshot in the distance, I would have believed I was in Japan when I was sitting on that hill, even though I have never been to Japan and don't really know what being in that particular country is like.

I sit down under a huge tree—on a dry spot of grass—and wait.

Rain clouds swallowed the sun a long time ago, but when I look at my watch, the numbers officially make it dusk.

My chest starts to feel tight; I notice that I am shaking and breathing heavily. I hold my hand out to see how bad the shakes are, and my hand is flapping like the wing of a bird, or maybe it is as if I am hot and trying to fan myself with my fingers. I try to make it stop, and when I can't, I shove both hands into my father's overcoat pockets, hoping Nikki will not notice my nervousness when she shows up.

It grows darker, and then even darker.

Finally, I close my eyes, and after a time, I begin to pray:

Dear God: If I did something wrong, please let me know what it was so I can make amends. As I search my memory, I can't think of anything that would make You mad, except for my punching the Giants fan a few months ago, but I already asked for forgiveness regarding that slip, and I thought we had moved on. Please make Nikki show up. When I open my eyes, please let her be there. Maybe there was traffic, or she forgot how to get to La Salle? She always used to get lost in the city. I'm okay with her not showing up exactly at dusk, but please let her know that I am still here waiting and will wait all night if I have to. Please, God. I'll do anything. If You make her show up when I open—

I smell a woman's perfume.

I recognize the scent.

I breathe in deeply to ready myself.

I open my eyes.

"I'm fucking sorry, okay?" she says, but it's not Nikki. "I never thought it would lead to this. So I'm just going to be honest now. My therapist thought you were stuck in a constant state of denial because you were never afforded closure, and I thought I might afford you closure by pretending to be Nikki. So I made up the whole liaison thing in an effort to provide you closure, hoping you would snap out of your funk and would be able to move on with your life once you understood that being reunited with your ex-wife was an impossibility. I wrote all the letters myself. *Okay?* I never even contacted Nikki. She doesn't even know you're sitting here. Maybe she doesn't even know you are out of the neural health facility. She's not coming, Pat. I'm sorry."

I'm staring up into Tiffany's soaking-wet face—wet hair, runny makeup—and I can hardly believe that it's not Nikki. Her words do not register at first, but when they do, I feel my chest heating up, and an episode seems inevitable. My eyes burn. My face flushes. Suddenly I realize that for the past two months I have been completely delusional, that Nikki is never coming back and apart time is going to last forever.

Nikki.

Is.

Never.

Coming.

Back.

Never.

I want to hit Tiffany.

I want to pound her face with my knuckles until the bones in my hands crumble and Tiffany is completely unrecognizable, until she no longer has a face from which she can spew lies.

"But everything I said in the letters was true. Nikki did divorce you, and she is remarried, and she even took out a restraining order against you. I got all the information from—"

"You liar!" I say, realizing that I am now crying again. "Ronnie told me that I shouldn't trust you. That you were nothing but a—"

"Please, just listen to me. I know this is a shock. But you need to face reality, Pat. You've been lying to yourself for years! I needed to do something drastic to help you. But I never thought—"

"Why?" I say, feeling as if I might vomit, feeling as though my hands might find Tiffany's throat at any moment. "Why did you do this to me?"

Tiffany looks into my eyes for what seems like a long time, and then her voice sort of quivers like my mom's does when she is saying something she really truly means. Tiffany says, "Because, I'm in love with you."

And then I am up and running.

At first Tiffany follows me, but—even though I am in my leather loafers and it is raining pretty steadily now—I am able to find the man speed she does not have, running faster than I ever have before, and after taking enough turns and weaving through enough traffic, I look back and Tiffany is gone, so I slow my running a bit and jog aimlessly for what seems like hours. I sweat through the rain, and my father's overcoat becomes very heavy. I can't even begin to think about what this all means. Betrayed by Tiffany. Betrayed by God. Betrayed by my own movie. I'm still crying. I'm still jogging. And then I'm praying again, but not in a nice way.

God, I didn't ask for a million dollars. I didn't ask to be famous and powerful. I didn't even ask for Nikki to take me back. I only asked for a meeting. A single face-to-face conversation. All I've done since I left the bad place was try to improve myself—to become exactly what You tell everyone to be: a good person. And here I am running through North Philly on a rainy Christmas Day—all alone. Why did You give us so many stories about miracles? Why did You send Your Son down from heaven? Why did You give us movies if life doesn't ever end well? What kind of fucking God are You? Do You want me to be miserable for the rest of my life? Do You—

Something hits my shin hard, and then my palms are sliding across the wet concrete. I feel kicks landing on my back, my legs, my arms. I curl up into a ball, trying to protect myself, but the kicking continues. When it feels as though my kidneys have exploded, I look up to see who is doing this to me, but I only see the bottom of a sneaker just before it strikes my face.

Mad Nipper

When I wake, the rain has stopped, but I am shivering. I sit up, and my whole body hurts. My overcoat is gone. My leather loafers are gone. All the money I had in my pocket is gone. My leather belt is gone. The new watch my mother gave me for Christmas is gone. I touch my fingers to my face, and they turn red.

Looking around, I see that I am on a narrow street full of parked cars. Row houses on either side. Some are boarded up, many of the porches and steps attached to the fronts are in need of repair, and the streetlights above are not on—maybe smashed by rocks—making the whole world look dark. I am not in a good neighborhood, with no money, shoes, or any idea where I am. Part of me wants to lie on the sidewalk forever, but I'm afraid those bad people might come back to finish me off, and before I can really think about anything, I'm on my feet, limping down the block.

My right thigh muscle feels locked in place, and I cannot bend my right knee very well.

One house on the block is decorated for Christmas. On the porch is a manger scene with a plastic Mary and Joseph—both black. I limp toward Baby Jesus, thinking that people celebrating the holiday are more likely to help me than people without Christmas decorations, because—in the Bible—Jesus says we should help shoeless people who have been mugged.

When I finally get to the decorated row house, a funny thing happens. Instead of knocking on the door, I limp over to the black Mary and Joseph because I want to look into the manger and see if Baby Jesus is black too. My cramped leg screams with pain and gives out just as I reach the Nativity scene. On my hands and one knee, between His parents, I see that Baby Jesus is really black and plugged in—his dark face glows like amber, and a stream of white light blasts up through His little baby chest.

Squinting, taking in the light of Baby Jesus, I instantly realize that I was mugged because I cursed God, so I pray and say I'm sorry and I understand what God is telling me—that I need to work on my character some more before I will be allowed to find apart time's end.

My pulse is pounding so hard in my ears that I do not even hear the front door open, nor do I hear a man walk out onto the porch.

"What you doin' to Aunt Jasmine's Nativity scene?" the man says.

And when I turn my head, God lets me know He has accepted my apology.

When they first brought Danny to the bad place, he wouldn't talk. Like me and everyone else, he had a scar, but his was much larger and on the back of his head, making a bright pink line in his Afro. For a month or so, he just sort of sat in a chair by the window of his room as speech therapists visited and left frustrated. Me and the boys would stop in and say hello, but Danny only looked out the window when we talked to him, so we thought he was one of the people whose brain trauma was so bad he was most likely going to be a vegetable for the rest of his life—sort of like my roommate, Jackie. But after a month or so, Danny started taking his meals in the cafeteria with the rest of us, attending music and group therapy sessions, and even going on a few group excursions to the shops by the harbor and the Orioles games down at Camden Yards. It was obvious that he understood words and even was pretty normal—he just wouldn't talk.

I don't remember how long it took, but after a time, Danny started talking again, and I happened to be the first person he spoke to.

A girl from some fancy college in Baltimore came in to provide what we were told were "non-traditional treatments." We had to volunteer for the sessions, as this girl was not a real therapist yet. We were skeptical at first, but when she came to promote the program, we were soon persuaded by her girlish figure and cute, innocent-looking face. She was very nice and quite attractive, so we all did whatever she said, hoping to keep her around—especially since there were no women patients in the bad place and the nurses were extremely ugly.

For the first week, our college student had us look into mirrors a lot as she encouraged us to really get to know ourselves, which was pretty out-there. She'd say things like, "Study your nose. Look at it until you really know it. Watch how it moves when you breathe in deeply. Appreciate the miracle of respiration. Now look at your tongue. Not just the top, but underneath. Study it. Contemplate the miracles of taste and speech."

But then one day she paired us randomly, had us sit facing each other, and told us to stare into our partner's eyes. She had us do this for a long time, and it was quite weird because the room was completely silent, and men do not usually look into each other's eyes for long periods of time. Then she started telling us to imagine that our partner was someone we missed, or someone we had hurt in the past, or a family member we hadn't seen for many years. She told us to see this person through our partner's eyes, until that person was in front of us.

Looking into another person's eyes for an extended period of time proved to be a powerful thing. And if you don't believe me, try it yourself.

Of course I began to see Nikki, which was strange because I was staring into Danny's eyes, and Danny is a six-foot-three black man who looks nothing like my ex-wife. Even still, as my pupils remained locked on Danny's, it was as if I were looking directly into Nikki's eyes. I was the first one to start crying, but others followed. Our college girl came over, said I was brave, and then hugged me, which was nice. Danny said nothing.

That night I woke up to the sound of Jackie's grunting. When I opened my eyes, it took a few seconds for my pupils to adjust, but when they did, I saw Danny standing over me.

"Danny?" I said.

"My name's not Danny."

His voice scared me because I was not expecting him to speak, especially since he had not spoken to anyone since he arrived.

"The name's Mad Nipper."

"What do you want?" I asked him. "Why are you in our room?"

"I only wanted to tell you my street name, so we could be boys. But we're not on the streets right now, so you can keep calling me Danny."

And then Danny walked out of my room and Jackie quit grunting.

Everyone in the bad place was pretty shocked when Danny began speaking regularly the next day. The doctors said he was experiencing a breakthrough, but it wasn't like that. Danny just decided to talk. We really did become boys and did just about everything together in the bad place, including our exercise routine. And little by little I found out Danny's story.

As Mad Nipper he was a rising gansta rapper from North Philadelphia who had signed on with a small record label in NYC called Tougher Trade. He was playing a club in Baltimore when some beef broke loose, and somehow—Danny often changed the details of his story, so I can't say what happened for certain—he was struck in the back of the head with a tire iron, driven to the harbor, and thrown in.

Most of the time Danny claimed that a Baltimore rap group—one that was scheduled to perform before Mad Nipper—asked him to smoke up in an alleyway behind the club, but when he went outside with these other rappers, they started giving him some shit about headlining in their neighborhood. When he brought up his superior record sales, the lights went out, and he woke up dead, which is actually true, as his file says he was dead for a few minutes before the EMTs managed to revive him.

Lucky for Danny, somebody heard the splash Mad Nipper made when he entered the harbor, and this person fished him out and yelled for help right after the other rappers left. Danny claims that the salt in the water kept his brain alive, but I don't understand how that could be, especially since he was thrown into the filthy harbor and not the ocean. After an operation that removed tiny parts of his skull from his brain, and a lengthy stay at the hospital, Danny was brought to the bad place. The worst part was that he lost his ability to rap—he just couldn't make his mouth rap anymore, at least not as fast as he used to—so he took a vow of silence, which he broke only after looking into my eyes for a very long period of time.

Once, I asked Danny who he saw when he looked into my eyes, and he told me he saw his aunt Jasmine. When I asked him why he saw his aunt Jasmine, he told me she was the woman who had raised him up until he became a man.

"Danny?" I say, kneeling before the manger.

"Who are you?"

"It's Pat Peoples."

"White Pat from Baltimore?"

"Yeah."

"How?"

"I don't know."

"You're bloody. What happened?"

"God punished me, but then He led me here."

"What you do to make God angry?"

"I cursed Him, but I said I was sorry."

"If you really Pat People, what's my name?"

"Mad Nipper, a.k.a. Danny."

"You eat Christmas dinner yet?"

"No."

"You like ham?"

"Yes."

"You wanna eat with me and Aunt Jasmine?"

"Okay."

Danny helps me stand, and when I limp into Aunt Jasmine's home, it smells of pine needles and baked ham and pineapple sauce. A small Christmas tree is decorated with popcorn strings and colorful blinking lights, two green-and-red stockings are hung on a fake fireplace mantel, and on the television the Eagles are playing the Cowboys.

"Sit down," Danny says. "Make yourself at home."

"I don't want to get blood on your couch."

"It's got a plastic cover, see?"

I look, and the couch is really covered with plastic, so I sit down and see that the Eagles are winning, which surprises me, since Dallas was favored.

"I've missed you," Danny says after he sits down next to me. "You didn't even say goddamn goodbye when you left."

"Mom came and got me when you were in music relaxation class. When did you get out of the bad place?"

"Just yesterday. Out on good behavior."

I look at my friend's face and see that he is serious. "So you get out of the bad place yesterday, and I just happen to run to your neighborhood and get mugged on your street and find you here?"

"Guess so," Danny says.

"It sort of seems like a miracle, doesn't it?"

"Miracles happen on Christmas, Pat. Everybody knows that shit."

But before we can say more, a petite, serious-looking woman—who is wearing huge black-rimmed glasses—walks into the living room and starts screaming, "Oh, my Lord! Oh, Jesus!" I try to convince Aunt Jasmine I'm okay, but she calls 911, and then I am in an ambulance being driven to Germantown Hospital.

When I arrive at the emergency room, Aunt Jasmine prays for me and yells at a lot of people until I am taken to a private room, where my clothes are removed and my wounds are cleaned.

I am given an IV while I tell a police officer what happened.

After X-rays, the doctors tell me that my leg is really messed up; my mother, Caitlin, and Jake arrive, and then my leg is put in a white cast that starts at my heel and ends just below my hip.

I want to apologize to Danny and Aunt Jasmine for ruining their Christmas dinner, but my mother tells me that they left soon after she arrived, which makes me really sad for some reason.

When I am finally released from the hospital, a nurse puts a purple sock over my bare toes and gives me a pair of crutches, but Jake pushes me in a wheelchair to his BMW. I have to sit sideways in the backseat, with my feet on Mom's lap, because of the cast.

We drive through North Philadelphia in silence, but when we pull out onto the Schuylkill Expressway, Caitlin says, "Well, at least we'll never forget *this* Christmas." She means it as a joke, but nobody laughs.

"Why isn't anyone asking me how I ended up in North Philadelphia?" I ask.

After a long pause, my mother says, "Tiffany called us from a pay phone and told us everything. We were driving around North Philadelphia looking for you when the hospital called your father. He called Jake's cell phone, and here we are."

"So I ruined everyone's Christmas?"

"That crazy bitch ruined our Christmas."

"Jake," Mom says. *"Please."*

"Did the Eagles win?" I ask Jake, because I remember that

they were winning and am hoping my father will be in a decent mood when I get home.

"Yeah," Jake says in a clipped way that lets me know he is upset with me.

The Eagles beat T.O. and Dallas—in Dallas—on Christmas Day, locking up a play-off spot, and Jake, who has not missed a game since he was in elementary school, misses perhaps the best game of the season because he was searching all of North Philadelphia for his mentally deranged brother. And now I realize why my father is not with the search team—there was no way he'd miss such an important Eagles game, especially against Dallas. I can't help feeling guilty, as it probably would have been a really nice Christmas, especially since my father would have been in a phenomenal mood, and I am sure my mother prepared food, and Caitlin is even wearing an Eagles jersey, and I keep messing up everyone's lives, and maybe it would have been better if the muggers had killed me, and . . .

I start to cry, but quietly, so that my mom won't be upset.

"I'm sorry I made you miss the game, Jake," I manage to say, but the words make me cry even harder, and soon I am sobbing into my hands again, like a baby.

My mother pats my unbroken leg, but no one says anything.

We ride the rest of the way home in silence.

How Is She?

My birthday falls on a Friday. December 29. In the afternoon, Mom helps me tape trash bags around my cast so I can take my first shower since I broke my leg. This is sort of embarrassing to talk about, but Mom has to help me keep my cast out of the shower, so she holds the shower curtain for me, protecting the cast, as I straddle the edge of the tub, trying to keep my weight on my good leg. Mom hands me the soap when I need it and also the shampoo. She pretends not to look at my naked body, but I am sure she gets a glimpse at some point, which makes me feel strange. I haven't worked out in days, so I feel very small and weak—but Mom doesn't say anything about my diminished girth, because she is a kind woman.

After my shower, Mom helps me put on a pair of sweatpants she has modified, cutting one leg off at the thigh so my cast can fit through. I also put on a button-down shirt from the Gap and my new leather jacket. I hop down the steps, crutch my way out the door and into the backseat of Mom's car, sitting sideways so my cast will fit.

• • •

When we arrive at the Voorhees house, I crutch my way into Cliff's office, pick the black recliner, prop my cast up on the footrest, and tell Cliff everything.

When I finish my story, Cliff says, "So you've been in bed since Christmas?"

"Yeah."

"And you have no interest in reading or watching television?"

"No."

"And you're not working out your upper body at all? No weights?"

"No."

"What do you do all day?"

"I sleep, or I think. Sometimes I write, but Danny has been coming to visit me too." I had already told Cliff all about God reuniting Danny and me, which even Cliff had to admit was a bit of a miracle and maybe the silver lining to my awful Christmas.

"What do you and Danny do when he visits?"

"We play Parcheesi."

"Parcheesi?"

"It's the Royal Game of India. How can you not know it?"

"I know Parcheesi. I'm just surprised you and Danny play board games together."

"Why?"

Cliff makes a funny face, but doesn't say anything.

"Danny brings his Parcheesi game all the way from North Philly. He rides the trains."

"That's good, right? It must be nice to see your old friend."

"I was sorry to learn that he still can't rap, even after a second operation, but his aunt got him a job doing the janitorial work at her church, which is also a day-care center. He wipes down the pews with pine oil and mops the floors and empties the trash and vacuums every night—stuff like that. He smells like pine trees now too, which is sort of a nice bonus. But Danny is quieter than I remember him being in the bad place."

"Did you tell Danny about what Tiffany did to you?" Cliff asks.

"Yeah, I did."

"What did he say?"

"Nothing."

"He didn't give you any advice?"

"I didn't ask him for any advice."

"I see." Cliff grabs his chin, which lets me know he is going to say something my mother has told him. "Pat, I know how you lost your memory. Everyone does." He pauses here, gauging my reaction. "And I think you remember too. *Do you?*"

"No."

"Do you want me to tell you how you lost your memory?"

"No."

"Why?"

I don't say anything.

"I know Dr. Timbers used to tell you the story every day as part of your therapy. That's why I never brought it up. I thought maybe you would talk about it when you were ready, but it's been almost five months—and now you have a broken leg, and things seem to have gotten worse. I can't help feeling as though we need to start trying other tactics. What Tiffany suggested about closure is true. I'm not saying her methods were honorable, but you really do need to come to terms with what happened, Pat. You need closure."

"Maybe my movie isn't over," I say, because sometimes moviemakers trick the audience with a false bad ending, and just when you think the movie is going to end badly, something dramatic happens, which leads to the happy ending. This seems like a good spot for something dramatic to happen, especially since it's my birthday.

"Your life is not a movie, Pat. Life is not a movie. You're an Eagles fan. After watching so many NFL seasons without a Super Bowl, you should know that real life often ends poorly."

"How can you say that now, especially since the Eagles have won four straight and are headed into the play-offs—*even after McNabb went down*!" Cliff just looks at me, almost as if he is scared, and suddenly I realize that I was just yelling. But I can't help adding, "With a negative attitude like that, it *will* end poorly, Cliff! You're starting to sound like Dr. Timbers! You better watch out, or you're going to be defeated by pessimism!"

There is a long silence, and Cliff looks really worried, which begins to worry me.

On the drive home, Mom tells me that people are coming over for my birthday. She is making me a birthday dinner. "Is Nikki coming?" I ask.

"No, Pat. Nikki is never coming," Mom says. "Never."

When we arrive home, Mom makes me sit in the family room while she cooks meat loaf and mashed potatoes and green beans and an apple pie. She keeps trying to talk to me, but I really do not feel like talking.

Jake and Caitlin arrive first, and they try to cheer me up by talking really enthusiastically about the Birds, but it doesn't work.

When Ronnie and Veronica arrive, Emily climbs onto my lap, which makes me feel a little better. Caitlin asks Emily if she wants to draw a picture on my cast, and when she nods, Mom finds some markers and we all watch little Emily draw. She starts off by making a wobbly circle, which is understandable, since the cast is not perfectly flat, nor smooth. But then she just scribbles all sorts of colors everywhere, and I cannot tell what she is up to until she points to her creation and says, "Pap!"

"Did you draw a picture of Uncle Pat?" Ronnie says, and when Emily nods, everyone laughs because it looks nothing like me.

When we sit down at the dining-room table, my father is still not home. Even after the win over Dallas, he has been pretty distant lately, hiding in his study again. Nobody mentions my dad's absence, so I don't either.

Mom's meal is delicious, and everyone says so.

When it is time for pie, they sing "Happy Birthday" to me, and then little Emily helps me blow out the candles that make the shape of the number 35. I hardly believe that I can actually be thirty-five, because I still feel like I am thirty—maybe I only wish I were thirty, because then I'd have Nikki in my life.

After we eat our pie, Emily helps me open my presents. I get a brand-new wooden hand-painted Parcheesi board from Mom, who says she invited Danny to my party, but he had to work. Ronnie, Emily, and Veronica give me an Eagles fleece blanket. Jake and Caitlin give me a membership to a gym in Philadelphia. The brochure in the box says the club has a pool and a steam room and basketball courts and racquetball courts and all types of weight-lifting equipment and other machines that build muscles. "It's where I work out," my brother says. "And I was thinking we could start working out together once your leg mends." Even though I'm not all that interested in working out so much anymore, I realize that the membership is a nice present, so I thank Jake.

When we retire to the living room, I ask Veronica about Tiffany. "How's Tiffany?" I say. I'm not really sure why I ask. The words just sort of slip out of my mouth, and when they do, everyone stops talking and a silence hangs in the air.

"I invited her to your party," Mom finally offers, probably just so Veronica will not feel badly about her sister being excluded.

"Why?" Jake asks. "So she can lie to Pat again? Set him back a few more years?"

"She was only trying to help," Veronica says.

"Your sister has a funny way of helping."

"Stop," Caitlin says to Jake.

And then the room is silent again.

"So how is she?" I ask, because I really do want to know.

I Need a Huge Favor

On New Year's Eve day, after agreeing to buy unlimited beer for our neighbors, Jake manages to trade seats with the season-ticket holder in front of me—and once Jake is seated, he props my cast up onto his shoulder so I am able to sit down during the Falcons game.

A few minutes into the first quarter, head coach Andy Reid pulls the starters, and the game announcer reports that Dallas has somehow lost to Detroit, which means that the Birds have clinched the NFC East for the fifth time in the last six years and the current game is meaningless. Everyone in the Linc cheers, high fives abound, and it is hard to stay in a seated position.

With the starting wide receivers out, I get my hopes up for Hank Baskett, and he actually does catch a few balls in the first half, each of which Scott, Jake, and I celebrate excessively because I am wearing my Baskett jersey over my winter coat, and we all like to root for the undrafted rookie.

It's 17–10 Eagles at halftime, and Scott actually leaves the game, saying that he promised his wife he'd come home for New Year's Eve if the Cowboys lost and the Eagles game became meaningless. I give him a hard time about leaving and am surprised that my brother does not join in with the ribbing. But shortly after Scott takes off, Jake says, "Listen, Pat. Caitlin has me going to this black-tie New Year's Eve party at the Rittenhouse Hotel. She was mad at me for going to the game today, and I was sort of thinking about taking off early so I could surprise her. But I don't want to leave you here with the cast and all. So how do you feel about leaving early?"

I'm shocked, and a little mad.

"I want to see if Baskett gets his second touchdown," I say. "But you can go. I'll be all right here with all the *real* Eagles fans—the people who are staying to see the whole game." It's not a very nice thing for me to say, especially since Caitlin is probably already dressed and waiting for Jake to come home, but the truth is, I need my brother's help getting out of the Linc on crutches. I have a feeling that Baskett will get the ball a lot in the second half, and I know Jake really wants to see the game anyway; maybe he'll be able to use his mentally ill brother as a good excuse for missing the first part of Caitlin's New Year's Eve party; maybe this is what Jake really wants and needs. "Beer man!" I yell to the Coors Light guy who is passing our row. When he stops, I say, "Only one beer because this guy here is leaving his crippled, mentally insane brother to go to the Rittenhouse Hotel so that he can swill champagne with non-Eagles fans in tuxedos." My brother looks like I punched him in the gut, and soon he is pulling out his wallet.

"All right. Fuck it. Make it two beers," Jake says, and I smile as my brother sits down in Scott's seat and helps me prop my cast up onto the back of the empty seat in front of me.

Through the second half, Baskett continues to catch A. J. Feeley's throws, and early in the fourth quarter my favorite player runs an out, catches the ball, and runs down the sideline eighty-nine yards for the second touchdown of his young career. Jake helps me stand, and then everyone in our section is high-fiving me and slapping my back because over my coat I am wearing the Baskett jersey my brother gave me when I first got out of the bad place.

I would later learn that Baskett is the first Eagles player to catch two touchdown passes longer than eighty yards in the same season—which is an accomplishment, even if number 84 has only been a marginal player this year.

"And you wanted to leave," I say to Jake.

"Go Baskett!" he says, and then gives me a one-armed sideways hug—shoulder-to-shoulder.

After the Eagles' backup players win the last regular season game, the Birds finish their season at 10-6, locking up at least one home play-off game in the process. I crutch my way out of the Linc with Jake as my fullback, parting the crowds, shouting, "Cripple coming through! Cripple coming through! Move out the way!"

We don't meet up with Cliff's gang until we get back to the fat men's tent and the Asian Invasion bus. But when we do, our friends greet us with a Baskett chant because number 84 had a career-high 177-yard day and an 89-yard TD.

With play-offs to discuss, everyone is reluctant to leave, so we drink beers and discuss the 8-8 Giants, whom the Birds will play in the first round. When Cliff asks me if I think our team will beat the Giants, I tell my therapist, "Not only will the Eagles win, but Hank Baskett will catch another touchdown."

Cliff nods and smiles and says, "You called it before the season even started: *Hank Baskett is the man!*"

Jake leaves first because he and Caitlin have that hotel New Year's Eve party to attend, so we all make fun of him and call him whipped—but even though he is leaving us for his woman, I give him a hug and thank him again for staying, getting me a season ticket, and paying for the play-off tickets too, which are pretty expensive. And I know Jake has forgiven me for making him miss the second Dallas game, because he hugs me back and says, "No problem, brother. I love you. Always. You know that."

After Jake leaves, we drink beers for another half hour or so, but eventually many of the guys admit they too have New Year's Eve plans with their wives, and I take the Asian Invasion bus home to New Jersey.

The Eagles have won the last five games and the NFC East, so there's no stopping Ashwini from blowing the Asian Invasion bus horn when he pulls up to my parents' house, and when he does, the chant blares loudly—"E!-A!-G!-L!-E!-S! EAGLES!"—which brings my mother to the door.

Standing on the front step, Mom and I wave as the green bus pulls away.

We eat a late New Year's Eve dinner together as a family, but even after another Eagles win and with Super Bowl hopes alive, my father doesn't say much, and he heads for his study before Mom finishes her meal, probably so he can read historical fiction.

• • •

Just before the ball drops on Dad's huge flat-screen television, Mom asks me if I want to go outside and bang pots and pans like we used to do when I was a kid. I tell Mom I don't really want to bang pots and pans, especially since I am tired from spending the day outside in the cold, so from the couch, we watch people celebrating in Times Square.

Two thousand and six becomes 2007.

"It's going to be a good year for us," Mom says, and then forces a smile.

I smile back at Mom, not because I think it is going to be a good year, but because my father went to bed an hour ago, Nikki never came back, there's not even the slightest inclination to suggest that 2007 is going to be a good year for either Mom or me, and yet Mom is still trying to find that silver lining she taught me about so long ago. She is still holding on to hope. "It's going to be a good year," I say.

When Mom falls asleep on the couch, I turn off the television and watch her breathe. She still looks pretty, and seeing her resting so peacefully makes me angry at my dad, even though I know he can't change who he is, but I wish that he would at least try to appreciate Mom more and spend some quality time with her, especially since he doesn't even have the Eagles to be grumpy about anymore, because the season is already a success regardless of what happens in the play-offs, especially after making it this far without McNabb. And yet I know my father is not likely to change, because I have known him for thirty-five years, and he has always been the same man.

Mom tucks her knees and elbows in close to her body and begins to shiver, so I push myself up, grab my crutches, and crutch my way over to the closet. I pull a blanket from the bottom of the closet, crutch my way over to Mom, and cover her—but she continues to shiver. Back at the closet, I see a heavier blanket on the top shelf, so I reach up and pull it down. It falls on top of my head just after I hear a little crash. I look down, and by my feet is a videocassette in a white plastic case that has two ringing bells on the cover.

I crutch my way over to my mother and cover her with the heavier blanket.

It is hard to pick up the cassette with my cast preventing me from squatting—I actually have to sit down on the floor to pick it up. After sliding over to the TV, I slip the cassette into the VCR. I look over my shoulder, checking to make sure that Mom is sleeping soundly, and then turn down the volume before I hit PLAY.

The video is not completely rewound, and the part that pops up on-screen is the beginning of the reception dinner. Our guests are seated in the banquet room of the Glenmont Country Club, which is near a golf course in a swanky little town just outside Baltimore. The camera is focused on the entrance doorway, but you can see the dance floor and the band too. Using the microphone, the lead singer says, "Let's introduce the wedding party Philly style," at which point the horn section of the band begins playing the opening notes of "Gonna Fly Now!" The guitarist and bassist and drummer soon begin playing, and even though it doesn't sound exactly like Rocky's theme song, it's close enough to get the job done.

"Parents of the groom, Mr. and Mrs. Patrick Peoples!"

Our guests clap politely as my mom and dad cross the dance floor arm in arm, and the painful expression on my father's face suggests that this was one of the worst experiences of his life—being announced at my wedding.

"Parents of the bride, Mr. and Mrs. George Gates."

Nikki's parents do a little skipping routine into the banquet hall, making them look sloshed, which they were, and I laugh thinking about how much fun my in-laws were when they drank. I really do miss Nikki's parents.

"Bridesmaid, Elizabeth Richards, and groomsman, Ronnie Brown."

Liz and Ronnie come out waving to our guests, as if they are royalty or something, which was strange, and the tactic all but mutes their applause. Ronnie looks young in the video, and I think about how he was not yet a father, how Emily did not even exist when this video was shot.

"Maid of honor, Wendy Rumsford, and best man, Jake Peoples!"

Jake and Wendy walk across the dance floor and directly toward the camera until their faces are life-size on my father's huge flat-screen television. Wendy just sort of screams like she is at an Eagles game or something, but Jake says, "I love you, brother!" and then kisses the camera lens, leaving a lip-shaped smudge mark. I see the videographer's hand emerge and quickly wipe the lens with a piece of cloth.

"And now, for the first time ever, allow me to introduce Mr. and Mrs. Pat Peoples!"

Everyone stands and cheers as we walk into the banquet room. Nikki looks so pretty in her wedding dress. She's holding her head in that cute, shy position, with her chin close to her chest, and seeing her now makes me cry because I miss her so much.

When we move to the dance floor, the band shifts gears, and I hear those sexy synthesizer chords, faint high-hat taps, and then the soprano saxophonist steps forward and "Songbird" takes flight.

Something in my mind begins to melt, and it feels as though I am experiencing an ice-cream headache—or as if someone is churning my brain with an ice pick. I'm not seeing the television screen anymore, I'm seeing the road through a fogged windshield, and it's raining something fierce. It's not even four in the afternoon, but it's as dark as midnight. I'm upset because we have a big game coming up and yet the gym roof is leaking again like a sieve, which has forced me to cancel basketball practice.

All I want to do is take a shower and then watch game tapes.

But when I enter my house, I hear a soprano sax moaning, and it's strange to hear Kenny G's smooth jazz coming from my bathroom at a time like this. Mr. G's notes are swirling all about. I open the bathroom door; I feel the steam lick my skin, and I wonder why Nikki is listening to our wedding song in the shower. Kenny G's solo has reached a climax once more. The CD player is on the sink, and two piles of clothes rest on the floor, and a pair of men's glasses are on the sink next to the CD player. Sexy synthesizer chords, faint high-hat taps.

"You fucking whore!" I scream as I rip the shower curtain off the rod, exposing so much awful, soapy flesh.

I'm standing in the tub. My hands are around his throat. I'm between them now, the shower is spraying the back of my coat with hot spokes, weighing down my sweatpants, and he is in the air, begging me with his eyes, pleading for a breath of air. His hands are trying to break my grip, but he is a tiny, weak man. Nikki is screaming; Kenny G is playing; Nikki's lover is turning purple. He's so small, I can hold him up against the tiles with one hand. I cock my elbow back, squeeze a tight, teeth-shattering fist, and take aim. His nose explodes like a packet of ketchup. His eyes are rolling into the back of his head; his hands have fallen away from mine. When I cock back my fist a second time, the music stops playing, and then I'm on my back in the tub and Nikki's naked lover has fallen out of the tub and naked Nikki is holding the CD player in her trembling hands. When I try to stand, she smashes the CD player over my head once more; my knees give out, and I see the silver faucet rise like some fat, shiny snake to strike the hard spot just above my right eyebrow, and then—

—I wake up in a hospital and immediately begin vomiting all over myself, until nurses arrive and tell me not to move my head. And I'm crying and calling for Nikki, but she does not come to me. My head hurts so badly. When I touch my forehead, I feel some sort of bandage, but then my hands are being forced to my sides. The nurses are screaming and holding me down, and then doctors are restraining me too. I feel a prick in my arm, and . . .

When I blink, I see my reflection in the blank television screen. The video has ended. I look life-size on my father's flat screen, and I can see my mother asleep on the couch, just over my right shoulder. As I continue to stare at myself, my little white scar begins to itch, but I do not really want to smash my forehead with my fist.

I find my feet and crutch my way into the kitchen. The address book is still in the cabinet above the stove. I place a call to Jake's apartment. As the phone rings, I look at the microwave and see that it is 2:54 a.m., but I remember that Jake is at a swanky hotel party and won't be home until tomorrow, so I decide to leave a message.

Hello, you've reached Jake and Caitlin's machine. Please leave a message after the beep. Beep.

"Jake, it's your brother, Pat. I need a huge favor . . ."

Best Intentions

Pat,

It's been a while, hopefully long enough.

If you haven't ripped up this letter already, please read until the end. As you have discovered, I am a much better writer than I am a speaker at this point in my life.

Everybody hates me.

Did you know your brother came to my house and threatened to kill me if I made contact with you? His sincerity scared me—enough to keep me from writing earlier. Even my parents have reproached me for pretending to be Nikki. My therapist says my betrayal might not be forgivable, and by the way she kept repeating the word "unforgivable," I could tell she was very disappointed in me. But the truth is, I did it for your benefit. Yes, I was hoping that once you found closure and got over Nikki, you would want to give me a shot—especially since we are such great dance partners, we both enjoy running, we are in similar housing situations, and let's face it, we're both fighting hard to maintain our grip on reality. We have a lot in common, Pat. I still believe you fell into my life for a reason.

Because I love you, I want to tell you something I have never told anyone—except my therapist. It's sort of screwed up, so I hope you will be able to handle it. At first I wasn't going to tell you, but I figured the situation couldn't get any worse, and maybe a little honesty could go a long way right now.

I don't know if you know this, but Tommy was a cop. He worked for the Meadowville Police Department and was assigned to the high school sort of as a counselor. So half of his hours were spent working with and counseling troubled teenagers, and the other half of his hours he was just a regular cop. I'm telling you this because it is important to understand that Tommy was a good man. He did not deserve to die, and his death absolutely proves that life is random and fucked-up and arbitrary, until you find someone who can make sense of it all for you—if only temporarily.

Anyway, Tommy was really good with teenagers, and he even started a club at the high school designed to raise awareness about the dangers of drinking and driving. Many of the parents thought the club condoned underage drinking, because it was not an anti-underage-drinking club but just an anti-drinking-and-driving club, so Tommy had to fight really hard to keep it afloat. Tommy told me that a lot of the high school kids drank every weekend, and underage drinking was even condoned by many of the town's parents. And the funniest thing to me was that the kids came to him and asked him to start the club because they were worried that someone was going to get hurt or die if their friends kept driving home after parties. Can you imagine talking to a cop like that when you were a teenager? That's the kind of guy Tommy was, people trusted him instantly.

So Tommy organized assemblies and even put together this

teacher karaoke night where students could pay money to hear their favorite teachers perform the current hits. Tommy could talk people into doing things like that. I'd go to these events, and Tommy would be up on the stage with all those teenagers, and he'd be singing and dancing with the other teachers, all of whom he had convinced to dress up in wild costumes—and parents, students, administrators would be all smiles. You couldn't help it, because Tommy was such a burst of positive energy. And he always gave speeches during these events—listing facts and statistics about drinking and driving. People listened to Tommy. People loved him. I loved him so fucking much, Pat.

A funny thing about Tommy was he liked to have sex a lot. He always wanted to make love. I mean, as soon as he got home from work, his hands were all over me. I'd wake up every morning and he'd be on top of me. We could hardly eat a meal together without his hands sliding under the table, searching for my legs. And if Tommy was home, there was no way I'd ever get through a television show, because as soon as a commercial came on, he'd be rock hard and giving me that look. It was pretty wild, and I loved it for the first ten years of our marriage. But after ten years of nonstop sex, I got a little tired of it. I mean—life is more than sex, right? So one bright sunny morning, after we had just finished making love under the kitchen table, the teakettle whistled, so I stood and poured two cups.

"I'm thinking maybe we should limit sex to so many times a week," I said.

I'll never forget the look on his face. He looked as if I had shot him in the stomach.

"Is something wrong?" he said. "Am I doing something wrong?"

"No. It's not like that at all."

"Then what?"

"I don't know. Is it normal to have sex several times a day?"

"Don't you love me anymore?" Tommy asked me with this wounded-little-boy look I still see whenever I close my eyes at night.

Of course I told Tommy I loved him more than ever, but I just wanted to slow down a little with the sex. I told him I wanted to talk with him more, take walks, and find some new hobbies, so sex could be special again. "Having this much sex," I told him, "sort of takes the magic out of it." For some odd reason, I remember suggesting that we go horseback riding.

"So you're telling me the magic is gone?" he said, and that question was the last thing he ever did say to me. So you're telling me the magic is gone?

I remember talking a lot after he said that, telling him we could have sex as much as he wanted and that this was just a suggestion, but he was wounded. He was looking at me suspiciously the whole time, as if I were cheating on him or something like that. But I wasn't. I just wanted to slow down a little so I could appreciate sex more. Too much of a good thing, was all I wanted to tell him. But it was clear I had hurt him, because before I could finish explaining, he stood up and went upstairs to take a shower. He left the house without saying goodbye.

I got the call at work. All I remember hearing was that Tommy was hurt and had been rushed to West Jersey Hospital. When I got to the hospital, there were a dozen men in blue uniforms, cops everywhere. Their glistening eyes told me.

Later I would find out that Tommy had gone to the Cherry Hill Mall during his lunch break. They found a Victoria's Secret bag full of lingerie in his cruiser—every piece was my size. On his way back to Meadowville, he stopped on the highway to help an elderly woman whose car had broken down. Tommy called her a tow truck, but then he stood at the nervous old lady's window chatting with her, keeping her company while she waited. Tommy was always chatting with people like that. The cruiser was behind him, the lights were going, but he was standing at the edge of the highway's breakdown lane. Some driver who had drunk his lunch dropped his cell phone, and when he bent down to pick it up, he pulled the wheel to the right, crossed two lanes, and . . .

The lead in the local paper read "Police Officer Thomas Reed—who was responsible for starting Meadowville High School's Anti-Drinking-and-Driving Club—was killed by a drunk driver." It was all so ironic, almost funny in a sadistic way. There were so many cops at his funeral. Kids from the high school made our front lawn into a living memorial—they stood on the sidewalk with candles and flowers. When I refused to go outside, these teenagers sang so sweetly to me through the first few evenings, a chorus of sad, beautiful voices. Our friends brought food, Father Carey talked to me about heaven, my parents cried with me, and Ronnie and Veronica stayed at our house for the first few weeks or so. But the only thing I could think about was how Tommy died believing I no longer wanted to have sex with him. I felt so guilty, Pat. I wanted to die. I kept thinking he would not have gone to Victoria's Secret on his lunch break if we had not had the fight, and then he would have never passed the old woman in the broken-down car, which meant he would not have been killed. I felt so guilty. I still feel so fucking guilty.

After a few weeks I went back to work, but everything in my mind got switched up. My guilt turned to need, and suddenly I was craving sex very badly. So I started to fuck men—any man who was game. All I really had to do was look at a man in that certain way, and within a few seconds I knew if they were going to fuck me. And when they did, I would close my eyes and pretend it was Tommy. To be with my husband again, I'd fuck men anywhere. In a car. In the coatroom at work. In an alley. Behind a bush. In a public restroom. Anywhere. But in my mind, it was always under the kitchen table, and Tommy had come back to me, and I had told him I wasn't tired of having sex, but would make love to him as many times as he needed, because I loved him with all my heart.

I was sick. And there was no shortage of men who were eager to capitalize on my sickness. There were men everywhere who—with glee—would fuck this mentally ill woman.

Of course this led to my losing my job, therapy, and many medical tests. Luckily, I did not contract any diseases, and I'd be happy to get tested again if that ever becomes an issue for us. But even if I had contracted AIDS or whatever, it would have been worth it to me at the time, because I needed that closure. I needed that forgiveness. I needed to live out the fantasy. I needed to fuck away my guilt so I could break out of the fog I was in, to feel something, to feel anything, *and begin to start my life again, which I am only now beginning to do—since we became friends.*

I have to admit that during Veronica's dinner party I only thought of you as an easy lay. I sized you up in your stupid Eagles jersey and figured I could get you to fuck me, so I could pretend you were Tommy. I hadn't done it in a long time. I no longer wanted to have sex with strangers, but you weren't a stranger. You were handpicked by my own sister. You were a safe man with whom Ronnie was trying to set me up. So I figured I would begin to have sex with you regularly, just so I could fantasize about Tommy again.

But when you held me in front of my parents' house, and when you cried with me, things changed—in a very dramatic way. I did not understand it at first, but as we ran together and ate raisin bran at the diner and went to the beach and became friends—simply friends, without any sex to complicate things—it was sort of nice in a way I hadn't anticipated. I just liked being around you, even if we didn't say anything.

I knew I had feelings for you when I began to cringe inwardly at the sound of Nikki's name. It was obvious you were not ever going to get back together with your wife, so I called your mom and got her drunk at the local bar, and she told me everything about you. You didn't see me, but I was in the driveway when she came home so loaded and you helped her into the house. I drove her home that night. After what happened to Tommy, I don't drink at all. We've been meeting every week since, Pat. She needed a friend; she needed to talk to someone about your father. So I listened. At first I was just using her for information, but now we are sort of girlfriends. She did not know about the letters I was writing as Nikki, and she was really mad at me for a while after the Christmas episode, but she knows about this letter obviously, since she delivered it for me. She is a very strong and forgiving woman, Pat. She deserves better than your father, and maybe you deserve better than me. Life is funny like that.

I wrote those letters hoping to provide you with the closure I somehow found through casual sex after Tommy died. Please know I began the liaison scheme only after I was certain that Nikki would never agree to talk to you again under any circumstance. Maybe you will never be able to forgive me, but I wanted you to know I had the best intentions—and I still love you in my own fucked-up way.

I miss you, Pat. I really do. Can we at least be friends?

Tiffany

Booyah!

When Danny finishes reading Tiffany's latest letter, he sighs, scratches his Afro, and looks out my bedroom window for a long time. I want his reaction because he is the only person I know who doesn't already have a strong opinion about Tiffany. Everyone else is obviously biased—even Cliff.

"So," I finally say from my bed. I'm sitting with my back against the headboard and my cast propped up on a few pillows. "What do you think I should do?"

Danny sits down, opens up the Parcheesi box, and takes out the hand-painted wooden board and pieces my mother gave me for my birthday. "I feel like being red today," he says. "What color you want?"

After I pick blue, we set up the board on the little table my mother put in the room for us when I first came home with a broken leg. We play Parcheesi like we always do when Danny visits, and it becomes obvious that he isn't going to weigh in with an opinion regarding Tiffany, probably because he knows that only I can make this decision—but maybe because he just wants to play the game. He loves Parcheesi more than any man I have ever met, and when he lands on one of my spots and sends one of my pieces back to the start circle, Danny always points at my face and yells, "Booyah!" which makes me laugh because he is so goddamn serious about Parcheesi.

Even though I don't really enjoy playing Parcheesi as much as Danny does—and he won't answer any of my questions about Tiffany—it's nice to have him back in my life again.

We play Parcheesi for so many hours—days pass, and my record against Danny grows to 32 wins and 203 losses. Danny is a supreme Parcheesi player, and the best dice roller I have ever met. When he says, "Papa needs a doublet," he almost always rolls two sixes. Whatever Papa needs, Danny rolls.

Break Free of a Nimbostratus

A week after my cast has been removed, I stand alone on the footbridge in Knight's Park, leaning my weight on the railing, gazing down at a pond I could walk around in less than five minutes. The water underneath me has a thin layer of ice on top, and I think about dropping rocks through it, but I do not know why, especially since I have no rocks. Even still, I want to drop rocks through the ice so badly, to puncture it, proving that it is weak and temporary, to see the black water below rise up and out of the hole I alone will have created.

I think about the hidden fish—mostly those big goldfish people stock the pond with so old men will have something to feed in spring and little boys will have something to catch in the summer—fish now burrowed in the mud at the bottom of the pond. Or are these fish burrowing just yet? Will they wait until the pond freezes completely?

Here's a thought: I'm like Holden Caulfield thinking about ducks, only I'm thirty-five years old and Holden was a teenager. Maybe the accident knocked my brain back into teenager mode?

Part of me wants to climb up onto the railing and jump off the bridge, which is only ten yards long, only three feet above the pond; part of me wants to break through the ice with my feet, to plunge down, down, down into the mud, where I can sleep for months and forget about all I now remember and know. Part of me wishes I never regained my memory, that I still had that false hope to cling to—that I still had at least the idea of Nikki to keep me moving forward.

When I finally look up from the ice and toward the soccer fields, I see that Tiffany has accepted my invitation to meet, just like Cliff said she would. She is only two inches tall in the distance, wearing a yellow ski cap and a white coat that covers most of her thighs, making her look like a wingless angel growing and growing—and I watch her pass the swing sets and the large pavilion with picnic tables inside. I watch her walk along the water's edge until she finally reaches her usual height, which is five feet and a few inches tall.

When she steps onto the footbridge, I immediately look down at the thin layer of ice again.

Tiffany walks over to me and stands so her arm is almost touching mine, but not quite. Using my peripheral vision, I see that she too is now looking down at the thin layer of ice, and I wonder if she also wishes she could drop some rocks.

We stand like this for what seems like an hour, neither of us saying anything.

My face gets very cold, until I can no longer feel my nose or ears.

Finally, without looking at Tiffany, I say, "Why didn't you come to my birthday party?" which is a stupid question to pose at this time, I realize, but I can't think of anything else to say, especially since I haven't seen Tiffany for many weeks—not since I screamed at her on Christmas Day. "My mom said she invited you. So why didn't you come?"

After a long pause, Tiffany says, "Well, like I said in my letter, your brother threatened to kill me if I made contact with you. Also, Ronnie came to my house the day before your party and forbade me to go. He said they never should have introduced us in the first place."

I had already talked to Jake about his threat, but I have a hard time imagining Ronnie saying such a thing to Tiffany. And yet I know Tiffany is telling the truth. She seems really hurt and vulnerable right now, especially because she is sort of chewing on her bottom lip as if it were a piece of gum. Surely Ronnie said these words against Veronica's wishes. His wife would never let him say something so potentially ego-damaging to Tiffany, and the thought of Ronnie keeping Tiffany from attending my party makes me a little proud of my best friend, especially since he went against his wife's wishes to protect me.

"Bros B4 Hos" is what Danny said to me every time I would lament Nikki, back when we were both in the bad place—before he had that second operation. In art therapy class, Danny even made me a little poster with the words written in stylish gold letters, which I hung on the wall space between my bed and my roommate Jackie's—back in the bad place—but one of the evil nurses took Danny's artwork down when I was not in the room, a fact Jackie confirmed by blinking and banging his head against his shoulder. Even though I realize the phrase is sort of sexist (because men should not refer to women as hos), saying "Bros B4 Hos" in my mind now sort of makes me smile, especially since Ronnie is my best bro in New Jersey, now that Jake and Danny live in PA.

"I'm sorry, Pat. Is that what you want to hear? Well, I'll say it again, I'm really, really fucking sorry." Even though Tiffany uses the f-word, her voice sort of quivers like Mom's when she says something she truly means, and it makes me think that

Tiffany might actually start crying right here on the bridge. "I'm a screwed-up person who no longer knows how to communicate with the people I love. But I meant everything I told you in my letter. If I were your Nikki, I would have come back to you on Christmas Day, but I'm not Nikki. I know. And I'm sorry."

I don't know what to say in response, so we stand there for many minutes, saying nothing.

Suddenly—for some crazy reason—I want to tell Tiffany the ending of the movie, the one that was my old life. I figure she should know the ending, especially since she had a starring role. And then the words are spilling out of me.

"I decided to confront Nikki, just to let her know I remember what happened between us but do not hold any grudges. My brother drove me to my old house in Maryland, and it turns out that Nikki is still living there, which I thought was sort of strange, especially since she has a new me—this guy Phillip who works with Nikki as a fellow English teacher and always used to call me an illiterate buffoon because I never used to read literary books," I say, leaving out the part about my strangling and punching naked Phillip when I caught him in the shower with Nikki, "and if I were Phillip, I probably would not want to live in my wife's ex-husband's house, because that is just sort of weird, right?"

Tiffany doesn't say anything when I pause, so I just keep on talking.

"When we drove down my old street, it was snowing, which is a little more rare in Maryland and therefore a big deal to little kids. There was only maybe a half inch on the ground—a dusting—but enough to scoop up in your hands. I saw Nikki outside with Phillip, and they were playing with two children—by the colors each was dressed in, I figured the one in navy blue was a little boy and the one mostly in peach was an even littler girl. After we rolled by, I told Jake to circle the block and park the car half a block away so we could watch Nikki's new family play in the snow. My old house is on a busy street, so we weren't likely to draw Nikki's attention. Jake did as I asked and then killed the engine but left the windshield wipers on so he could see. I rolled down my window, as I was in the backseat because of my cast, and we watched the family play for a long time—so long that Jake finally started the car back up and turned on the heat because he was too cold. Nikki was wearing the long green-and-white-striped scarf I used to wear to Eagles games, a brown barn coat, and red mittens. Her strawberry blond hair hung freely from under her green hat, so many curls. They were having a snowball fight; Nikki's new family was having a beautiful snowball fight. You could tell the kids loved their father and mother, and the father loved the mother, and the mother loved the father, and the parents loved the children—as they all tossed the snow at each other so lovingly, taking turns chasing each other, laughing and falling into one another's heavily bundled bodies, and . . ."

I pause here because I am having trouble getting the words out of my throat.

"And I squinted hard trying to see Nikki's face, and even from a block away I could tell she was smiling the whole time and was so very happy, and somehow that was enough for me to officially end apart time and roll the credits of my movie without even confronting Nikki, so I just asked Jake to drive me back to New Jersey, which he did, because he is probably the best brother in the entire world. So I guess I just want Nikki to be happy, even if her happy life doesn't include me, because I had my chance and I wasn't a very good husband and Nikki was a great wife, and . . ."

I have to pause again. I swallow several times.

"And I'm just going to remember that scene as the happy ending of my old life's movie. Nikki having a snowball fight with her new family. She looked so happy—and her new husband, and her two children . . ."

I stop talking because no more words will come out. It's as if the cold air has already frozen my tongue and throat—as if the cold is spreading down into my lungs and is freezing my chest from the inside out.

Tiffany and I stand on the bridge for a long time.

Even though my face is numb, I begin to feel a warmth in my eyes, and suddenly I realize I am sort of crying again. I wipe my eyes and nose with my coat sleeve, and then I am sobbing.

Only when I finish crying does Tiffany finally speak, although she doesn't talk about Nikki. "I got you a birthday present, but it's nothing much. And I didn't wrap it or get you a card or anything, because, well . . . because I'm your fucked-up friend who does not buy cards or wrap presents. And I know it's more than a month late, but anyway . . ."

She takes off her gloves, undoes a few buttons, and pulls my present from the inside pocket of her coat.

I take it from her hands, a collection of ten or so heavily laminated pages—maybe four by eight inches each and held together by a silver bolt in the top left corner. The cover reads:

SKYWATCHER'S
CLOUD
CHART
An easy to use,
durable identifying chart
for all outdoor enthusiasts

"You were always looking up at clouds when we used to run," Tiffany says, "so I thought you might like to be able to tell the difference between the shapes."

With excitement, I rotate the cover upward so I can read the first heavily laminated page. After reading all about the four basic cloud shapes—stratus, nimbus, cumulus, and cirrus—after looking at all the beautiful pictures documenting the different variations of the four groups, somehow Tiffany and I end up lying on our backs in the middle of the exact soccer field I used to play on when I was a kid. We look up at the sky, and it's a sheet of winter gray, but Tiffany says maybe if we wait long enough, a shape will break free, and we will be able to identify the single cloud using my new Skywatcher's Cloud Chart. We lie there on the frozen ground for a very long time, waiting, but all we see up in the sky is the solid gray blanket, which my new cloud chart identifies as a nimbostratus—"a gray cloud mass from which widespread and continuous rain or snow falls."

After a time, Tiffany's head ends up on my chest, and my arm ends up around her shoulders so that I am pulling her body close to mine. We shiver together alone on the field for what seems like hours. When it begins to snow, the flakes fall huge and fast. Almost immediately the field turns white, and this is when Tiffany whispers the strangest thing. She says, "I need you, Pat Peoples; I need you so fucking bad," and then she begins to cry hot tears onto my skin as she kisses my neck softly and sniffles.

It is a strange thing for her to say, so far removed from a regular woman's "I love you," and yet probably more true. It feels good to hold Tiffany close to me, and I remember what my mother said back when I tried to get rid of my friend by asking her to go to the diner with me. Mom said, "You need friends, Pat. Everybody does."

I also remember that Tiffany lied to me for many weeks; I remember the awful story Ronnie told me about Tiffany's dismissal from work and what she admitted to in her most recent letter; I remember just how bizarre my friendship with Tiffany has been—but then I remember that no one else but Tiffany could really even come close to understanding how I feel after losing Nikki forever. I remember that apart time is finally over, and while Nikki is gone for good, I still have a woman in my arms who has suffered greatly and desperately needs to believe once again that she is beautiful. In my arms is a woman who has given me a Skywatcher's Cloud Chart, a woman who knows all my secrets, a woman who knows just how messed up my mind is, how many pills I'm on, and yet she allows me to hold her anyway. There's something honest about all of this, and I cannot imagine any other woman lying in the middle of a frozen soccer field with me—in the middle of a snowstorm even—impossibly hoping to see a single cloud break free of a nimbostratus.

Nikki would not have done this for me, not even on her best day.

So I pull Tiffany a little closer, kiss the hard spot between her perfectly plucked eyebrows, and after a deep breath, I say, "I think I need you too."

Acknowledgments

Special thanks to the kin, friends, mentors, and professionals who helped me along the way and made this read possible: Sarah Crichton, Kathy Daneman, Cailey Hall, and everyone else at FSG; Doug Stewart, Seth Fishman, and everyone else at Sterling Lord Literistic; Al, Dad Dog, Mom, Meg, Micah, Kelly, Barb and Peague, Jim Smith, Bill and Mo Rhoda, "Peruvian Scott" Humfeld, "Canadian Scott" Caldwell, Tim and Beth Rayworth, Myfanwy Collins, Richard Panck, Rachel Pollack, Bess Reed Currence (B), Duffy, Flem, Scorso, Helena White, "The WMs"—Jean Weitz, Wally Wilhoit, Kalela Williams, Karen Terrey, Beth Bigler, and Tom Léger—Dave Tavani, Lori Litchman, Alan Barstow, Larz and Andrea, Corey and Jen, Ben and Jess, Uncle Dave, Aunt Carlotta, Uncle Pete, and my grandparents, Dink and H.